"Thank you for sharing your past with me."

Lucas's expression conveyed his sincerity, and for the first time, Addy did not regret opening up to him. Somehow her confession had broken through that barrier of solitude he'd worn when she first approached.

Addy propped her foot on the bottom step of the porch and gave him a little smile, wanting their solidarity to continue. "Ready to double-team some kids?"

Lucas shook his head. "I'm not cut out for this."

"Who is?"

He walked down the steps and she didn't back away. She'd never been attracted to someone like Lucas before...someone so raw and masculine, so big and Marlboro Man–like.

Stopping in front of her, he reached out and tucked a strand of hair behind her ear. The gesture was both tender and intimate. She lifted her gaze to his. Those dark eyes were soft, and a flicker of hunger ignited within them.

"You're such a rare beauty, Addy Toussant."

Dear Reader,

I'll never forget one morning while folding clothes, I saw a young woman on a national news program talking about the horror of living with a stalker. Never had I seen such absolute terror on a person's face, and the image haunted me. I'd never contemplated being terrorized by another person set on having power over me. In that moment I wanted to give that sweet woman a happy ending. So the character of Addy Toussant was born.

To help Addy learn to trust and love again would take a special man, and Lucas Finlay fits the bill. A loner rancher/photographer, Lucas is no stranger to heartache—his high school sweetheart and brother betrayed him, leaving a gap in his life...and nephews and a niece who don't know him. Lucas is my take on one of my favorite movies—*Uncle Buck.* Nothing complicates and demands all hands on deck like being forced to take care of three children, an incontinent dog, a devil cat and two hamsters. Lucas and neighbor Addy must unite, and in the process, they fall in love.

So join me down where the Mississippi is lazy and the food is crazy good for a story of healing and facing the past. As always, I'd love to hear what you think about the story. You can contact me at www.liztalleybooks.com or find me on Facebook at www.facebook.com/liztalleybooks.

Happy reading!

Liz Talley

His
Brown-Eyed
Girl

—

Liz Talley

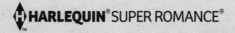
HARLEQUIN® SUPER ROMANCE®

Recycling programs
for this product may
not exist in your area.

ISBN-13: 978-0-373-71878-8

HIS BROWN-EYED GIRL

Copyright © 2013 by Amy R. Talley

HARLEQUIN®

™ www.Harlequin.com

Printed in U.S.A.

ABOUT THE AUTHOR

A 2009 Golden Heart Award finalist in Regency romance, Liz Talley has since found a home writing sassy Southern stories. Her book *Vegas Two-Step* debuted in June 2010 and was quickly followed by four more books in her Oak Stand, Texas series. In her current books, she's visiting one of her favorite cities—New Orleans. Liz lives in north Louisiana with her hero, two beautiful boys and a passel of animals. She enjoys laundry, paying bills and creating masterful dinners for her family. She also lies in her biography to make herself look like the perfect housewife. What she really likes is new shoes, lemon-drop martinis and fishing off the pier at her camp. You can visit her at www.liztalleybooks.com to learn more about the lies she tells herself, and about her upcoming books.

Books by Liz Talley

HARLEQUIN SUPERROMANCE

*The Boys of Bayou Bridge

Other titles by this author available in ebook format.

For my dear departed friend Katie Sue Morgan
who taught me so much about being a writer.

And a special dedication to the
best editor around—Wanda Ottewell.
Her name should be right underneath mine on
every book...or maybe before it.
I'm blessed by her guidance and support.

CHAPTER ONE

ADDY TOUSSANT STUDIED the fading bloom of the Pauwela Cloud orchid. Such a shame to snuff out the white-ruffled beauty, but the withered edges of the petal bore the tale. The bloom was off the—snip!—orchid.

Irony didn't escape her as she tucked the petals into the waste bag she wore hooked on her gardening utility belt.

Not that Addy was old. Or unhappy about having her bloom fade. She rather liked the emerging lines around her eyes. Gave her character and all that.

Besides, thirty-two wasn't "old"—it was practically the new twenty-two. Or so a magazine she'd read yesterday in the optometrist waiting room had declared. Still, so many of her high school friends were married and starting families, and though Addy didn't feel empty, something about being so behind the curve made her feel, well, old.

But she shouldn't feel that way. After all, not everyone wanted to be a wife and mother. Some women liked being exactly who they were. She'd always embraced that notion, a lifestyle her aunt Flora had modeled for her.

Addy stood and ignored the cracking of her knees, stretching her back and looking up at the plastic skylight in the greenhouse she'd had built in her yard. Afternoon was giving over to evening. She could see the moon peeking out from behind the pink clouds. Another Tuesday nearing conclusion, but at least it had been filled with sunshine and a warmer breeze.

Then her peace shattered.

A blur of motion rocketed into the structure, rending the heavy plastic sheeting. A scream caught in her throat as she pitched herself to the side, away from the roar. A corner of the greenhouse collapsed under the assault as Addy rolled away. The black rubber tire missed her nose by inches and the reverberation of an engine thundered in her ear. Gasoline fumes choked her and she coughed, raising herself up on an elbow amidst broken pottery. The spinning wheel of the motorbike snagged her sleeve.

"Oh, my sweet Lord," Addy said, her voice drowned by the noise, tugging her loose-sleeved yoga shirt from the grip of the tire and trying to get her bearings. Pushing herself upward, she caught sight of a Converse sneaker and jean-clad leg draped over the seat of the still-rumbling bike.

Addy turned the switch on the handle to the off position. How she knew exactly where the switch was stymied her, but the engine died.

A groan emerged from beneath the wooden shelf that had collapsed onto whoever had driven a small motorcycle into her newly constructed greenhouse.

Addy shoved the splintered wood away to find a small boy. Or—to be more specific—a small boy who'd run through her daylilies on the same motorbike a month ago; a small boy who was the middle child of her irresponsible neighbors; a small boy whose name was Chris.

Or Michael. She got them mixed up.

Okay, so her neighbors weren't necessarily irresponsible, merely overwhelmed with a lot of kids and pets running amuck.

"Chris?"

"What?" he mumbled.

"Are you okay?"

The child moved, pulling his leg to him and lifting himself from the yellowed-grass floor. He blinked and his face crumbled as he realized what had occurred. "Oh, no. My bike."

His bike?

Addy looked at the torn plastic, bent frame, busted shelves and pottery shards. Yeah, she was totally concerned about the stupid bike. Precious, no, valuable, orchids lay scattered on the ground, roots dangling, stems crushed, petals bruised.

Dirt smeared the boy's cheek, and if Addy hadn't been so troubled by the fact the accident-prone child had nearly decapitated himself and destroyed her orchid collection, she might have thought it endearing. But she *was* upset… and mad…and scared the boy had nearly broken his fool neck.

"My arm hurts," he said, cupping his shoulder. "And my handlebars are all bent."

Addy struggled to her feet, carefully lifting the bike off him and pushing aside. "Let me see."

The boy scooted back, wincing as he cradled his right arm. "Owww."

Addy knelt beside him and gently placed her hand on his forearm. "Can you wiggle your fingers?"

Big tears hovered on his thick lashes. He dashed them away with his other hand. "I don't know."

"Try."

He looked at the arm he held tight against his torso. The grubby little fingers moved. Slowly, he uncurled his fist and wiggled his fingers.

"Good."

He smiled slightly, obviously happy he'd not lost use of his fingers. Carefully, he extended his arm, moving it so his elbow resembled a hinge. "It still hurts a little."

"Well, yeah, you fell on it. Can you stand up?"

He nodded and scrabbled to his feet, wincing only slightly as he moved his shoulder.

Addy rose as the new flap in her greenhouse flew open. A huge man stood in the blinding sunlight. She stumbled back, knocking another shelf to the ground. More pottery broke as irrational fear exploded within her. Unable to gain traction, she hit the heavy metal pole supporting the greenhouse and nearly tripped over the discarded bike.

"What in the hell happened here?" the mountain asked, his voice strong as the shoulders filling the space where plastic sheeting had once stretched tight.

Fear rose in Addy's throat as her body prepared to fight. Instinctively, her mind cleared and she noted in mere nanoseconds the exits and the tools around her. She'd been preparing for this day for a long time. But even as her instinct took over, reason clawed its way into her head.

He wasn't a stranger.

She'd seen this man before—he'd been in and out of the Finlay house the past few days, obviously minding the kids. He wasn't there for her. He was here for the boy.

She steadied her breathing, but remained aware…just as she'd practiced.

Chris started crying. "I'm sorry. I really am, Uncle Lucas. I forgot she put this dumb house on my bike path." Tears weren't wiped away. Snot followed. He looked pathetic…and was blaming her for the crash.

She was fairly certain she could build a greenhouse on her own property. Or technically Aunt Flora's property. Addy stared at the kid, wondering if she should say something, wondering how he'd managed to turn into a sobbing mess in a matter of seconds.

The large man jabbed a finger at the boy. "No excuse. I told you to stay off that bike when I wasn't around. I had to wipe your sister, and you disobeyed."

The kid ducked his head, sniffling, tears falling on his New Orleans Saints jersey. "I want my momma. I want my momma."

"Okay, stop yelling at him," Addy said, ungluing herself from the now-sagging plastic and propping her hands on her hips. Remain assertive. Protect the victim. "It's obvious the child is hurt. And scared."

The man flicked dark eyes toward the boy. "Are you hurt, Chris?"

"Mmm-hmm." The boy wiped his face on his sleeve, using the uninjured arm. "I hurt my shoulder."

The man stepped inside, crowding the area, making Addy's heart race…and not in a good way. More in the way large male strangers had been doing for over fifteen years. The fear never went away. She merely had to control it.

Breathing deeply, she stretched out a hand, shifting some of the power. "I'm Addy Toussant. This is my aunt Flora's house, but I live with her."

The man the kid had called Lucas didn't tear his eyes from the boy as he placed a humongous hand on the boy's shoulder. "And I'm Chris's uncle Lucas. I'm taking care of him for a while."

"And Charlotte. And Michael," Chris said, his brown eyes meeting hers as he allowed his uncle to move his arm.

"Yeah, them, too," Lucas muttered, his eyes screwed up in concentration as he poked and prodded the boy. "Stand up so I can get a better look at your shoulder."

Chris allowed Lucas to lift him to his feet. Addy watched for signs of pain in the boy's face, but didn't see anything alarming.

Chris hobbled a little. "My ankle hurts, too."

Lucas stepped back so his shoulder brushed hers. Addy dropped the hand he hadn't shaken and scooted away, ignoring the piece of splintered shelf jabbing into her thigh. "Are you surprised? You drove your bike through this nice lady's, um, house thing."

Chris peered over at her. "Sorry, Miss Abby. Really. I forgot you put this on my trail."

Addy didn't say anything. She probably should say something inane like "It's okay" or "My name's Miss *Addy*," but she didn't. Mostly because the child had destroyed part of her newly built greenhouse…and plenty of poor, helpless orchids.

"I'm glad you're sorry because you're going to help her rebuild it." This from the tall, dark and somewhat handsome man.

"What? No." Addy turned to the giant glowering at the boy. "It's really not necessary."

"The hell it isn't. I told him to stay off that damn bike while I went in to help his sister. He disobeyed, nearly killed himself and destroyed property in the process. *He's* helping fix this."

"You're cussing," Chris whined, making a god-awful face. "I don't know nothin' about fixin' stuff."

"Well, that's the way you learn." The man picked up the motorbike as if it were a small toy and rolled it toward the split in the plastic as the older boy arrived on scene.

"Holy shit, Chris, what did you do? Mom's going to freak."

"Watch your mouth," Lucas said, shooting the older boy a stern look, blatantly ignoring his own naughty word moments before.

Michael crossed his arms and gave his uncle a go-to-hell look. "Whatever. Like you don't cuss."

The man ignored him and shoved the bike toward Michael. "Take this to your house."

Michael caught the bike and glowered. "Why do I have to clean up his messes? I always have to—"

"Do what I said," Lucas said, his tone brooking no further argument. "Where's your sister? I left her in the bathroom."

And that was when Charlotte showed up sans pants.

"I'm through," she trilled with a smile, thrusting a wad of toilet paper in the air toward Lucas.

For a moment, all were stunned silent.

"Where are your pants?" Lucas asked as the two older boys started laughing.

"I couldn't put them on. You hadda wipe me." She looked about three or four years old. Old enough to know better than to go outside with a bare behind. Young enough not to care.

The man lifted his eyes heavenward and took in a deep breath. Addy wasn't sure if he was praying or trying his best not to bolt toward the huge truck he'd parked in the narrow drive the day before. She didn't know why he'd gotten saddled with the Finlays' three kids, dog, cat and whatever else they sustained in the rambling shotgun house next door, but he was more of a champ than she.

Or was that chump?

"For crying out loud, Lottie. You're not supposed to leave the bathroom without clothes on. And you can wipe yourself. You know it and I know it," Chris said looking like a small parent. "Wipe yourself."

"But not when I go poop," Charlotte said, twisting cherub lips beneath bright blue eyes, corkscrew blond curls and a bow askew on her snarled ponytail. Tears filled her eyes and that bottom lip trembled.

The man's mouth moved.

Definitely praying.

"Uh, hi, Charlotte. Remember me? I'm Miss Addy," she said, darting a look toward Chris so he got the message about what her name actually was. "Why don't you go with your brother Michael to your house and let him help you find your pants."

She heard Michael's bark of protest and shot him a look that said "Shut it" before turning to the darling pantless girl. "When you're done, you can come back and I'll give you a homemade chocolate chip cookie Aunt Flora made for her bridge club."

Charlotte made a little smile adorable enough to melt the sternest of hearts.

Lucas sighed. "Please, Charlotte, go with your brother."

The little girl looked up, up, up at the big man above her and her body literally shook. "Mmm'kay."

Michael rolled his eyes, shifted the dirt bike to Chris and took his sister's hand—not before carefully inspecting it—and tugged her out the hole in the greenhouse. Toilet paper trailed behind the barefoot child.

Lucas gave Addy his full attention for the first time. "Thank you."

"You're welcome."

"Think I'll just go, too," Chris said, slinking past his uncle, rolling his bike toward the entrance.

"Wait," Lucas said.

The boy stopped and looked at his uncle with frightened eyes. Addy watched as the man forced himself to relax.

"You need to help Miss—" He struggled for her name.

"Toussant," Addy said.

"—Toussant clean up. And then we'll arrange a time for you to help repair the damage you've done."

"A boy can't fix this." Addy's gaze roved over the rubble. "I have to replace some beams and most of the sheeting. Plus several of the shelves are broken. And pots. And several plants will need replacing…" Her voice faded as the enormity of the task set in.

"*I'm* going to help, too," Lucas said, his dark eyes sweeping her from foot to crown, but not in a skeevy way. No hair raised on her neck. The look was appreciative, but not harmful. There was something else—a tingly awareness that made her swallow the misery of the situation and avert her eyes from the broad shoulders and hard jaw. Her thoughts needed to stay away from the overt maleness of Uncle Lucas.

"I'm sure you don't have the time what with taking care of the children."

"I *need* to help." His eyes relented in hardness, giving her a glimpse of something else within the depths. Was it desperation? "In fact, I'll get Michael to help, too. We can make short work of the cleanup."

"He's not going to like it," Chris muttered. "He doesn't like helping with anything. He's lazy."

Addy smiled. Most thirteen-year-old boys were lazy when it came to chores. Michael was not lazy, however, when it came to lacrosse. The boy tossed balls all over his yard. And Addy's and Mr. Linnert's and every house within a one-hundred-yard radius. "I don't care what he likes or doesn't," Lucas said, toeing a piece of wood hanging haphazardly from the metal framework of the shelves. "He's helping us rebuild Miss Toussant's shed."

"Greenhouse," Addy said, accepting the fact she'd have three males and a sometimes pantless toddler invading her world…whether she wished it or not. Lucas didn't seem the sort to take no for an answer, which was somewhat alarming. But Addy couldn't deny it would be good for Chris to learn how to right the wrong he'd created. And something about the pleading in the man's voice had her conceding to what would likely be more trouble than aid. "And you might as well call me Addy since we're embarking upon a project together."

"And I'm Lucas."

"Lucas," she repeated, holding out her hand again.

This time he took hold of her small hand with something roughly the size of a grizzly paw. But his grasp was warm, friendly even, for a man who seemed made of hard corners.

No zaps of attraction.

No weird tingly crap like in all those movies. Just heart-felt and firm. She inhaled slowly and exhaled with a smile.

Something about his handshake allowed for respite, for some measure of conviction. She knew Courtney and Ben Finlay well enough to know they wouldn't leave their children with anyone who wasn't trustworthy. She pulled her hand from his. "I don't have time this week to rebuild the greenhouse, but I work only until noon on Saturdays. Should be home by one o'clock. I'll make a list of materials, and if you can get them from a home improvement store…"

Lucas's eyes traveled over her again. "I can and will. I'm sorry this happened to your greenhouse. I should have made sure he didn't get on the bike. From here on out, until his mother returns he will not be terrorizing the neighborhood because the bike will be in the garage."

"But I gotta ride in the Nola Classic in a couple of weeks. I gotta practice."

Lucas gave the boy a look that should have been hard, but somehow looked sympathetic. "Not while I'm here. Take that up with your—"

"Like that's going to happen. Why won't Mom come home? Why won't you tell us where she is?"

"That's not my call, kid. My job is to make sure you don't kill yourself before she gets back…something in which I'm obviously close to failing. Take up complaints with her when she calls."

"All she does is ask how our day was. She don't say nothin' about nothin'," Chris grumbled.

The whole conversation sounded tense and personal, so Addy bent and started stacking shards of pottery in the plastic rolling bin she used for compost. Her action directed the attention of both males to the task at hand.

Chris carefully set down the bike outside the greenhouse while Lucas shifted unbroken pots of delicate blooms to a concentric area in the one sturdy corner of the house. Wordlessly he picked up broken boards and handed them to Chris, jerking his head toward the two empty trash cans sitting behind her house. He moved elegantly for such a large man and the trepidation Addy had felt earlier returned. She didn't like being penned inside with him.

"Better get moving. Sun's about to set." He moved the cans beside the rent plastic and got to work in a business-like manner that chased away her fear. She pulled a rake from the small cupboard on which part of the damaged greenhouse rested and did as he suggested.

After so many words spoken, silence was welcome, allowing each to his or her own thoughts. They worked easily together to clear away the mess and restore some order to the broken greenhouse.

"Luckily we're not expecting frost," Addy commented, placing the final ruffled pink-and-green orchid in the rows sitting shiva over the pile of poor unsalvageable plants.

Lucas agreed, picking up her ring of keys that held the small canister of pepper spray. He eyed it before passing it to her.

"I'm a single woman." Her declaration wasn't an invitation. Wasn't a status update. It was explanation—she protected herself. Lucas was damn lucky she hadn't had the keys in hand when he'd burst through the plastic earlier.

"Smart," he said.

Chris sighed, obviously bored with the adult talk. "Can I take my bike home now?"

Lucas nodded. "I'll take this pile out to the bin."

A disturbance at the torn entrance drew Addy's eye. Blond curls followed by one blue-green eye studied her.

"And then we can have chocolate chip cookies."

"Don't both—" Lucas turned as he saw Charlotte emerging in the opening. Her big eyes were fastened on

Addy and she looked hungry…maybe for more than chocolate chip cookies.

Addy was accustomed to being around kids—she had
a dozen nieces and nephews—but she'd hardly said "boo"
to the kids next door, though her aunt Flora liked to chat
them up occasionally. Charlotte looked a little lost under
her uncle's care, and an invisible string inside her heart
plinked at the girl in her juice-stained T-shirt and mis-
matched pants.

Holding out a hand, Addy beckoned the girl. "You ready
for some cookies?"

"Mmm-hmm." Charlotte nodded, reaching small
grubby fingers toward Addy. "I wike cookies."

The adorable speech impediment cemented the intent
in Addy's heart. Lucas needed help. "I like cookies, too."

"Uncle Wucas don't wike cookies. He wikes beer."

Addy couldn't stop the smile. She heard Lucas grunt as
he bent to scoop the discarded plants into the rolling bin.
"Please don't tell Sister Regina Maria. She already thinks
I'm the very devil," he said, pushing the bin out into the
encroaching darkness. Michael stood at the end of Addy's
drive, tapping on his cell phone, but casting glances toward
where Lucas tugged the plastic sheeting closed.

"Sister Regina Maria is my principal," Charlotte said,
looking at Addy with eyes the color of sea glass. Clear
blue mottled with bottle green. Beautiful and trusting.
But not when she looked at Lucas. Something about the
big man scared the girl. Normally, Addy would agree. As
a former victim of violence, she avoided large men. Even
though she knew it was wrong to judge a man on his size,
she couldn't seem to help herself. Lucas was an oak tree.

"Sister Regina Maria sounds like a good principal. Is
she nice?"

Michael joined them. "If dragons are nice."

"She's not a dragon," Charlotte admonished, her plump

lips straightening in a line, her brow wrinkling into thunderclouds. "You a fart head. Chris said so."

Michael laughed. "He'd know."

Charlotte didn't seem to know what to say. But Lucas did. "Michael, did you finish your schoolwork?"

The boy gave his uncle a withering look.

"Did you?"

The boy still didn't answer, but instead tugged Charlotte's hand. "Let's go home, Lottie."

"Nooo," the toddler screeched, pulling away from Michael. "I want cookies."

"We got cookies." The boy leaned over and picked his sister up, shooting Lucas a funny look. "If you don't come with me, I'll leave you with Uncle Lucas all by yourself."

The little girl froze and slid her gaze to her towering uncle. "Nooo! He eats little kids' fingers. Did he eat Mommy?"

Michael's eyes sparked. "Probably. He hates Mom and Dad."

Charlotte started crying, but her older brother didn't seem to care. He charged toward the gap in the camellia bushes, not bothering to listen as his uncle shouted "Stop!"

"That little—" Lucas bit down on the expletive sure to explode from his mouth. He shoved the rolling bin to the side and started toward the gap.

But Addy did something unexpected.

She reached out and laid a hand on his arm.

And Lucas stopped, turned to her and arched a dark eyebrow. "What?"

"Let him go."

The man shrugged off her touch. "He's being—"

"Lucas Whatever Your Name Is, I think you need to tell me what's really going on."

CHAPTER TWO

Lucas Finlay looked at the small woman staring expectantly at him with eyes the color of aged wheat—not quite golden but not wholly brown—and stilled himself.

What was really going on?

How about total incompetency in dealing with kids?

Or helplessness?

Or guilt?

Or all of the above?

All those would likely cover the past forty-eight hours spent in the company of three kids he knew nothing about, a house that creaked and moaned and had weak pipes, and pets that needed constant feeding and walking. He'd encountered more poop in the past two days than in his entire lifetime...and he raised cattle on his ranch.

Not to mention, Michael had been correct.

Not about eating small children. Lucas might be tall, but he'd given up devouring tiny tots long ago...when he'd sold the golden-egg-laying goose. But the boy had been right about him hating his brother and sister-in-law. Unequivocally correct.

"It's a long story."

Addy hooked a dramatic eyebrow. "Yeah?"

"I need to go."

"Where are Ben and Courtney?"

For a moment, he didn't answer. Was it any of her business? She was a neighbor. Neighbors carried tales and Lucas wasn't sure what Courtney wanted to reveal about

Ben's injuries…about the fact Lucas's younger brother lay in a hospital bed miles away, knocking on death's door. "They're in Virginia."

Not a lie. Walter Reed Army Hospital was in Virginia.

"Ben's deployed to Afghanistan. Was he injured?"

Lucas didn't move a muscle. "I can't give out information without their permission."

"What about your parents? Why aren't they here instead of you?"

"Mom and Dad are in Europe, trying to get back so they can meet Courtney in Virginia. There was no one else to stay with the kids on such short notice."

The woman didn't say anything. Just studied him, which made him uncomfortable. This is what he didn't like about being back in New Orleans. People lurked around every corner and there were so many things in his way—trees, bushes, grass, lushness. Yes, everything was so damn plush and suffocating.

Not like West Texas where a man could breathe. Where a man could stretch out and see for days what came toward him. There were no corners…and very few people. And those very few people left him the hell alone. Just as he wished.

Here in New Orleans, he drowned in all the *stuff* surrounding him.

Mostly in dog piss because Kermit the golden retriever had bladder issues. The vet was on the list for tomorrow, but if he had to go to Home Depot…

She cleared her throat.

He glanced at her again. She hadn't warmed up to him, but most people didn't. There was something hard in his demeanor, something off-putting that sent people away from him rather than toward him. Probably his size. He stretched six foot four inches and filled up most doorways with his breadth. He wasn't fat, but neither was he slim. Solid. Thick. And unlikely to smile. Charm was his antonym.

But he liked the look of her. Petite but not mousy. Brown hair that caught in the waning sunlight. Pleasant heart-shaped face. Very natural—no caked-on makeup or weirdly patterned shirts with spiky high heels. Just simplicity. Yeah, this woman looked simple. His fingers itched to photograph her. He'd use the new Nikon and catch the natural light falling soft against her golden skin.

Then he remembered where he was.

"Look, I don't feel comfortable talking about the situation. Courtney hasn't told the kids what issues she and Ben are facing." Damn. Even that was too much to say. He could tell Addy knew the situation wasn't good, but he couldn't take back his words. Yet, somehow he knew this woman wouldn't spread them around.

She nodded, mink hair falling over slim shoulders. He wondered what she'd do if he reached over and felt it between his thumb and finger. Scream?

Then he remembered the pepper spray on her key ring and shoved his hands into his pockets.

"Okay, I'm smart enough to realize it's something bad otherwise you wouldn't be here. I've never seen you before so that means you're not close to your brother. The children seem scared of you, likely perpetuated by Michael who is locked in a power struggle with you. So I'd say—"

"You a counselor?"

She smiled and her face transformed into beauty. Not an overblown, sexy beauty, but the kind a person observes as a swan glides over the water on a still morn, the kind reflected in a pool sitting taciturn beneath a towering mountain pass. Serene beauty. Peaceful beauty. "I'm a floral designer."

His expression must have betrayed the question.

"Fine. It's a fancy way of saying I'm a florist."

At this he gave a rare smile. "So you arrange things. Pull apart, reassemble and create something that makes sense…just as you're doing now?"

She made a face. "I don't think anyone has ever put it in such a way, but I suppose that's accurate."

A scream erupted from the house. Chris or Charlotte? He couldn't tell.

"That's my cue. Need to go, but I'll send over whichever child's not bleeding for your list." His strides ate up the distance between her drive and the gap in the bushes. For some odd reason he didn't want to leave her just yet.

Or maybe he merely tried to avoid the slap of reality awaiting him. He'd learned kids were fantastic at delivering those particular slaps.

Before he disappeared, Lucas turned and held up his hand. "Good to meet you and sorry about—"

Another scream.

Addy jerked her gaze to the blue house. "Go."

So he did.

Of course when he saw what awaited him when he stepped through the front door, he wished he'd stayed awhile longer basking in the serenity that was his brother's next-door neighbor.

Charlotte stood in the living room screeching like a parrot, pointing at a huge puddle of something.

"What?" he shouted, stomping onto the area rug.

Charlotte froze.

"Where are your brothers?"

She didn't say anything. Just looked at him like he had horns. Like he might be looking over the plumpest parts of her for his nighttime meal.

"Michael!" He called up the stairs.

No answer.

Kermit, the ancient golden retriever, slunk past, quick-stepping it toward the kitchen and back door.

"Oh, no," Lucas muttered, glancing at Charlotte. "Is that dog pee?"

She slowly nodded. "I stepped in it. Gross."

Chris came in holding a large plastic storage bag filled with ice, sank into the leather recliner and propped his ankle up, plunking the ice on his bare foot and grabbing the remote control. "Looks like Kermit the Dog peed again."

Lucas closed his eyes and counted, throwing in a Hail Mary and the Serenity prayer for good measure. When he opened his eyes, the things he couldn't change were still there. Dog pee, three-year-old and a ten-year-old watching Cinemax.

"Hey, turn that to a kid's channel or something," he said, giving Chris the same eyeball job his father had given him when he sneaked off to watch shoot 'em up movies.

"But it's PG-13. No sex or nothin'."

"You're not thirteen. You're barely ten. Turn the channel. Now." Lucas skirted the pond of pee and looked at his niece who balanced on one foot.

"It gotted on me," she said by way of explanation.

"Of course. It's nearly time for your bath, so we'll take one early, okay?"

"'Kay. Can I have frooty-ohs for dinner?" she asked, allowing him to lift her. She didn't even shudder, but she didn't hold on to him, either. Maybe they were making progress. "You weally ain't a monster, are you?"

"No. I'm your uncle. Your daddy's older brother. I'm just big."

Her blue eyes didn't blink.

"You're little. Does that make you a fairy?"

She smiled and something near the rock that was his heart stirred. Felt like gas but not as sharp. "Like Tinker-bell?"

"Who's Tinkerbell?"

The little girl relaxed against him as he climbed the stairs. "You don't even know who Tinkerbell is?"

Music blasted from behind Michael's closed door. Lucas knocked but got no response, so he kept moving toward the kids' bathroom. Courtney had obviously taken pains to make it bright and kidlike, but the boys seemed to care little, tossing their socks, undies and wet towels on the floor and leaving streaks of toothpaste in the sink.

"Here. I'll start your bath then I'll get Michael to help you while I clean up the mess Kermit made."

Charlotte balanced on one foot, holding aloft a tiny foot with chipped pink polish on her little toenails. "'Kay."

Lucas banged on Michael's door.

No answer. Of course.

"Michael!" Lucas raised his fist to pound on the door once more but it jerked open.

Music battered him and an angry thirteen-year-old with sullen brown eyes met him. "What?"

Lucas lowered his fist because the kid's eyes darted to it and there was a hunted look in them. "I need you to bathe your sister."

"That's not my job. I did my homework and took out the trash. Plus, I already wiped her and put her pants on."

"Fine. I'll bathe her. You clean up your dog's pee. Use the steam cleaner." Lucas turned toward the bathroom.

"Fine. Whatever. I'll bathe the flea." There were equal parts disgust and resignation in Michael's voice.

Good. Lucas didn't want to bathe Charlotte again. The first night she'd sung songs about spaghetti at the top of her lungs and insisted on using something called Dora the Explorer shampoo...which he could not find. He'd also thought she'd bathe herself, but that didn't seem to be the case. Seems he was supposed to bathe her. And it felt weird because he'd never washed a little girl before. Big girls and a bottle of bath gel? Sign him up. Little girls with Strawberry Shortcake soap and a Mardi Gras party cup to rinse her hair? Not so much.

He'd take dog pee any day of the week.

Chris quickly changed the channel when Lucas entered the room so he tossed him another *Father Knows Best* stern look and went in search of the paper towels stored in the half bath under the stairs.

Fifteen minutes later he stood in the kitchen looking at the retriever who sat innocently at the back door, tongue lolled out, happiness pouring out of sweet brown eyes. He sort of wanted to kick it…and he sort of wanted to take it for a walk. Or maybe fishing. He'd always wanted a dog to take fishing.

"Out, Kermit. And don't piss in the house again."

The dog lumbered out into the fenced yard. And the Wicked Cat of the West darted in.

Mittens. Meaner than a two-headed snake.

Lucas sighed and leaned his head against the smooth painted wood of the door.

He needed help.

He didn't know what in the hell he was doing as evidenced by being yelled at in the carpool line while picking up Charlotte from school. Sister Regina Maria had actually scared him…and she was barely five feet tall.

Why did he tell Courtney he would come to New Orleans and watch the kids?

Of course, he knew the answer. But it was complicated…and tied around the fact the brother he'd once loved and now hated was teetering on the precipice of death. Nutshell.

But all the other shit he felt cluttered around that reason made it harder than he'd ever thought to be here in the world he'd left behind.

Long ago.

Courtney's voice. *Please, Lucas. I know you hate me,*

*but please. I don't know what else to do. I have to be with
Ben. Have to. Please, he's your brother. This is me begging you.*

Words he'd longed to hear, but never in such regard.
He'd wanted to punish Courtney. Wanted her to grovel.
To regret. To know what she'd given up.

But her words hadn't been filled with regret.

They had been for her children, the ones she'd had with
his brother. The family she loved more than her pride. So
she'd begged him to help her. Begged the man she'd betrayed so she could go to the man she'd cheated on him
with—his own brother.

Lucas banged his forehead against the door.

"Uncle Wucas?"

Charlotte stood in the doorway clad in a nightgown
with ponies on it. Her wet hair hung nearly to her waist,
but he knew now from experience it would curl up to her
shoulders when it dried. Her blue eyes looked so much
like Courtney's—big and ready to be filled by life. She
still looked frightened of him, but he couldn't do anything about it.

He tried to smile but it probably looked as if he were in
pain. She took a step back.

"Do you want some cereal?" He walked to the fridge.
"Uh, I think your brother must have drank the last of the
milk." He looked at her. Would she pitch a fit? He'd seen
kids her age in the grocery store lying on the floor, scream-
ing and kicking. Lucas wasn't up for handling that at the
moment, not after the dirt bike crash and the dog piss.

Chris hobbled in. "What's for dinner?"

Good question. "How about pizza?"

"Yes!" Chris pumped his fist in the air. Oddly enough,
he landed on his "injured" foot without a grimace telling
Lucas all he needed to know about a trip to the doctor.

Charlotte didn't say anything, but several crystalline tears hung on her thick blond lashes.

"You don't like pizza?" Lucas asked, using the voice he used on his mares when they were foaling.

Charlotte shook her head.

"Shut up, Lottie. You like pizza," Chris said, hopping to the pantry, grabbing a bag of potato chips and shoving a handful into his mouth. Pieces fell, sprinkling the floor and his T-shirt.

Lucas grabbed the bag and rolled it shut. "If you want pizza, you need to lay off the chips."

"But—" Chris made a swipe for the bag, but when he realized he had no chance, he dropped his arms and glared at Lucas. "Why are you here anyway? We don't even know you."

Good question. Lucas didn't know the answer. On the drive from West Texas to Louisiana the same question had bounced around in his head. Why was he going to help out a family he knew nothing about?

Well, he knew a little.

His mother had forwarded him Christmas cards of this perfect family year after year. Lucas had watched his nephews and niece grow up in the happy, shiny photos, gummy grins shifting into painful half smiles. But other than a Christmas card and what he gleaned from his parents, Lucas knew nothing about his brother's family. "Because your mother needed help."

"But you hate my dad." Statement. Delivered with anger. From the affable Chris.

Charlotte stopped swinging on the doorknob.

Michael appeared, face dark as a thundercloud, arms crossed. Tension hung like wet flannel. "Yeah, you do. We're not stupid. So why don't you clue us all in on why we've never seen you before now?"

Another good question.

But the truth was too hard for children.

"Where's the number for a pizza place nearby?"

Flickering within the dark depths of Michael's eyes—so similar to Ben's—was an unspoken line scratched between them. "Find it yourself, *Uncle*."

ADDY STARED at the dregs in her chai tea. She should have had decaffeinated tea or a nice glass of wine. The past few hours had left her unsettled and sucking down caffeine hadn't been a good idea. She lit the chamomile-and-honey-scented candles on the shelf above the ancient claw-foot tub and tossed some dried lavender in the water pouring from the arched faucet.

Surely a bath would wash her cares away and later she'd get back to reading about the sensual Arabian sheikh and the woman who defied him…only out of bed of course.

"Addy?"

Addy set the empty teacup on the marble vanity and pulled on her worn terry-cloth robe as her aunt Flora burst into the bathroom.

"Oh, there you are," Aunt Flora said, readjusting a sombrero on her gray locks. "I hollered for you for a good five minutes. Thought you were out for a run."

"You know I don't run at night. The faucet must have masked the sound of you calling. What the heck are you wearing?"

"What does it look like?" Aunt Flora asked. "It's one of those Mexican hats. Doris got it for me for the Zumba class. We're doing a Latin routine that requires a sombrero."

"Mexican Hat Dance?" Addy cracked.

Aunt Flora twisted her lips and sent her eyes toward the pressed-tin ceiling. "Well, I don't know the song, but it's very sexy. You should come to class with me."

"I'll stick to yoga and running. I'm hopeless at sashaying."

Aunt Flora snorted and sat on the toilet lid. "We don't sashay. We rumba, salsa and do kicks. But stick to your boring exercise. Zumba is for the young at heart."

"There's an insult in there somewhere."

"Phooey. The insult was right out front." Aunt Flora smiled, revealing the gold crowns in the back of her mouth. The woman had a Cheshire cat smile and a wicked sense of humor…when she could still find it. "I saw that tall drink of water next door. Who is he? And where can I get one?"

"He's Ben's brother. I think. At any rate, he's the kids' uncle Lucas. And I don't think he's for sale." Addy tamped down the odd feeling stirring inside at the thought of the man who had so recently invaded her world. She felt an attraction toward him, which seemed at odds with the perpetual fear she clung to whenever a large man lumbered into her periphery. That contradiction unsettled her.

Not that she couldn't use a man in her life.

Again she reminded herself she wasn't unhappy without a man to stomp bugs and fix the hinge on the laundry room door. Still she wouldn't mind a date or two…but this man had his hands full enough without worrying with her. And he'd be leaving eventually. Of course she didn't know where he'd return to, just that he would. So not a good idea to open herself up to the idea of Lucas.

"Pity. I'd take a dozen. I could use some help around here. And he's a good-lookin' tall drink of water, if you ask me," Aunt Flora said, plucking at the tight Lycra covering her thin legs. Honestly, the tight leggings weren't appropriate on a seventy-five-year-old woman, but when had something like propriety ever stopped her flamboyant aunt?

"I didn't ask you." Addy shut off the water and cocked an eyebrow at her aunt.

Flora didn't budge. "You could use a drink of water."

"I could use a bath. I'm dirty and the middle Finlay kid destroyed my new greenhouse two hours ago."

"What?" Aunt Flora rose and jerked the blinds open, peering out in the inky darkness to where Addy's greenhouse tilted like a drunk.

"Hey! I'm naked under this robe," Addy said, pulling the collar closed and moving out of line of sight in case anyone peeped out the upper window of the blue house next door. Which never happened. That she knew of.

"Heh." Flora shook her head and pulled the blinds closed. "Wouldn't want anyone to see you nekkid, now would we? Might lead to dangerous things."

"Aunt Flora." Addy shook her head.

"Just saying."

"I'm not afraid of it leading to dangerous things. I just don't want to scar those poor Finlay children for life," Addy said, trying to deliver her aunt the message she wanted to get on with her bath so the woman needed to skedaddle.

"You have a beautiful body and there's a thirteen-year-old boy next door. If he should catch sight of a nekkid Addy Toussant, then he'd be set up for failure his entire life, for you, my dearest, are the loveliest of women. It's a good thing he hasn't caught sight yet. I don't need boys with binoculars falling out of trees."

Addy snorted. "That's so inappropriate. And you're too good at flattery."

"I'm a pro. It's what I do." Aunt Flora grabbed Addy under her chin and gave a squeeze. "But I'm not a liar."

"I left you some soup on the stove. Should still be warm, but if you need it hotter, use the microwave."

Aunt Flora stilled. "I know very well how to light a fire on that stove. Been doing it since you were knee-high, and I didn't cause that fire."

"I know," Addy said, laying a soothing hand on her aunt's forearm. "Put that out of your mind. I'm going to take a bath and then we'll watch that cutie pie Mark Harmon in *NCIS,* okay?"

Aunt Flora nodded, but the damper remained. Addy wanted to kick herself but knew her role as semicaretaker of her aunt meant she had to step on Flora's toes at times. Her aunt had been diagnosed with Alzheimer's disease— still in its early stages—and though she functioned well enough to drive familiar distances and conduct her daily living, she had suffered some setbacks, most recently, a small fire when she'd left the oven mitt on the burner. "Yes, that sounds nice. Enjoy your bath, dear."

The door closed and Addy twisted the lock, craving the solitude of fragrant water and her own thoughts. She stepped into the water, settled in the claw-foot tub and allowed the warmth to embrace her. The scent of lavender soothed her and almost made her forget the intensity of Lucas's dark eyes.

Lucas.

Why did the man intrigue her?

Maybe because he looked like a man who needed help. Three kids, a bunch of pets and a chaotic household? She'd likely need a bottle of wine in hand to muddle through, and she'd been raised with four brothers and sisters, along with assorted pets.

But Lucas had never asked outright for assistance.

So maybe it wasn't the fact he looked like a man who needed someone to toss him a lifesaver.

Maybe she was intrigued by those broad shoulders, the jaw hewn from marble, the slightly full bottom lip that pressed into a stern line when he looked troubled... which was frequent in her limited experience. Besides, he'd looked pretty spectacular in those worn Wranglers.

Yeah, she'd noticed the brand of jeans.

Cowboy jeans.

Boots.

Callous hands and—

A knock sounded on the door.

"Yes?" she called out.

"A little boy hobbled over here with a paper and said he wants a list. What am I to do with it?" Aunt Flora's tinny voice asked. "Oh, and…well, dearest, another letter from Angola."

Addy's heart plunged as she shot upright, sloshing water onto the tile floor. Fear's fingers squeezed hard. She sucked in air, closing her eyes and counting slowly as the alarm sounded inside her.

Windows locked? Yes.

Door bolted. Always.

Or maybe not. Aunt Flora had answered the front door, allowing Chris to hand off something. What if she hadn't relocked it? Her fading memory allowed for such gaps in the house's security.

Addy stood, water sluicing down her body, and jerked her robe from the hook.

"Addy?" Aunt Flora called. "You're not answering me, and that little boy is waiting down in the foyer."

The front door was definitely unlocked.

"Just a minute, Aunt Flora," Addy called, scooping up a towel and rubbing at her legs.

Breathe, Addy. Robbie Guidry still sits in a prison cell a hundred miles away. Breathe.

Addy hurried across the bathroom, twisted the bolt and jerked open the door. Aunt Flora chirped a surprised oh and stepped back, holding a yellow legal-size paper that said List at the top. She also held a letter that stuck out to the side. A stamp declared it sent from a prisoner at Angola State Penitentiary. Not Robbie. He wouldn't risk jeopardizing his parole. He used a friend, no doubt.

Addy's heart stopped.

"Sorry," she said, by way of apology when Aunt Flora

clasped her free hand to her chest. "Did you lock the front door?"

Aunt Flora blinked. "The front door? Well, I think I did. Chris is standing there, and—"

"You have to always lock the front door, Aunt Flora. You know that," Addy said, sliding past her aunt while tightening the sash of her bathrobe. Normally, she wouldn't venture out in front of anyone in such a state, but desperate times and desperate measures called for showing the legs she hadn't had time to shave.

She jogged down the stairs so fast Chris jumped when she hit the landing.

"Hey, uh, Addy," the boy said, nervously shifting his eyes around the foyer she'd painted Wedgewood blue last spring. He'd never been in her aunt's house before. Not many people had. "Uncle Lucas sent me over to get your list. I have to get my homework done and everything, uh, soon."

Addy reached over to twist the dead bolt, but just as her hand touched the handle the door opened.

She screamed and stumbled back.

Chris frowned and pulled the door open to reveal Charlotte standing on the porch in a pink nightgown and bare feet. "It's just Charlotte."

Addy's racing heart didn't slow. She clasped her chest and closed her eyes. "Oh, God, you scared me to death, Charlotte."

"You wearing a wobe," Charlotte said, sidling in, damp curls bouncing. "I have one. It's purple."

"Go home." Chris flung out an arm and pointed toward their house. "You're not supposed to go outside without permission. And never out the front door, Lottie."

"I came with you," Charlotte said, looking at her brother with eyes pure as snowbanks at midnight. "I love you. You're my best brother."

Chris hesitated, brown eyes flickering down at his little sister. "Well, I don't care. You still can't leave without telling—"

"Charlotte!" Lucas shouted, taking the porch steps two at a time. "What the hell do you think you're doing running off like that? Do you know what could have happened?"

The man's eyes blazed and even Chris stepped back, bumping into an antique table holding figurines her aunt had bought in Italy.

Charlotte screeched and scampered behind Addy, where she proceeded to crank up a good wail.

Addy curved a hand around the child's shoulder and held her to the back of her thigh. Charlotte wrapped her chubby arms around Addy's leg, causing the terry cloth to part. Addy felt the cool night air on her bare thighs and tried to tug the robe closed. As she jerked the bottom closed, she felt the bodice part. She let go of the child, pulling both parts closed and clutching them as she faced the huge man filling up her doorway. "Stop yelling at her. Please."

Lucas stilled, shifting in his boots, eyeing the exact spot where she held tight to the fabric. His gaze lowered slightly before rising to her face. "I'm sorry, but she scared me. I sent Chris over for your list, and after I paid the pizza guy, I couldn't find Charlotte."

The little girl still cried, holding fast to Addy. "As you can see, your yelling is not helping the situation."

"She's not supposed to leave our house without Momma," Chris said, folding his arms, very adultlike. He was quite the little parent.

"Mommy! I want my mommy!" Charlotte wailed, her little body trembling against Addy's leg.

"Here." Addy bent and scooped the child into her arms, praying she had not just shown her promised land to the two males in her foyer, and strode toward the living room on her left. Making calming noises, she stroked the little girl's back. "Shh, shh, Charlotte. Your mommy will be home soon."

The child hid her face in the curve of Addy's neck and squeezed her tighter. Addy sank onto the flowered couch, carefully tucking her robe around her and glanced at the two men standing silently in the foyer. She jerked her head, indicating they follow her, and tried not to worry about the front door standing wide-open, an invitation to the outside world.

Lucas pulled the door shut and nudged Chris toward where Addy sat.

"What?" Chris pulled back. "No, I wanna go. I'm hungry. Besides, I still gotta do some math."

Lucas nodded. "Go then. Three slices of pizza only. No soda."

"Cool. Later, Addy." Chris didn't wait for her response as he slid out the door, closing it with a loud bang.

Addy couldn't stop herself from eyeing the unlocked dead bolt. A second later she lifted her gaze to Lucas who noticed her preoccupation with the door, but hopefully thought she worried about the force the ten-year-old had used.

He walked into her living room, gaze darting left then right before once again landing on her.

"I'm sorry," Lucas said, ducking his chin slightly. "I didn't mean to scare her. Or you."

The irony was Addy wasn't scared.

Nervous to be practically naked in the room with a man she felt an uncanny attraction toward? Yes. Scared? No.

And that thought surprised the hell out of her.

She should be terrified of a man storming into the place she felt safest, yelling, disrupting, darting glances at the places that made her very much different from him.

Moments before she had been terrified.

The letter from Angola had been sent to terrorize her, and her heart still thudded from the adrenaline of pounding down the stairs and being startled by Charlotte. But Lucas arriving, filling up the foyer with his strength and somewhat sweet failing at being a caregiver stilled her. So odd, yet so welcome in the face of what she'd experienced earlier.

Lucas quieted her trembling.

"I know you didn't," Addy murmured, stroking Charlotte's back again. "But you are a large man and somewhat frightening to a small girl."

"I apologized. I don't know what else to say."

Addy shook her head and cuddled the little girl who sank into her, snuffling but no longer sobbing. Something sweet and tender toward the child awoke within Addy. Having her mother leave her with someone Charlotte didn't know had to be traumatic. "I know you don't know what to say, but you have to try on her shoes. She's young and missing her mother. She doesn't understand what's going on, only that you scare her with your scowls and anger."

Something in his eyes softened, something different glowing within. "But I don't scare a big girl like you?"

CHAPTER THREE

LUCAS WATCHED ADDY as she held Charlotte, her elegant fingers stroking the child's back. Rich hair fell in dark hanks around her serious face, and he had to practice extreme self-discipline not to slide his gaze to her bare thighs. Something about the turn of a calf, the delicacy of a knee and the sleekness of a woman's thigh got him every time. Total leg man.

And the glimpse of soft curve of breast covered by the child's golden ringlets wasn't helping any.

"*Should* I be afraid of you?" Addy asked, her gaze earnest and steady. Flirty hadn't worked on her.

"No."

"But *Charlotte* is afraid, Chris is out of control and, from what little I've seen of the oldest, he's declared you the enemy," Addy said.

He chewed on that nugget. Of course she was right, but could he out and out admit he was a failure? "Charlotte *has* said time and again I'm big…but I'm not much larger than her father."

"But Ben's her father. You're a stranger to her."

He shoved a hand through hair in need of a trim—he hadn't had time to pop by the barber before he'd left Rotan. Moment of truth. "Okay. You've got me. I don't know what the hell I'm doing."

Addy's lips twitched but her gaze didn't hold victory. Wasn't like she hadn't clued in to his incompetence within seconds of meeting him. "Takes a big man to admit it. No pun intended, of course."

He allowed his lips to curve upward by a centimeter. "It's obvious."

"Pretty much." The child had stilled in Addy's lap and lay heavy against her body, seemingly content to have her warmth and calming influence. Again, he was struck by the way Addy soothed those around her even as she herself often looked spooked.

Why did she continue to look toward the door? Maybe he made her nervous and she was subconsciously ushering him toward the exit? Yet her words didn't rush him out, and she'd invited him into the living area.

"I thought I could handle a few kids—maybe not the evil cat that jumps on my legs in the middle of the night. It's not like the kids are in diapers. I should be able to—"

"You think they're easier when they can move around independently and back-talk you?"

"Point made."

"So I'll see what I can do to help you out a little."

His gaze jerked to hers. "You'll help?"

"Sure. As much as I can."

"How?" Sweet relief blanketed him. Addy seemed capable and sincere—two qualities he appreciated in his fellow man, or rather woman. If there was any lemonade to be had after the lemons Chris had given by crashing into a greenhouse, this was it.

"Well, all the children should help us rebuild the greenhouse for two reasons—first, they can get to know you better with a like purpose in mind and, second, they'll be easy to keep an eye on. At some point, you and I can sit down and go over their schedules and see where I, or even my Aunt Flora, can help out. For example, Aunt Flora's an excellent cook and would likely be happy to save you from pizza every night."

"Who's Aunt Flora?"

"I'm Aunt Flora."

Lucas swiveled his head to where an older woman stood wearing a sombrero, a pair of pajama pants and a sweatshirt that read "I may be old but you're a moron." She looked a little like an older Lucille Ball, replete with red lipstick…and a little like she might have escaped from an asylum.

"Lucas, this is my aunt, Flora Demarco," Addy said, nodding toward the woman.

Aunt Flora raked him with a speculative gaze, lingering on particular parts. Like a connoisseur of men, she weighed and measured him…then gave him a smile that might have worried a lesser man. But Lucas was accustomed to such smiles.

He stuck out a hand. "A pleasure to meet you, Mrs. Demarco. I'm Lucas Finlay, Ben's brother."

"Miss Demarco, please. Or rather Flora." She wiggled a finger at Charlotte who peeked out from her resting spot on Addy's small breasts. Lucky child.

"I just told Lucas that we would be glad to help him. Courtney and Ben are undergoing some hardship, and Lucas has his hands more than full with the kids and the running of a household."

"Of course," Flora said, reaching toward Charlotte. "I'll start with taking this moppet into the kitchen for some milk and, perhaps, a cookie? I remember chocolate chip is your fav, right?"

Charlotte raised her head and nodded, lifting chubby arms to Flora. Addy shifted the child, trying in vain to cover her thighs, and set the girl on the floor. The little girl took the older woman's hand and allowed herself to be led from the room. She didn't look back. Addy cleared her throat and looked at the brass fireplace tools on the hearth.

Taking the child away gave an unsettling intimacy to the situation.

"Thank you," he said sincerely, trying to pull his mind away from the way her damp hair winged away from her delicate neck and the fact she probably wore not a stitch of clothing beneath the terry cloth.

A fierce hunger bloomed within him when he thought of her taut stomach and uptilted breasts. He could just make out the outline of her nipples and imagined their pliant puffiness growing hard beneath his fingers. Beneath his mouth.

"You're welcome," she said, jarring him from the kinky dream world he'd leaped into when thinking about her naked body.

He should be ashamed since the woman volunteered to help him with the kids, but Lucas Finlay rarely felt shame for wanting a woman.

And this one he wanted.

But he'd have to resist.

Something in Addy's demeanor told him she wasn't a woman to trifle with a man. Not that she looked beyond hot, fast sex on, say, the very couch on which she sat, but something he quite couldn't put his finger on warned a tumble with the florist wouldn't be wise.

"So you'll help me with the kids?" he asked, refocusing on the reason he was even in the same room with Addy.

"Sure, and if Aunt Flora isn't tied up for tomorrow evening, we'll see if she can whip up some dinner for the kids, distracting them, while you and I look over their schedules. We can't do anything about Charlotte's fear of you or Michael's resentment, but we can make the space in which they operate more efficient. Sound good?"

His mind flitted toward alone time with Addy. He'd like that. Would love breathing in her clean soft scent, feeling the accidental brush of her hand and the anticipation of what could happen between them…if he would allow it. "Sounds perfect. I think Michael has something at his church tomorrow night, so it will only be Charlotte and Chris for the evening."

"See, one occupied. Two to go." She smiled as she smoothed the fabric over her thighs. He clearly made her uneasy, but not in a fearful way.

Something crackled between them and she held his gaze for a moment, licking those pink lips nervously.

Heat poured into his pelvis and he felt himself harden. Hell.

"Uh, sorry about being in such a state of undress. I was in the middle—"

"Don't give me any fodder for my imagination."

Her face pinkened and Lucas thought it adorable. A blush in a world where women asked men out on dates and carried their own condoms was to be savored. Addy was refreshing and he wanted to breathe her in.

"I don't know what to say to that other than…okay." She gave a nervous laugh.

Silence fell between them, prodding him to grab the kid and haul his cookies to the house next door. Well, not his cookies, but if he brought a few of Aunt Flora's chocolate chip cookies, he'd have some bribery at the ready.

"I'd better go. It's almost Charlotte's bedtime and I still have to fight with her to brush her teeth. Plus, Michael has to be at school early for tutoring, and wrestling Chris into bed is somewhere in the middle of all that."

"Use a timer for Charlotte and see if you can't make it a game."

"What?"

Addy stood and gave him another glimpse of thigh. *Thank you, dear Lord, for that small gift.*

"Brushing her teeth. I have a funny chicken timer you can use. Set it for a minute and make it a game."

"That will work?"

Addy shrugged. "Worked for my little sister. She hated brushing her teeth. Now she's in dental school."

Lucas followed Addy to the kitchen, trying to control the impulse to grab her, whirl her around and kiss the devil out of her. He craved her mouth. Wanted to touch her, hold her—

"Here," Addy said, plopping a chicken timer into his hand, totally destroying his visions of kissing her. Chicken timers had a way of curbing horniness.

Or maybe it was Aunt Flora and Charlotte sitting at a retro silver table happily discussing cookies dissolving the desire.

The kitchen was pleasantly old-fashioned with white tile counters and a black-and-white-patterned floor. Touches of red and yellow dotted the palate, giving a homey feel to the slightly industrial stainless steel appliances that were very much of this century. A comfortable place as evident by Charlotte's swinging legs and chocolate-smeared face.

"I don't wanna leave," Charlotte said.

Addy squatted, tucking the terry cloth against her behind. Damn, she was sexy as hell in that raggedy bathrobe.

Lucas had to turn away to contemplate something besides the curvy brunette with her sexy bare feet and delicate wrists. He needed to get a grip...or get laid.

"You must go home so you can come again tomorrow. Uncle Lucas said you can come and play."

Could he come play, too? He knew of a few games to play with Addy...but she'd have to take off that—

Curb it, bud.

Swallowing hard, he studied the badly painted rooster perched upon the cabinet and focused on withering the erection growing in his jeans.

Okay, Luke ol' boy, think about the dog piss. Or the overflowing garbage can you forgot to set out at the curb.

*Or the claws of the Wicked Cat of the West sinking into
your balls. Yeah. That works...*

"I'll come tomorrow. For a cookie," Charlotte said.

Lucas heard the chair scrape against the tile and turned.
Charlotte slid from the chair and wrapped her arms around
Addy's neck.

"Good girl," Addy murmured, catching his gaze and
giving him a little smile.

And this time it wasn't his manhood that stirred.

It was something closer to his heart.

Must be gas from the pizza.

Had to be. Except he hadn't had any yet.

Because Lucas Finlay was a man who didn't want to
feel little plinks near his ticker. Love or anything near it
wasn't something he wanted cluttering up the clear horizon in his life.

"Let's go home, Charlotte."

The little girl looked at him. "It's not your home, Uncle
Wucas."

Point taken.

ADDY PLACED the freesia between the Stargazer lilies and
squinted. Too much? Or just right?

"About to deliver the bouquets for the Richard wedding.
Are there any deliveries you need made downtown? I'm
headed that way," Shelia Guillory asked as she hefted the
long box containing the bridal bouquet and walked toward
the back door.

"Nope. Slow day for flowers."

"About time. We've been busier than a one-legged man
in a butt-kicking contest," her assistant and sometimes delivery person said with a chuff of relief. "Valentine's Day
nearly did me in."

"Busy is good." Addy murmured her standard reply.

"Says the owner," Shelia said using her droll voice. It

was one Addy was well acquainted with because Shelia lived for sarcasm, biting irony and fuzzy kittens. The latter she wasn't droll about, merely passionate.

"You like eating?"

Shelia indicated her lush figure. "What do you think?"

The topic Shelia had brought up weeks ago about her buying into the business sat fat between them, but Shelia had sworn she wouldn't leave if Addy didn't accept her offer. Addy had told her she'd think about it and get back to her later…but she knew she didn't want to sell part of the shop to Shelia. Fleur de Lis floral was her life, something she'd worked hard to buy from her aunt Flora after she'd retired. Addy had opened the business to a new market with her creative designs and couldn't imagine letting even a small part of Fleur de Lis go. Luckily, Shelia hadn't pushed nor said anything more about it.

Addy smiled. "I love the way you look, Shelia. Wish I had some of those dangerous curves. I'm a straight drive."

"Eh, you do all right. I see the way Tom looks at you when he comes in for deliveries. If there were ranch dressing lying around, he'd dip you in it before he devoured you."

"Wait, the UPS guy? Ranch dressing?"

"Yeah, Tom. And everything is good dipped in ranch dressing."

"That's trite, huh?"

"The dressing or Tom?"

"The cute UPS guy."

Shelia raised eyebrows she'd penciled to perfection. "He looks pretty damn good in those shorts if you ask me. But I'm too old for him."

"Bah." Addy tilted her head. "His knees are nice, now that you mention it."

Shelia's robust laugh filled the shop as she scooped up

the other boxes for the chapel. "You know what they say about a man with sexy knees, don't you?"

Addy made a face, bracing herself for the sexual innuendo sure to follow.

"Wears a lot of shorts."

Addy rolled her eyes and focused on the arrangement. "I'm outta here. You got that last delivery?"

"Yes, and I can't wait until Herbert is back. I hate knocking on strangers' doors."

"I know you do, baby. You going to the meeting tonight? I'll be there." Shelia paused, her dark eyes softening. Shelia wore a caftanlike shirt and jean stretch pants accessorized with three gold chains around her broad neck. Shelia called her look "ghetto funk" and Addy couldn't imagine her friend and employee without a little bling. But as loud, sarcastic and bossy as Shelia was, Addy knew her to be the kindest of women, as evidenced by the love for the kittens she rescued and helped place in good homes for the past few years.

But Addy wasn't the type to rescue things. Never felt compelled to pull someone from the fire…most of the time she tended her own fire, struggling to keep the flames of fear from consuming her. She wasn't selfish, merely protective and cautious. So why had she agreed to help Lucas?

She knew. Something in his tone, his manner, his damned dented pride pulled her toward him rather than away. And there *was* that weird attraction thing between them.

"Actually I'm having company tonight." Addy grinned, enjoying stringing her friend along.

Shelia's thinly drawn eyebrows settled into a straight line as she eyeballed her. "Oh?"

"Yes, a big hunk of a man."

"You watching *300* again?"

Addy laughed. "No, this one is real."

"Really?"

Addy swept the stem trimmings into the plastic-lined garbage bin. "No. Well, not really. You know my neighbors?"

"The ones with that cute tabby that has white paws?"

"Yeah, and a proliferation of kids, lawn ornaments and sticky fingers. Ben deployed to Afghanistan but was injured. Courtney went to him in Virginia—I'm assuming Walter Reed—and left the kids in the care of Ben's brother. Yesterday, the middle kid destroyed my new greenhouse. So—"

"The thing you just had built?" Shelia's eyebrows made an even tighter line of outrage. Leave it to Shelia to be pissed off for her.

"Yeah, they're coming over on Saturday to repair it, but tonight I'm sitting down with the hunky uncle to go over the kids' schedule and see if Flora and I can't help him out a little."

"*Really?* Baby, I like the way you say *hunky uncle,* and it's nice you're helping your neighbor. Just tread careful." Shelia's wide, always glossed lips curving into a smile. She wasn't one to push Addy to date, like some of her other friends, because she knew what it was like to have trust twisted and stomped upon. Shelia had married an abusive man, a man who had beaten her so severely she'd miscarried their child and had been forced to undergo an emergency hysterectomy. After years of enduring the abuse, she left him, only to have him stalk her and torture her for many more years. The abuse and terror had ended when Alfred ran his car into a tree. A bottle of Crown Royal and a wet New Orleans street saved Shelia from the gun the man had in his glove box…the same gun he'd already fired at her once before.

So, no, Addy's assistant didn't trust easily.

But she hadn't given up on Addy finding love. She

pushed gently, but she pushed. Just like Aunt Flora. And Addy's mother. And her sisters. And…well, Addy could go on and on with the people who wanted to see her with a man and a baby on her hip.

But Addy wouldn't be moved until she was ready. She'd learned long ago to listen to her instincts and step carefully where men were concerned. It took her a long time before she trusted. Which was why she couldn't figure out why there was a sort of auto-trust when it came to Lucas.

"He's hunky, but it's not a date."

"You've got weekend plans."

"We're rebuilding a greenhouse…with three kids."

"Who knows what can come of some innocent hammering, nailing, screwing…uh-huh." Shelia bobbed her head and performed the wave…which was hard to do holding a floral box.

"Go."

Shelia's laughter trailed behind her as she left. Addy locked the door behind her friend. Shelia had vacuumed the indoor-outdoor carpet and then locked the front door, but Addy scooted out of her back workstation and double-checked.

Like she did every day.

Then she located her purse, cell phone and pepper spray.

Like she did every day.

Fighting against fear wasn't for the fainthearted. Addy's nerves shredded every time she saw an unlocked window, a door left cracked or a shadow falling over her when she was alone.

Most people never thought about their personal safety, but ever since the day in November fifteen years ago, Addy had thought of little else.

Being stalked and attacked did that to a gal.

Of course, Addy knew she was likely safe in her corner of the world. Wednesday evenings in St. Denis Shop-

ping Center in Uptown New Orleans was busy enough
with shoppers, diners and looky-loos enjoying the early
spring weather. No dark alleys or lonely stretches inviting violence. None of that comforted her. After all, danger lurked on the sunniest of days, in what seemed to be
the safest of places.

Her safety routine complete, Addy's mind turned to last
night. Her thoughts had been haunted by Lucas and the
feelings he stirred in her. Hungry, sweet thoughts claimed
by the normal Addy, the woman who wanted to find love
and peace with someone who completed her, who made
her feel at home.

But the other Addy had pulled her mind from that hope-
ful thought to the letter she'd received from Angola State
Penitentiary. From some random inmate named Jim Mc-
Dade. Some decoy who likely owed Robbie Guidry a favor
and most likely had no clue why he'd been asked to send
the missive. Probably didn't even care.

Inside the envelope was a drawing—well done—of a
field of brown-eyed Susans. The cheerful yellow flowers
with the brown center seemed to dance in the picture, their
little faces turned toward the fading sun sinking against a
streaked horizon. It had been folded carefully, a crisp tri-
fold. Innocuous. Innocent.

But the image had caused Addy's hand to shake so violently she'd dropped the paper to the floor.

Brown-eyed Susans.

A favorite flower for a brown-eyed girl.

Her father had sung that song to her when he strummed
his guitar, winking at her, making her feel like the safest,
most-loved girl in the world. Brown-eyed Addy. Daddy's
girl.

And Robbie Guidry, the twenty-five-year-old man who
lived across the street from her family, three doors down

on the left, had listened, smiling like the rest of their neighbors as he carefully absorbed everything about her life.

So the drawing wasn't innocent.

It was a reminder.

An instrument of terror plied to take her to that sunny afternoon fifteen years ago—the day Addy learned what fear was, the day the darkness settled into her bones and refused to leave her. Before she went home she would drop off this latest drawing with Lieutenant Andre, who had worked her original case. The man kept a file of the "gifts" sent to her over the years, even though no physical evidence could tie the missives to Robbie Guidry. The nutso stalker wasn't stupid and never, never allowed what he sent to be traced to him.

Picking up the bouquet of spring flowers, Addy scooped up her purse, her car keys in hand, her thumb firmly on the fob's alarm, and turned out the lights. Her heartbeat sped up, but she was accustomed to that reaction. She inhaled, exhaled and became hypervigilant to the world around her as she pushed out the door that led to an open parking lot used by the employees of the shops. Open and in sight of a half dozen businesses. Safe. The rational part of her brain overrode the irrational.

Addy walked to her blue Volkswagen Bug, parked against the curb, noting her car needed a wash. Maybe she could get the kids next door to wash it. She could pay Michael and Chris fifteen or twenty bucks.

Three steps from her car, she froze.

Tucked beneath the windshield wiper was a single brown-eyed Susan.

The shattering of the glass vase made Addy jump and stumble backward. She hadn't realized she'd dropped the flower arrangement. Instinctively she pressed the alarm on her fob, and the chirping wails bounced around the near-empty lot.

Breathing hard, Addy rifled through her purse for her cell phone. The purse-size canister of pepper spray was already in her hand.

The owner of the monogramming shop stuck her head out the rear door with a questioning look, but Addy ignored her and instead focused on the innocent flower sitting bright against the blue of her car. Another reminder from a man who hated her, a sharp left hook of a message meant to do exactly what it had done—scare her.

Addy sat on the curb, clutching her cell phone, not bothering to stop the car alarm. The world tilted, and she concentrated on taking deep breaths, rather than the short panicked ones sounding in her ears.

Breathe, Addy.

Think, Addy.

Robbie Guidry still sat behind bars, but Addy sat in a safe area. No one was an immediate threat. She stood, and looked around the parking lot.

Safe.

Who could have left the flower on her car? Who, either knowingly or unknowingly, could be aiding such a horrible man? She doubted she would get answers, but she would report it…not that it did much good. Without proof Robbie Guidry instigated the gifts sent her way, she had no leg to stand on in prosecuting him for harassment. It had been almost six months since she'd received anything from him. She'd hoped her lack of response had done its job.

But two things within twenty-four hours?

She shivered despite the sun on her shoulders and turned off her alarm. The woman at the monogram shop closed her door and Addy took out her phone to photograph the flower, sending it immediately to Andre's email along with the date and time of the incident. She'd long since ceased bothering to call the NOPD with the threats—the responding officers made her feel stupid for wasting their time.

Addy tore the flower from beneath the wiper and tossed it onto the pavement where it would wither and be crushed beneath the wheels of the vehicles going in and out of the lot.

If only she could toss her fear the same way.

She looked at the cell phone she still clutched and, for some crazy reason, she wished she had Lucas Finlay's phone number.

CHAPTER FOUR

LUCAS LEARNED the hard way that taking three kids to Home Depot was living hell on earth. As soon as they waltzed under the orange sign, Charlotte had to go to the bathroom. At first Lucas panicked. How was he supposed to take a little girl to a public restroom? Thankfully he spied something called a "family bathroom" and sent Chris in with her. Of course, Michael disappeared before he could be nabbed.

After a full ten-minute wait while Charlotte did her business, Lucas met Chris's demand—a sports drink as payment for taking care of his sister's "business" in a place where "any of the hotties from my school could see." The kid drank three sips then asked Lucas to carry it. Michael remained MIA while Lucas juggled locating the right wood screws with pushing Charlotte in a race-car cart. Charlotte insisted he make engine noises like her father. Lucas found the whole thing embarrassing, but if it kept her from climbing out and playing on the lawn furniture display then he'd gladly rumble like a NASCAR engine.

He needed a drink…and it was only nine-thirty.

Not the ideal way to spend a Saturday morning, especially after Addy had canceled their Wednesday dinner, sending over Aunt Flora's gumbo without a word on why she couldn't meet. Flora had taken Chris to karate on Thursday, and outside of catching a glimpse of Addy wrapping her orchids in what appeared to be wet newspaper, he hadn't seen her.

So much for finding a haven in the chaos. He'd been in survival mode for the past five days and now only wanted to get the damn greenhouse repaired and then get on with keeping the plates spinning, balancing on sticks he knew little about.

At the truck, Michael finally appeared with earbuds in, frown on his face. "Where have you been?" Lucas asked, hefting the lumber into the back.

"I've been sitting on that bench." Michael pointed toward the front of the store.

"With the smokers?"

"I wasn't smoking."

Charlotte skipped past the truck and climbed onto the cart return. "Jeez, Chris, pull your sister down. I told you to watch her. Chris?"

"He's over there looking at lawn mowers." Michael flung an arm toward the side of the store.

"Chris!"

The ten-year-old froze, looked around to make sure no one had witnessed then jogged toward them.

"Why did you yell at me across the parking lot?"

"Because you are supposed to be watching your sister while I load this lumber, and I'm pretty sure there aren't any 'hotties' at Home Depot on a Saturday morning."

Chris shot him a withering look. "Girls are prisoners just like me. We get dragged everywhere by our parents… even to Bed Bath & Beyond. No one cares what a kid wants. Besides, I've already seen Josie Dupont."

"You're wasting your breath, plague. She's too hot for you," Michael muttered.

Chris rolled his eyes. "This from the biggest social piranha at St. Mark's."

"Shut the hell up." Michael reached for Chris, but Lucas caught his arm.

"Okay, I've had enough. Chris, fetch your sister and stop

calling your brother an Amazonian fish." Lucas heaved another load into the truck.

"What?" Chris asked.

"Look, stupid, if you're going to insult me, at least use the correct terminology. It's social *pariah*." Michael's voice dripped with venom…and a shade of hurt.

Lucas turned Chris toward where his sister dangled. "Go."

Chris sighed and did as bid.

Lucas faced Michael who had fixed his gaze on the cars whizzing down Veterans Boulevard. "What did he mean by that? You having trouble at school?"

His oldest nephew stiffened. "What's it to you?"

Lucas looked at Michael. Dark hair swooping low across a forehead that bore the hallmark of being thirteen. Acne also marred his cheeks and chin, but not so much that it took away from his handsomeness. He was thin and gawky, but so were many boys that age. He looked like the quintessential young teen but with Ben's smile and brown eyes. It was as if Lucas saw his own brother twenty-two years ago.

"Just trying to hel—" Lucas bit down on his tongue because that sounded lame even to him. "Never mind. But if you want to talk or if anything is going on that can't wait until your mother gets home, you know where I am."

"Yeah, I do. You're sleeping in my parents' bed. A virtual stranger who doesn't know me or anything about my life."

Lucas nodded. "True, but I'm here."

"Yes. You're here." Without another word, Michael started to unload the cart.

Such anger and frustration was to be expected when going through puberty. Lucas could remember how awkward the age was. One moment he wanted to hit his father, the next crawl into his lap and hide from the cruel world.

So Lucas would give Michael space. No doubt he dealt with something at school, but the boy didn't trust him enough to seek help or advice. Lucas would keep his eye on his nephew…in case he needed to intervene.

After loading the truck, he drove through a doughnut place and picked up a couple dozen to pacify the kids. Screw never rewarding kids with food. This was survival for Lucas and he'd "pick his battles" like the article in the parenting magazine on the back of the toilet had suggested. Ben and Courtney had no hunting, fishing or sports magazines lying around their house, but obviously liked knowing the ten best snacks for their toddler.

The entire way to Uptown, Michael was silent, noshing on doughnuts, earbuds in as Chris and Charlotte quietly worked on a sugar high Lucas knew he'd pay for later. Every time he glanced in his rearview mirror, he caught sight of the three-year-old, who looked like a commercial for everything cute. At one point she caught his eye and smiled, sugary doughnut gumming up her face, looking so like her mother he couldn't help but soften.

Which was strange since he'd spent years being angry at the woman who had ripped out his heart and left her high heels embedded within its depths.

He remembered the first time he'd seen Courtney. She'd been eleven years old, all legs and glorious blond hair, dangling from a branch of an old oak tree in the front yard of the house her parents had moved into days before. Lucas had been cutting through on his way to his friend Matt's house to shoot hoops when he'd seen her fall from the tree. He'd scrambled over some bushes, hopped the low fence and found her in a tangle, laughing like a loon. She'd looked up, grabbed the book that had also fallen and smiled. "This is exactly how these two met."

"Huh?"

She pointed to the cover of a book that had a Native

American woman entwined in a cowboy's arms. "These two, Small Dove and Colt. She fell out of a tree and he caught her. Crazy, huh?"

Lucas took several steps back wondering why a kid was reading a book that seemed to have sex in it. "I just came to see if you were okay."

She beamed at him. "You rescued me. You're my *siuleehu*. That means soul mate in Cherokee."

He hadn't known what to say to that. Or to her every time she boldly rode her bike to his house, stalking him with sunshine and silly smiles, all skinny-legged and browned by the sun. Then one day, she stopped following him. And six months later, he started following a new Courtney. One whose flat planes had developed into curvy wonderfulness, a girl who smelled like a meadow, wore lip gloss and tossed her golden hair over her shoulder. She'd been gorgeous, still funny but not so silly anymore.

For ten years they'd played tag with each other, giving each other their first kiss, accompanying each other to school dances, taking long walks down shady streets, sneaking in kisses, practicing moves on each other and cementing the idea Courtney had offered up that day years before—that they were soul mates.

To be together, build a life with a home, children and successful careers had been the plan...until Ben had come home from college with a hard body and a charming smile. While Lucas had been busy studying for law exams, his brother had been sending out resumes and schooling Courtney around town. Lucas had actually felt gratitude toward his brother for taking care of his soon-to-be fiancée while he studied. After all, they would be family within a few years.

But while he slaved over the intricacies of tax law, Ben and Courtney had been falling madly in love over lattes and late night movies.

Lucas hadn't had a clue until he'd shown Ben the carat-and-a-half square diamond he planned to surprise Courtney with and watched the blood drain from Ben's face. At that moment, he began to suspect the distance between him and Courtney had been because of Ben. A kernel of suspicion had bloomed, only to be confirmed days later when they had come to him, contrite, tears in their eyes as they explained how the impossible had happened, how they'd tried to fight against it, but hadn't been able to stop fate. They were in love…and expecting a baby.

Lucas glanced over at that baby, thirteen now, and disdainful of the man who had stayed away from him because it hurt too damn bad to be in the same room with the two people he'd once loved so well, but who had betrayed him. Made a fool of him.

"You missed the turn," Michael said.

"Sh—" Lucas bit off the curse word. He had to be careful with his language, but minding his tongue when he felt stressed to the limit was hard. "Easy fix. I'll take the next exit. Little sightseeing."

Except it wasn't great sightseeing on the detour—most of the houses were dilapidated and lonely. Like a neighborhood time forgot…or more like politicians forgot after Hurricane Katrina. Lucas's artist eye saw opportunity for some emotional photos. Maybe when the kids were in school, he'd come with his camera and play around with some shots. Wasn't stark landforms against a barren landscape, but the beauty peeking from beneath the cracks and weathering had a rare quality.

Fifteen minutes later, they were on State Street. Ten more and they were in Addy's driveway unloading bags containing the wood screws and other supplies. Michael, without being asked, hefted a roll of heavy-duty plastic from the bed of the truck and dropped it onto the grass next to the greenhouse.

"Careful," Lucas said. He wished he'd brought his worn work boots, but the newer, shinier cowboy boots would have to do. "We don't want to tear that plastic."

Michael's mouth flattened into a line. "I don't know why I have to help do this. I didn't tear it up."

"Because it's Saturday, the sun is out and a neighbor needs help."

No response came from the kid.

Lucas glanced into the backyard where Chris ignored his younger sister who balanced on her stomach on the swing dangling from the massive wooden play set. His finger swooped across the small screen he held, his concentration centered on the iWhateveritwas in his hand. "Chris, please keep an eye on your sister while we unload everything," Lucas called.

"Okay," the boy said, not looking up.

"That means put away that thing you're tapping on."

Grumbling, the boy slid the electronic device into his jacket pocket.

"I can watch Lottie." Michael crossed his arms.

"Chris isn't strong enough to unload this."

Michael made a sound that might have been a muttered "whatever" but Lucas chose to ignore it, picking his battle once again.

A small car pulled into the driveway and Lucas glanced at his watch—1:20.

A little late, but that could be expected of a business owner. Things came up and had to be addressed before closing for the day. Besides he hadn't been counting the minutes until Addy arrived.

Or at least that was what he told himself.

Lucas wasn't accustomed to keeping shopkeeper's hours. As a landscape photographer, he didn't have steady hours. Though his art brought in plenty of money, he never allowed the business to overshadow the passion, so often he worked in spurts, obsessively working days on end then taking weeks off before beginning the artistic cycle again. Usually after working with no rest and little food, his body demanded the restoration. Then at some point he had to meet with Chavez about the running of the ranch. But he liked his world, liked being able to embrace his passion whenever the mood struck him.

Addy parked in the spot sitting kitty-corner from the back door, her posturing proving she'd forgotten they were to reconstruct the greenhouse that day.

How could she have forgotten?

He tried to deny he'd thought about her over the past few days. Heck, that morning while walking Kermit and scooping cat litter, he'd vowed the attraction he'd experienced nights before had been a figment of his imagination.

But he knew he lied to himself. Addy was a cool drink of water after walking a desert…otherwise known as Home Depot with three kids.

Maybe the kids were driving him bonkers, but he suspected the desire to see Addy was more than craving an adult's company. If he had wanted that, he would have taken Shannon Something-or-other up on her coffee invitation after dropping Charlotte at St. George Day School yesterday morning. Of course, the married and bored Shannon had had more than caffeine on that agenda. Her expression had said, "Let's have a playdate."

But he didn't want to have a playdate with Shannon or any other "single" mother in Charlotte's preschool class. He wanted a workday with Addy.

"Hey," Addy said, as she climbed from the cute little Volkswagen that somehow looked too cartoonish for such a serious woman. "I'd forgotten we said we'd work on repairs today."

Disappointment gave him a little sock. He'd thought she was attracted to him several nights ago. Something had ignited between them…but maybe his lack of sleep from being kicked by Chris, who had climbed into bed with him that first night—probably forgetting his mother wasn't there—had his mind playing tricks on him.

Addy's shoulders were tight and something in her expression worried him. She looked so different from the way she'd looked before. Sure, she'd seemed guarded—a private woman with a side of mystery.

But today she looked spooked.

What could make a woman look so hunted?

ADDY PUSHED A few tendrils of hair from her eyes and studied the big man. She hadn't actually forgotten Lucas. She had, however, temporarily forgotten about the greenhouse and repairs. Messages from Robbie Guidry tended to do that. Rattled her so that she forgot to stop for eggs or pay her water bill on time. When she got reminders from the man who had stalked her, attacked her and nearly killed her, it put her off balance for several days. So she'd canceled on Wednesday night and stayed inside. Even taking the letter by Lieutenant Andre's office stirred anxiety and it took time for the reality that Robbie was behind bars and she had control of her life to permeate her brain.

But how much longer would he remain behind bars? She inhaled and exhaled, knowing she had no control over when Robbie Guidry would be released from prison.

Lucas approached her as if she were made of glass. She willed her thoughts to settle.

"You okay?"

"Of course, I am. Busy morning at the shop." She hated lying but didn't want to talk about her life. About how she'd been a victim. That was her past.

"No, I don't think so. Something's wrong."

"Not really. Just have a lot on my mind."

"What do you have on your mind?" His question wasn't

soft. He pried into her thoughts and she didn't want him there.

"Nothing you need to worry about. Let me change and then we'll get started." Addy pulled her purse out of the car, pausing to slide the cell phone out of a side pocket. She'd texted her father to let him know she'd talked with Lieutenant Andre yesterday, but he hadn't replied. But then again he didn't check text messages often—they seemed beyond him. She didn't want to call because then her mother would know something was up, and Addy hated when her mother worried. Maybe she would drive out to New Orleans East to corner her father and share what Andre had told her.

Addy's father was her go-to man. When she'd first received an anonymous drawing of a single brown-eyed Susan, she'd reported it, but with no evidence the drawing came from Guidry, there was nothing to be done. Still, Don Toussant kept track of the evidence and haunted the parole hearings making sure Guidry didn't get out until he paid his entire twenty-five-year sentence for assault with a deadly weapon, attempted rape and attempted murder. They were a team...a team who couldn't do much but wait.

Addy dragged her gaze to Lucas, whose dark eyes weighed and measured her.

"Something's off with you, Addy. You seem...scared. Did something happen—"

She pushed by him. "My life is none of your concern. I don't like people shoving their nose in my business. I said I was okay, so leave it."

Lucas raised his eyebrows. "Wow. Defensive."

She yanked her keys from her purse as she turned toward him. The anger pressed beneath the fear slipped out. "Maybe I *am* defensive, but I didn't invite you to examine me. I didn't even invite you to fix my greenhouse. You're the one who insisted. I said I would help you with the kids because I'm trying to be a good neighbor to Ben and Courtney. That's all I offered and there is no reason for you to think you can dig into my past, looking for a reason I don't want to talk about my day with a stranger."

Lucas didn't say anything. Merely studied her more intently.

Something about the way he looked at her made her want to apologize. He'd tried to help and she'd been a bitch. Then again, guys trying to help, not taking no for an answer and buddying up to a woman who hadn't opened the door either literally or figuratively—all were indicators of a man being potentially harmful. Even so, she knew in her bones, Lucas wasn't harmful to her. At least not in that way.

"Look, I know you're trying to be nice, but I'm good. Okay? I'll change, we'll fix the greenhouse and then we'll talk about how I can help with the kids."

Lucas nodded. "I didn't mean to pry. Guess I thought I was being neighborly."

"But you're not my neighbor."

Something flashed in his eyes and she knew she'd pissed him off a little with that one. "Good point."

Then he walked away from her. Just like she wanted.

CHAPTER FIVE

ADDY'S WORDS HAD surprisingly hurt him. They shouldn't have. He didn't know her beyond a couple of hours spent together. But somehow meeting her defensiveness when he'd tried to be helpful, tried to nurture a stable relationship with the only rational nearby adult, made him feel less than what he was.

He was honorable, damn it. And no one had ever called him nosy.

Aunt Flora bumbled out the back door and gathered the children, directing Michael and Chris to unload pots out of Addy's car and giving Charlotte a spoon for worm digging. The three-year-old made a strange face, but allowed the older woman to lead her to the compost pile in the corner of the yard.

For a moment, Lucas fought feeling inferior. What the hell was wrong with him anyway? He was a man who rarely cared what others thought of him, a man who rarely cared if he pleased others.

But he knew one thing—Addy's past had made her fearful.

The phone attached to his belt rang, and Lucas glanced at the screen. He was waiting on his manager at the Manhattan gallery to call about some pieces for a renovation. But it wasn't Gerald. It was Courtney.

Dread knotted in his stomach.

Was she calling merely to check on the kids or had his brother worsened?

"Hey," he said, as Addy reemerged from the house still wearing the dark dress and casting an apologetic glance at him. Something moved within him at that look in her eyes. Something weak. He turned away.

"Hey," Courtney said, her voice weary…almost defeated. "Thought I better call and check on the kids while I had a chance. They're changing Ben's bedding and I'm in the waiting room."

"The kids are fine."

"Are they? I've been worried. I left without saying goodbye."

"Wasn't ideal." He'd arrived early Monday morning. Courtney had taken a cab to the airport minutes later, leaving him with sleeping kids and a page of instructions that didn't cover jack.

"No, it wasn't but it was the best way."

"Not sure about that, but you can smooth things over a bit if you tell the kids about Ben's condition. It would be easier—"

"On you?" Her voice also held anger. "All I asked was for you to be their caretaker. That's it. I'm truly grateful, but I can't tell them their father may be dying over the phone, Luke."

He hadn't been called Luke in many years and the sound of his name on her lips confused him. On one hand it swept him back to a time when he'd loved hearing her say his name, and on the other hand, it caused the anger of betrayal to eat away at any pleasure left in hearing her voice. "And I complied, Courtney, but I'm a stranger. Not knowing what's going on makes it harder on them. Not me. Them."

Michael came around the corner of the house followed by Flora. He caught sight of Lucas on his phone and some kind of internal homing signal went off and the boy started walking toward where Lucas had slipped into the shadows.

"Hey, is that my mom?" Michael asked.

Courtney dropped a curse word. "Tell him no. Please, I'm not ready to talk to him about Ben."

Lucas pulled the phone from his ear and turned to head off Michael. "This is my call and you're being rude interrupting it."

Michael's chest expanded in outrage. "If that's my mother, I have a right to talk to her. It's her, isn't it? Let me have the phone."

Lucas shook his head and pointed toward where Chris held a stack of planters. Addy appeared, her forehead crinkled in concern. Chris watched his brother, mouth slightly open, anticipation of the confrontation in his eyes. Charlotte happily dug in the compost heap looking for worms, which she promptly dumped into a can sitting beside her. The girl didn't seem to know there was anything else in the world except fat, squiggly earthworms that probably both fascinated and repelled her.

"Go help Addy's aunt with the wheelbarrow." When Michael didn't budge, Lucas added, "Now."

"This is bullshit. If that's my mom, I want to talk to her. She won't text me or call me. *Her*. Not *you*."

Courtney said with a sigh, "Give him the phone."

Lucas didn't want to concede to Michael. He'd read in one of the parenting magazines consistency was the solution to many behavior problems in children of all ages. He wanted to stand firm on telling Michael no, but he wasn't the kid's parent. Courtney was, and maybe she'd finally tell the boy about his father's condition.

"Mom, what's going on? Why did you leave us with him?" Michael said into the receiver. He plodded toward the low screen of bushes lining Addy's home.

Lucas watched as Michael nodded, made a defiant face then shook his head. Several heated words were exchanged before the boy's shoulders sank in defeat.

Lucas knew Courtney hadn't told him about Ben's injury and complications from the surgery. If anything, Michael swelled even more with resentment as he handed Lucas the phone and stalked away.

"Courtney?"

"What?" She was crying.

"Why won't you at least tell Michael about Ben? He's old enough to understand."

"Shut up, Luke. You don't understand how vulnerable Michael is. He and his dad are close. If I tell him Ben might die, it will be real. So shut up, feed them, make sure they brush their teeth, but don't tell them anything about their father. You hear me?"

"Avoiding reality doesn't help Michael."

"Ben is going to get better. I have faith. This can't happen to me again, and I'm not going to put them through what I went through with Mom and Dad. You understand? Just tell them I'm with their father and everything is okay."

"I know what you went through, Courtney. I was there. Remember?"

"Of course I remember. It was excruciating seeing my mother the way she was, seeing my daddy die. Those memories are in my head, Luke. I can't get them out, and I don't want my children to have that same hopelessness."

"But what if you hadn't been there? What if you'd been kept in the dark? It's not pleasant to be lied to."

He hadn't intended to throw the extra meaning in, but it was there nevertheless. It would always be between them. Lucas had been in the dark, Courtney and Ben had kept their affair in the shadows, skulking around, betraying him.

No, it did not feel good being lied to.

Courtney's crying grew louder. "Ben's going to get better. I know it, Luke. He's got to. Just give me a little more time, that's all. Time will fix it. The doctors said the antibiotic might be working. His blood work looks better."

"Is he still on the ventilator?"

A choked sob was his only answer.

"Okay, okay. I won't say anything to the kids, but consider it…for Michael's sake. He's hurting with the unknown and somehow that seems worse than knowing the truth about his father."

"The truth is not always best, Luke. Don't you remember how much it can hurt?"

Oh, he remembered. The truth about Ben and Courtney had crushed him, not so much with what he lost in a future with Courtney, but in the loss of faith in his brother, in a girl he'd grown up loving. Yeah, the truth hurt, but it was a hell of a lot better than pretense. "Just think about it."

"I will. How's my girl?"

"Right now she's digging for worms."

"Worms?" The sob ended with a choke of laughter. "Well, I guess there are worse things. Why's she digging for worms?"

"Well, Chris had a little accident a few days ago. Don't worry, he's fine."

"An accident? How?"

"He forgot your neighbor had a greenhouse built in her yard and took the dirt bike for a spin while—"

"He's not supposed to ride the bike without adult supervision."

Lucas started to mutter *No shit* but bit down on the smart-assed comment. "I went inside to wipe Charlotte."

"Charlotte knows how to wipe herself."

He allowed silence to speak for itself.

"She likes attention." Courtney sighed. "I wish I could have given you a handbook instead of a page."

"Me, too."

"I know it's not easy, but I knew if any single guy could swoop in and take care of three kids, it was you. You've always been so competent, never messing up in life. Really, Luke, I don't know what I would have done. With your parents in Europe, I—"

"I make plenty of mistakes, Courtney, and I don't know shit from shinola about raising kids, but we're all making do."

"What about Flora and Addy? And the greenhouse?"

"We're working together on the repairs now. Chris's dirt bike is in the garage and I've hidden the key. We're good."

"Okay, apologize to Addy for me and keep the receipts for the repairs. I'll make sure you're reimbursed."

Lucas said goodbye and hung up, not feeling at all comfortable with continuing to lie to his brother's children. But he wasn't their parent. He was merely their caretaker, not involved enough in their lives to offer an opinion. He opposed what Courtney was doing, but he understood.

When Courtney had been in high school, her parents had been shot in a convenience store theft. Neither had died in the actual robbery, but they'd been gravely injured. Courtney's father died from his wounds the day after the robbery, but her mother had held on for days, undergoing several surgeries before succumbing. Courtney had lived at the hospital, Lucas with her, bringing her food and comforting her as best an eighteen-year-old kid could. The loss had devastated the sunny Courtney, turning her into a shell of what she'd been, maybe even driving the wedge between them that allowed for the betrayal.

Lucas walked to where Michael sat tapping on his phone. "Guess we better start demoing the damaged parts of the greenhouse. I'll grab Chris. Can you dig the shears out of the bag so we can cut away the torn plastic?"

Michael looked up. "So you're finally going to make him do something?"

The kid's tone was feral.

Courtney's secrecy had created an angry monster of a

boy…one Lucas had to deal with. And he tired of dealing. "Why don't you watch your tone, Michael?"

"Why don't you leave?"

"I wish I could." Lucas shoved his curled fist into his front pocket and walked away. Toward the front of the house. Away from Michael. Away from Chris and Charlotte and the dotty old lady trilling encouraging words to the kids. Away from Addy and her prickly demeanor.

He needed air. And space. And peace. And quiet.

And maybe a shot of bourbon.

ADDY SET THE ORCHIDS she'd gathered on the newspaper. She wrapped the roots in wet newspaper and tucked them beneath the blooming azalea bushes framing the back stoop. Thankfully, Cal, the guy who made gorgeous pottery along with inexpensive clay pots, had plenty of selection. She liked terra-cotta for the orchids.

For the past few minutes, she'd tried to forget about Lucas and the guilt she felt about being overly defensive. She hadn't meant to be so forceful, but the fear inside her over the stupid wildflower tucked beneath her windshield wiper had hooked into her gut and seeped into her bones. When fear came knocking, it was hard to not open the door. So she'd lashed out at Lucas, which was ironic considering her first thought at discovering the "gift" was to call Lucas. Something about the man with broad shoulders and a hard jaw struck something within her, something that told her he could help her.

Out of the corner of her eye, she caught Lucas pocketing his phone and approaching Michael who sat sullenly beside the lumber. A few words were exchanged then Lucas walked away, moving to the Finlay house. Toward his truck. Something in the slant of his shoulders had her dumping the orchids and following him.

Surely he wasn't going to leave?

True, dealing with kids was tough, but he'd made a commitment, right?

He heard the crunching of the gravel beneath her feet as she followed him, but he didn't slow or turn his head. She nearly breathed a sigh of relief when he passed his truck and hooked around the front of the house. Lucas climbed the porch steps and sank into a rocking chair that needed a new coat of paint.

Hesitating on the steps, she looked at him, not knowing what to say.

Lucas studied the floating clouds beyond her head. "This was a mistake. I've got to get out of here. I'm not the right person to take care of these kids."

Addy started to deliver platitudes but snapped her mouth closed. "Maybe not, but right now you're all they have."

"I need clean air and a clear landscape sitting outside my door. I can't breathe here."

The longing in his voice touched her. He felt trapped by the world he now occupied. She knew a little about being confined to a smaller world.

A few minutes ticked by as the sounds of the neighborhood waned and an even smaller world was formed on the porch. A line of black ants squiggled across the top step. A spider clung to a web in the camellia bush, and the rocking chair creaked with the slight motion Lucas gave it. Small, closed in. Intimate in a way she hadn't experienced the other night. Raw emotion pulsed and she knew it was seldom Lucas admitted defeat, admitted any weakness.

He didn't look at her, at where she stood near the line of overgrown bushes that had needed pruning last fall. Addy knew Lucas was mentally picking up the scattered bits of his emotions and trying to tuck them into an airtight box he kept in his soul.

Like recognized like.

Something inside her stirred, then stilled. Certainty of what she needed to say settled in her gut.

"I'm sorry about the way I acted earlier. Something happened on Wednesday that shook me up, and I allowed a remnant of that emotion to spill over into today."

He waved away her apology. "No problem. You were right. I don't have any business prying into your life. We're not friends, not really anything to each other. You're a nice person trying to help me. Bottom line."

The casual dismissal pricked her. She didn't want to be nothing to him, and that surprised her all over again. "I'd like to think we are friends."

His gaze swept to hers. "I suppose we are. In a way."

"Then you should understand something about me. Not even Courtney or any of my other neighbors know this, but somehow, I think you need to know who I am."

She saw the muscles in his neck move as he swallowed, as his eyes softened. She didn't understand the need to tell him about Robbie, about the fear that sometimes ate at her. Just knew it would make things better.

"When I was senior in high school, a neighbor, a man I thought I knew, held a knife to my throat and tried to rape me."

Lucas's hands tightened on the rocker. "What?"

Acid ate at her stomach and her hands trembled. She tucked them behind her and met Lucas's gaze. "I was stupid, a good girl, a quintessential overachiever with a pretty face and a bright future, but I had this need inside me, a little part of myself who wanted to rebel. Down the street lived this older guy. He was in his mid-twenties, cute in a boyish way, rode a Harley and sometimes hung out at my dad's garage. He flirted with me, I flirted back and then one night I snuck out my bedroom window and climbed on his Harley with him."

Lucas's eyes narrowed. "You seem so levelheaded. I can't imagine you sneaking out with an older guy."

"Of course not. I've changed. But we all have some wildness inside us. I just chose to be wild with the totally wrong guy."

Silence sat for a moment.

"Eventually, being a naughty girl got old. I didn't really like him as much as I liked the feeling of being disobedient, of having some say-so in my own life. Eventually, I stopped opening that window. But Robbie wouldn't accept I wasn't into him. I tried to tell him I had prom coming up and college. I told him we had no future together. And it got ugly."

"What did he do?" His voice was soft as the day, like sunlight falling on the emerging green of spring.

"At first he said ugly things. Then he showed up at my high school and watched me with my friends. He slashed my tires, wrote me violent letters and called my cell phone and hung up several times a day. I didn't tell my parents because I knew they'd be so disappointed…and that I'd be grounded for life." She offered him a wry smile.

He didn't smile back.

"Then one day I came home from cheerleading practice. No one was around, and I didn't think twice about taking a shower. That's when he broke in. Luckily my father had left something at the house—a flyer he needed to print for the Rotary Club. Funny how I remember exactly what was on that flyer—seems silly to remember—but I can't forget anything about that day. The soap I'd used in the shower, the way my uniform lay crumpled on the bathroom floor, the way that blade felt at my throat. I ran into the kitchen and grabbed a knife—I'd seen too many B movies and thought I could protect myself—but Robbie took it from me. The knife cut me here." She rolled up her right sleeve to reveal the pink line that ran from midforearm to her bicep. It had faded, but the memories had not. Then she pulled down the collar of her shirt to show him the scar on her shoulder. "And here."

"Addy." Lucas leaned forward, hands clasping the broad wood arms of the chair. He looked as if he might get up, as if he needed to do something.

She tugged her sleeve over the reminder of what Guidry had given her—not just the wound, but fear itself. "My dad saved me. Hit Robbie with the baseball bat my brother left in the corner of the kitchen. My mother must have told Mike a million times to put it up. Thank goodness my brother had selective hearing. All this happened long ago, but it changed me. I'm cautious, and I fight being afraid. I go to group therapy and I function quite well, but the fear is always there. It's part of who I am."

"Jesus."

"I don't know why I'm telling you this."

His face softened. "Don't you?"

"Watching you struggle, feeling trapped and very much, I don't know, alone? Guess I wanted you to understand why I'm private. Why I'm not a girl who can open herself to just any guy."

Lucas watched her, his hands still clasping the chair. Strong hands with hair sprinkled on his knuckles, hair that caught the sunlight. Lucas's reaction was odd, almost as if he took it personally. "I assumed something had happened to you by the wariness you displayed, but not…that."

She pressed her lips together, embarrassment creeping in. Or maybe not embarrassment so much as vulnerability. She hated feeling an eternal victim.

He ran a hand through his dark hair, making it stick up and softening his normally hard look. "So is this guy in prison?"

She nodded, anxiety once again filling her at the thought of Robbie Guidry and the scare tactics he employed from behind bars. Seemed ironic he could still bait her from that locked cell.

An overwhelming feeling crept over her. She shouldn't have said anything to Lucas, should have marched her hind end up those stairs, changed into work clothes and rebuilt the stupid greenhouse with him. "Good fences make good neighbors"…even if he wasn't her true neighbor.

After all, what did she care if he thought her a rude bitch? He might pack up and leave the next day, so why bother giving him a glimpse into her world?

"Good. I hope he rots."

Addy swallowed the inclination to give him more details. She'd said enough. The less she gave Lucas, the more she held of herself. "So now you know why I get a little rattled when strangers burst into my world. I try not to allow the past to affect me, but I accept sometimes it does."

He nodded, his gaze dipping. She knew his thoughts. She dressed to fade into the background. Her long black dress wasn't particularly flattering and the comfy Mary Janes weren't anything close to sexy. She'd pulled her dark hair into a low ponytail and tasteful silver hoops dangled from her ears. Her only cosmetics consisted of a good moisturizer, under eye concealer and cherry ChapStick. Plain and unassuming. Designed to be overlooked.

So different from that seventeen-year-old girl with her teased hair, red lips and tight clothing. The Chalmette High School Homecoming Queen 1997 had faded into a shadow of her former self.

But Addy embraced that change. She owned her neurosis about standing out, drawing attention to herself. Many would say she limited herself, but she valued her comfort over being some symbol. So she didn't buy miniskirts, highlight her hair or get tipsy at bars, dancing in killer high heels in front of strangers. Once she'd done so, and she couldn't make her brain accept that what had happened with the man down the street years ago wouldn't happen again.

"I'm sorry he hurt you," Lucas said.

"Yeah, I am, too. But our past doesn't have to dictate our future. It's hard to remember that, but sometimes you have to leave the past behind so you can live."

Lucas held silent, a lone figure once again contemplating the horizon, the puffy clouds of an early-March afternoon. "The past defines us, becomes part of us. We can't change that."

"No, we can't. We have to accept what happened and move on, trying to be the best we can and still be comfortable within our parameters. That's what I do."

"Thank you for sharing your past with me."

"I wanted you to see it wasn't you. It's me."

"That's a breakup line."

Addy smiled. "Yeah, but it stands true in this situation and I needed you to know my prickliness is part of my protection."

"I see that now."

"Good, so can we move forward with repairing the greenhouse?"

He nodded, but the troubled expression on his face didn't ease. His escaping to the porch wasn't only because she'd lashed out at his questions. The kids and the situation he found himself in had pecked at his confidence, had sent him scurrying for space.

Addy propped a Mary Jane on the step and gave him a smile. "Ready to double-team some kids?"

Lucas shook his head. "I'm not cut out for this."

"Who is? Taking care of kids is like herding cats—you come away with a few scratches and hair on your clothes, but it's not impossible."

Lucas walked down the steps and Addy didn't back away. He wore a blue work shirt that stretched across his broad chest, sleeves rolled up, biceps bulging against the crinkled fabric. One pearl button in the middle of his shirt was chipped and she longed to touch it, if only so she could step closer to him and learn his smell.

She'd never been attracted to someone like Lucas before…someone so raw and masculine, so big and Marlboro Man–like.

Stopping in front of her, he reached out and tucked a strand of hair behind her ear. It was both tender and intimate. She lifted her gaze to his. Those dark eyes were soft and a flicker of hunger ignited within.

"You're such a rare beauty, Addy Toussant."

Addy had been called beautiful before, but it had been a very long time. Something warm and liquid swirled within her, twisting together, making her body soften, crave his touch.

"Thank you," she whispered as his hand lingered at her jaw.

A tug on her skirt jarred her from the wonderfulness of the moment.

A pair of blue-green eyes attached to a child with a hand thrust between her legs and a desperate look on her face blinked at her. "I gotta go tee-tee bad."

Lucas lifted his chocolate eyes heavenward. "Dear God, grant me the serenity to—"

"Take Charlotte to the bathroom?" Addy finished for him with a laugh. She longed to step back into that sensual moment with Lucas, but was relieved she didn't have to. Something about the unexplained intensity with him scared her. "I can do it."

"If you'll take her inside to the restroom, I'll round Chris and Michael up."

"Be consistent with both those boys," she said, jogging up the steps, tugging Charlotte with her.

"And you know this how?"

"I don't."

"Right," he said, heading toward the rear of the house.

"Hey, Addy. You wike my Uncle Wucas?"

"He's all right."

Charlotte twitched the I-gotta-go dance on the end of Addy's arm like a fish on the end of a line. "He's scary."

"No, he's a man just like your daddy."

"Michael says he's a giant like in my book."

"You don't believe everything Michael says, do you?" Addy pushed open the door and entered the family room. It was a mess, with socks on the floor, pillows off the couch and the television projecting cartoons into an empty room.

"Him's the oldest," Charlotte said with conviction, tugging Addy toward an open door in the hallway. "Michael says he knows why Uncle Wucas hates us...because Mommy was his first."

Mommy was his first...what?

Addy frowned. Did Courtney and Lucas have a past? That could explain why she'd never seen the man around the Finlay house. Sounded a bit soap-opera-ish but wasn't reality stranger than fiction?

"Your uncle doesn't hate you, Charlotte." Addy helped the little girl slide down the elastic-waist jeans and sit on the potty. "He just isn't used to children."

"Then why did Mommy leave us with him?"

That was a good question...and Addy didn't have an answer.

CHAPTER SIX

THE SUN FELT HOT on Lucas's shoulders, making sweat trickle down his back. He shrugged out of the long-sleeved shirt he'd donned that morning and worked in his T-shirt. He'd found a table saw in Ben's workshop and had created a makeshift station to cut the boards, which he handed to a sullen Michael. Chris and Charlotte helped Addy and Aunt Flora replant the orchids in the new pots. The three-year-old seemed to be wearing more soil than was in the pots and was happy digging around in the yard and checking on her worm farm.

"I think this ought to do it," Lucas said to Michael, handing off the last board. "I bought some premade shelving we'll put together after we get these boards in place. The instructions are in the box if you want to get started."

"I don't. I need to shower. I'm going over to Jase's house." Michael set the board on his shoulder and walked to the greenhouse, setting it carefully against a small Japanese maple.

"Who's Jase? And how come I don't know anything about this?"

"He's a friend and it's his birthday. Mom should have told you I had this planned." Michael squared his shoulders, ready to fight Lucas on the point.

"Fine. I'll drop you off so I can talk to his parents."

Michael made a face. "Whatever."

"That's your favorite word, huh?" Lucas pointed toward

the box. "If you'll open that and lay out the parts according to the directions, I'll put it together after I get back."

The boy sighed. "Whatever."

"What's the problem, Michael?"

The boy turned, his expression fierce. "What do you think?"

Lucas said nothing for a minute—merely studied the lanky boy with the crappy attitude. "I never sent you twenty bucks in a birthday card?"

The boy sneered. "Yeah, because that would have made this all better. Me getting a card from you."

Okay, humor wasn't going to work on the iceman.

Lucas cast a glance to where Addy lugged a bag of soil to the patio, liking the way she looked in her faded jeans. Her aunt helped Chris to gently tuck the roots of a plant into the terra-cotta pot. "You don't understand the big picture, kid. There's a lot of choppy water under a bridge that burned years ago. I had my reasons for staying away from New Orleans."

Michael set the box at his feet. "I'm sure those reasons are comforting to Grammy and Grampy when you're not here at Christmas…or for anything else. I'm sure it's totally cool to ignore the family you have."

A punch to the stomach would have had the same effect. Lucas tried not to react to the guilt. His mother had always said she understood—he didn't have to come for Thanksgiving, for his father's heart catheterization, for their fiftieth wedding anniversary. So Lucas had stayed away…selfishly. "That's not what I was doing."

Michael glared at him before giving him a familiar sardonic Ben smile. "Okay. Sure."

Something broke in Lucas and anger flooded him. How dare this brat accuse him of being the bad guy? Did he know what his mother and father had done? Did he know the hurt that had fishhooked his heart and festered there for years? This wasn't just a pride thing—he'd hurt, damn it.

The kid didn't know shit about him.

But Michael obviously didn't care because he continued. "Chris, Lottie and I had nothing to do with whatever happened between you and Mom and Dad, so I don't give a flip. I'm going to help Addy. I'll send Chris over to fix *his* mistake."

Lucas's fist curled, so he gave his idle hand work, stooping and picking up the shelves. He didn't know how to handle the smart-ass Michael. He'd given the kid a pass on his rudeness for the first couple of days because Courtney had left without telling them goodbye and told them diddly-poop about their father, but his patience flagged.

But part of him knew Michael was correct. The rift between Lucas and Ben wasn't the kids' fault. Lucas shouldn't have spent the past thirteen years pretending the children didn't exist. He'd been at a loss for how to reach out to them when he still simmered with anger at their parents.

Or maybe it hadn't been anger as much as wounded pride. Like a sucking wound, the injury done to him had chafed and poisoned him against children who had nothing to do with what had happened all those years ago.

"Michael said I have to help you." Chris rubbed at the smears of soil on his forehead. "What you want me to do?"

"Just hold the boards in place while I use the drill."

"Can I use the drill?"

"We'll see."

Chris pulled on the small gloves Lucas had bought him at the home improvement store. "That means no. Every kid knows that."

"Fine. I'll show you how to use it and let you try."

"Really? 'Cause Dad never lets me around power tools

and stuff." Chris grinned and reached for the orange drill sitting on the board resting on two sawhorses.

Lucas beat him to it. "Probably with good reason. First, let's take a break, okay?"

Lucas had caught sight of Aunt Flora emerging from the house balancing a tray with lemonade and what looked to be a plate of cookies. Chris caught sight of food and all thought of drills flew out of his mind. He disappeared faster than beer at Oktoberfest.

Lucas watched as the kids surrounded Aunt Flora. Addy unwound from her seated position and stretched. She'd changed into an old T-shirt with a Mardi Gras 10K run on the front and a pair of jeans that fit her nicely even with the hole in the knee. She pointed her worn tennis shoes toward him and he got a warm feeling that had nothing to do with the sun bearing down.

"You're making good progress. We'll finish today," she said as she wiped perspiration from her forehead. "Whew, it's warm for a change."

"That's New Orleans for you."

For a moment they watched Aunt Flora tease the children while refilling their cups. He liked the way Addy felt beside him. Small enough to fit under his arm, but she had a presence that made her feel so solid. Maybe it was because he now knew what she'd faced, how brave she had to be every day.

"Hey, walk with me a minute," he said, motioning her toward Ben and Courtney's house.

She followed. They slipped between the large camellia bushes and walked onto the covered patio scattered with toys and outdoor furniture that needed a good scrubbing. "What's up?"

"I've been thinking about what you told me earlier, and I want you to know you can trust me."

Addy made a face. "That's what you wanted to tell me? You could have done that back there."

"You seem private, and those kids are nosy. Well, Chris is."

"He is a little nosy. When I told him I'd pay him for washing my car tomorrow, he asked how much money I had in my checking account."

"Dear Lord. He's—"

"Precocious?" she said, lifting her eyebrows in an endearing way. Heck, everything she did was endearing.

"I was going to say cheeky." Lucas watched the smile playing about her lips and thought about how much he wanted to taste her. He wanted to touch her smooth skin, maybe trace her bottom lip with his thumb as he cradled her head in his hands. He wanted to soak her in, feel her against him, make love in the cool grass out back in the moonlight. This woman stroked the poetry in his soul. She made him feel lighter, younger and really horny.

But Addy's confession changed things. Oh, he still wanted her, but he wasn't going to do anything about it. Obviously she needed time to trust a man, and that was something he didn't have. No need to pursue something he couldn't finish.

"Is that all you wanted?" she asked.

Hell, no. He wanted more and maybe that was why he'd pulled her away from the others.

"Yeah. I needed a break." *Or just wanted you to myself.*

"You definitely need a break." Addy smiled and her gaze lowered to his sweaty chest. In those pretty brown eyes he thought he saw interest and it struck something in him. *Maybe...*

No. Even if she were interested, it wasn't a good idea to start anything. Even flirtation felt as if it could get out of hand quickly. Better to maintain friendship.

"Yeah, I'm seeing single mothers in a whole new light. How do they manage showers or going to the bathroom? Charlotte walked in on me in the shower last night. It was traumatizing."

Something devilish danced in Addy's eyes. "Oh, really?"

"Yeah, I screamed like a little girl."

She gave a snort of laughter. "That's not what I expected you to say."

He moved a little closer, not able to resist a smidgeon of flirting. "Oh, yeah. What did you think I'd scare her with?"

"What a flirt you are, Lucas Finlay. Very unexpected from a man who looks like he could tangle with the devil and come out without a single burn."

Lucas tucked a strand of hair behind her ear. Addy inhaled and suddenly the air crackled with tension. Desire flared like diesel fuel poured on a small flicker of fire.

Screw keeping his distance. He had to kiss her. Had to.

"I have my moments of weakness, times where I show the gooey center beneath the…the…" He inched closer.

"Leather?"

"Leather?" He made a face.

"Uh, steel?"

"I like that better. Man of steel," he murmured, studying her pink lips. He loved her full bottom lip and the way it contrasted against the slight bow of the top one. Not balanced, but definitely kissable. Her skin glowed, not pale and pasty like so many women, but with warmth and vitality. Her warm brown eyes sparked beneath brows that reminded him of that chick in that sappy love movie from the '70s his mom was crazy about. Sad movie with Ryan O'Neal. Ali somebody. Yeah, Addy looked like that actress. Serene, calm with that same jaunty smile.

Addy studied him, not seeming alarmed as he moved closer, but not necessarily welcoming. "So beneath the machismo you're a nerdy, soft-spoken beta boy?"

"Maybe I am. Maybe you need to find out for your—"

"Uncle Lucas!" The voice cried from their right.

"Of course," he whispered at the shrieking voice of reason interrupting a weak moment, a moment he really, really wanted to have with Addy despite his admonitions to himself seconds earlier.

Lucas stepped back and gave Addy a regretful smile.

"Hey," Chris shouted, loping toward them with cookie crumbs stuck to his chin. "Michael pushed me down and made me break one of the pots. I didn't do nothing but ask him about—"

"Shut up already," Michael said, climbing the three steps to the back porch, studying them with some extra-perceptive knowledge that he'd interrupted something intense.

"You two boys are at it again, huh?" Lucas asked.

"He's overdramatizing," Michael said. Quick as a cat, he disappeared, the click of the back door the only sound on the porch besides Chris hitting the toe of his sneaker against the step.

"He's a butt head. And mean. I wish mom would come home. He'd be grounded for acting like that," Chris said, turning his gaze upon them.

"Won't be too long, Chris."

The boy grew quiet, still for once. "Is my dad okay, Uncle Lucas? I know he got hurt in Afghanistan, but Mom won't tell us nothing. She said he was coming home, but he didn't."

Lucas didn't want to lie, nor did he want to let on how badly Ben fared. The actual IED explosion had happened three weeks ago and Ben had done well with the surgeries. But no one had seen the vicious infection winging in from left field. "Your mother is with your father, and that's the most important thing."

Chris nodded and resumed kicking the step.

Addy rubbed her hands on her jeans before heading toward her house. "I better get back. We'll talk about the kids' schedules later—I think Aunt Flora's got something in the oven, so we'll do dinner tonight for y'all. And I should be able to help this upcoming week. Picking up or dropping off. Whatever you need."

Whatever he needed, but not what he wanted.

But that was for the best. He truly believed it.

"Well, Charlotte has her school Spring Fling tomorrow. Someone's gotta take her to that," Michael said, reappearing with a backpack slung over his shoulder and a football. He tossed the ball into the air, flicking it toward his brother who snatched it out of the air with one hand. Impressive.

"I don't want to go to Spring Fling. It's lame," Chris said, tossing the ball to Michael who missed it. It clattered onto the glass table knocking over a cup of red juice. "Oops."

Lucas frowned, wondering how much more of the whining, bickering and just plain-out difficulty he could handle. A departing Addy noticed. "Hey, why not let the boys stay here with me? I have some things I need some strong men to help with. I'll pay, too."

Chris's eyes grew big. "More money than just washing the car?"

"Sure, after you wash the car, you can help me rake out the flower beds."

Michael nodded. "I can do that."

"Me, too," Chris shouted.

"Guess you're Charlotte's date to the Spring Fling," Addy said, smiling as she sauntered away like a sexy vixen. Okay, so she didn't exactly saunter, but the sexy part was dead on. There was something deliciously sexy about her subtleness.

But he'd think about kissing Addy later.

Maybe that evening over whatever Flora served for dinner.

Or the next day.

Or…

Addy hurried toward him. "Charlotte just threw up."

LUCAS CLIMBED OUT and jogged around to the passenger side of the extended cab truck. Opening the rear door, he found Charlotte already out of her car seat. Rather than giving him a mistrustful look, she held out her arms and allowed him to lift her and place her on the ground in the school's parking lot.

"Do you wike snoballs, Uncle Wucas? 'Cause Sister Tewesa said they was gonna have 'em here."

He looked at her and nodded. "I loved snoballs when I was little. Your daddy and I once had a contest to see who could eat theirs the fastest. Gave us both horrible headaches. But since your tummy was upset, maybe we'll skip snoballs today."

"But I want one."

"We'll see." He surveyed the scene for a moment, wondering how one proceeded at a school fair.

"Come on," his niece said, tugging the tail of his shirt toward the field where the Preschool Spring Fling had been set up. The brightly colored tents and milling laughing families made him feel a bit lonely…and sad for Charlotte that she had to experience the event with an uncle she didn't know rather than her parents.

Ben.

If he survived, he'd face many obstacles with the loss of his leg. Ben had always taken great pride in being active—running in marathons, training for triathlons and hiking in the Ozarks—or so Lucas had gleaned from their mother. But even navigating a small school fair would be a challenge until Ben adjusted to a prosthetic.

That thought made Lucas's sadness over his brother more pronounced.

There was a gulf between them wide enough to make Lucas doubt it could ever be bridged. It still hurt to think about how sick his brother was, about how unsettled he'd feel if Ben died without either of them extending the olive branch.

If Ben continued to worsen, Lucas might never have a chance to find forgiveness. If he recovered, there was no guarantee it would matter. Lucas wasn't ready to forgive Ben or Courtney. Or maybe he was. He couldn't sift through his feelings fast enough. Things felt too cluttered in his life at the moment. It was enough to survive until the next day.

"Hey, Charlotte's uncle," a voice called.

He turned to find the blonde who had offered to buy him a coffee that first morning he'd attempted carpool and found himself on the receiving end of nun fury. It wasn't Shannon, the bored housewife—she had red hair—but he couldn't remember a name for this one. "Yeah?"

"Just saying hello. I'm Tara Lindsay, Sheldon's mom. Remember?"

He nodded, but didn't want to encourage chitchat with the woman who wore tottering heels and carried a big purse he'd be willing to bet cost more than his monthly truck payment. Yet he didn't want to be a total ass. He held out a hand. "Lucas, and, of course, I remember. So I'm guessing I'm supposed to, what, let Charlotte play all the games? Never been to a Spring Fling with a three-year-old."

"I'm about to be four," Charlotte piped up.

"I bet you haven't," Tara drawled, ignoring Charlotte, her voice flirtatious, her gaze likely illegal in three states. He squelched the inclination to wriggle in jeans that felt too tight under her perusal.

"I wanna get my face painted," Charlotte said, pointing toward a tent where teenage girls swiped paintbrushes against the cheeks of preschoolers. Maybe he should have brought Michael after all. The boy might find someone who made him smile. It could be a miracle at St. George's.

"The tickets are over there." Tara pointed a long manicured finger toward a small red booth. "I'll walk with you. My ex is taking Sheldon around and I'm waiting for father-and-son time to wind down. I'm sure Sam will be out of here as quickly as possible."

Lucas didn't have anything to say to that very personal revelation.

"Maybe seeing me with tall, dark and cowboy will rub salt in a wound or something," she continued, snaking a hand through the crook of his arm and steering him toward the ticket booth.

He took Charlotte's hand. "Let's get some tickets, then I'll take you to the face-painting tent, okay?"

Charlotte didn't pull away, though her blue eyes did dart to Tara tottering beside him. For some reason, he gathered Charlotte didn't like the woman latching onto them. Maybe his niece was coming around to having him in her life. She'd even let him hold her after she'd gotten sick yesterday afternoon. Seemed that many cookies and two glasses of milk was a bit too much for a child her age.

"I want Addy," Charlotte said as they stopped in the short line. "Why wouldn't she come?"

"She wanted to finish planting the flowers. Flowers have to be put in soil or they'll die."

"And you gotta water 'em." Charlotte nodded in a serious manner. "I'm gonna feed my worms when I get home. Addy said she'd find out what they wike to eat."

"Oh, my gosh, she's just so cute," Tara trilled, refusing to let go of his arm even though they'd arrived at their destination. He really wanted her to let go. Looked weird to have her cuddled up to him when he barely knew her.

Lucas pulled his arm from Tara's so he could remove his wallet from his back pocket. Ten seconds later and twenty dollars lighter, he had a strip of blue tickets and his arm back.

"I wanna a butterfly with sparkles," Charlotte said, dropping his hand and running toward the tents.

Lucas sighed and followed. He wasn't exactly thrilled to spend his Sunday afternoon at the Spring Fling for Charlotte's preschool, especially when the Spurs were playing on TV. And with Tara tagging along touching him and cooing over Charlotte, he really longed for the recliner, a remote and some Michelob time. Not that he'd likely get it in that particular household.

"So how is everything going? You seem to be doing okay with the kids…outside of the carpool incident."

"It's going okay. Taking care of three children isn't for the weakhearted."

"No shit." Tara shoved her hands into the back pockets of her jewel-encrusted jeans, making her breasts tighten against the small animal-print T-shirt she wore. He noticed only because she had a pretty nice rack, and even though he wasn't interested in Tara, he wasn't dead.

To his right, he spied a concession stand offering beer and wine. Silver lining.

"If you'll keep an eye on Charlotte, I'll buy you a drink."

"Now you're talking, cowboy." Tara smiled and he noted

she had a lot of teeth. Straight white expensive-looking teeth.

"Beer or wine?"

"White wine," Tara said, keeping her breasts front and center while rubbing together her glossy lips and sliding her gaze down his body.

Made him feel like a deer in a rifle sight but he'd been in more uncomfortable situations. There had once been a woman named Delilah in a New Orleans nightclub who wasn't exactly Delilah beneath her skirt. Beer goggles and overzealous hormones had given him that vivid memory, so, yeah, he'd been way more uncomfortable in being pursued by the, ahem, opposite sex.

Lucas checked on Charlotte, who balanced on a stool under the ministrations of a teenage girl and went to grab a beer and white wine. A few minutes later he returned and Tara wasn't alone. A slender man with a receding hairline and a glowering expression stood beside her, holding the hand of a boy whose face was smeared with cotton candy.

"Way to be obvious, Tara. You're forty, for Christ's sake, and you're dressed like a whore at your son's school fair," the man said.

"Shut up," Tara hissed. "I've seen what you've been dating. You're lucky you're not in jail."

"Ah, someone's jealous…not to mention past her shelf date." A mean smile played about his lips. "And suddenly my afternoon is more enjoyable."

Lucas wasn't interested in Tara, but he could tell her ex-husband was a jerk. Something cruel lurked in the man's eyes.

"Here you go, babe," Lucas said, curving an arm around Tara's waist. She stiffened before relaxing against him. The gratitude in her eyes in that moment was enough to outweigh the difficulty he knew he'd have convincing her he was not into her.

"Thank you, Lucas," Tara said, smiling at him.

"You ready to move to the duck pond? Charlotte's finished," Lucas said, nodding toward the ex-husband. The man's self-satisfied smile vanished, and he stepped back quickly, releasing the boy's hand. Tara picked up her son's hand, rubbing some of the candy gunk off his chin.

"I'm Sam Lindsay," the man said, holding out a hand.

Lucas took it and gave him a punishing handshake. "Lucas Finlay."

Sam resisted wincing, but Lucas knew he'd gotten the message. Nothing Lucas hated worse than a bully. Sam had pretentious prick written across his forehead. In fact it was almost a blinking marquee.

"Okay, let's go," Tara said, tossing her ex a smile that said "eat shit and die."

Charlotte ran to Lucas, skidding to a stop in front of him. Preening, she put her little hands on either cheek and asked, "What am I, Uncle Wucas?"

"A sparkling butterfly!" he proclaimed.

"Yes!" Charlotte bounced up and down…and nearly hit the dirt.

"Let's go with Sheldon to the duck pond," Lucas said to his niece.

Charlotte looked over at the boy who wore paper bunny ears and hadn't stopped chowing down on his cotton candy and said, "This kid wooks weird."

Sheldon dropped his candy and slapped Charlotte right in the face. "You're a dumb booger head!"

Then both kids started crying.

And that was how Lucas ended up not having to worry about Tara clinging to his arm. He bought Charlotte extra tickets and let her eat two snoballs as a thank-you.

CHAPTER SEVEN

ADDY TRIED TO CONCENTRATE on the computer screen where the accounting program was doing its best to defeat her, but it was no use. She wasn't in the mood to reconcile her bank statement…but then again who was ever in the mood to reconcile her bank statement?

Her mind kept tripping back to the afternoon she'd spent yesterday with Lucas and the kids next door. How they'd eased her fear over Robbie's "gifts," allowing her to place her energy in something much more worthwhile. Charlotte had glowed from the attention, Chris had laughed and entertained and even Michael had smiled…once. Just that afternoon, the work she'd done with the boys while Lucas took Charlotte to her school fair had filled her with an odd contentment.

And then there was Lucas.

Lucas, a man of the broad-shoulder, rugged type.

Lucas, a man she'd never have chosen in a million years.

Something about him reminded her of the sheriff in the naughty erotic romance she started reading the night before. She'd set aside the book with the sheikh and helpless English virgin for the Western knowing she shouldn't play with fire. But something about those wranglers and boots, about the hard line of his mouth she wanted to feel against hers had her opening a new book about a cowboy.

How would Uncle Lucas look tied up to her bed? Reclining against ruffled pillows and lavender quilt? She could see his muscles, long and sinewy, beneath golden skin. She wanted to touch his hair, trial her fingers along his chest, down to—

What was she doing fantasizing about a man who looked at her like a box of doughnuts that once he'd taken his fill of would mosey back to Texas?

But then again maybe Lucas was exactly what she needed in her life at that moment. A big—what had Flora called him?—tall drink of water. Yes, maybe she needed a drink from that well.

Or maybe she should stop trying to make her naughty books real.

Addy pushed back in her rolling chair, just as Aunt Flora passed carrying her bedding down the hall.

"Hey, Auntie dearest, what are you doing with those sheets?" she called, rising and trailing down the hall behind her aunt.

"Washing 'em," her aunt answered.

"Why? Did you spill something? You washed them a few days ago," Addy said, propping her hands against the doorjamb of the laundry room. Aunt Flora set the bundle of sheets in the wicker laundry basket and turned to Addy. "I didn't wash my sheets a few days ago. A few days ago was Wednesday or Thursday. I never do laundry midweek. I'm too busy."

Alzheimer's reared its ugly head. Her aunt had done laundry midweek after spilling an entire cup of tea on her bed. "I thought you had—" Addy snapped her mouth closed.

"Wait, did I?" Aunt Flora looked blankly at the sheets. "I could have sworn…"

"Well, it won't hurt to wash them again. You'll be back on schedule." Addy offered with a wry smile.

"Don't baby me," Aunt Flora snapped, slamming the lid on the washer. "I'm not an idiot. I forgot. No use trying to spin it for me."

Addy stood there silently, not knowing how to respond to the fact her aunt's mind deteriorated more and more each week. The medicine had helped for a while, but over the past few months, her aunt had worsened. They needed to talk to the doctor about trying something different. "I'm not—"

"Yes, you are. I'm not a child. Don't treat me that way."

What could she say? She tried hard not to treat her aunt any different from before she'd been diagnosed, but she couldn't ignore the signs…nor the fact her aunt's forgetfulness made Addy feel vulnerable, feel as if she needed to check behind her. "I'm sorry."

Addy turned to go.

"Wait," her aunt said. "I shouldn't have gotten angry. I'm not mad at you. I'm mad at myself. At this stupid disease that's making me feel so…so weak."

Turning, Addy stepped toward her aunt and took the laundry basket from her. She grabbed her aunt's hands and forced her to look at her. "You're not weak. You're the same person you've always been. I shouldn't have said anything. Doesn't hurt if you wash your sheets again. In fact, I wish you'd wash mine, too. I haven't had time."

"Please," Aunt Flora muttered.

"Don't overthink this, okay?"

Aunt Flora's eyes reflected agony. "Why is this happening to me? All these years I've waited to turn the shop over to you, waited until I could do all those things on my bucket list—skydiving, driving out West to see the Grand Canyon, taking painting classes. I'd put all those things off until I retired, and now look at me. My mind is being eaten away and I can't even remember when I washed my damn sheets last. Or where they moved the dry cleaners I use. Or what the Harringtons named that ugly dog of theirs."

"Freddy Bear."

"Huh?"

"Their pug's name is Freddy Bear. Ridiculous, huh?"

"Yes. Very ridiculous."

Addy squeezed her aunt's hands. "Look. It sucks. No way around it. But you are still you. You're not weaker or any less of a person. So suck it up, buttercup."

Her aunt smiled at the adage she'd often muttered to Addy over the years. "I've never considered myself a buttercup kind of a gal."

"No?"

"I'm a Bird of Paradise."

"I can see that," Addy said, giving her a quick hug before turning back toward the office and ledger awaiting her. "And wash my sheets while you're at it…or come help me with balancing the books."

"I don't remember how to do the books. You're on your own, kiddo," Aunt Flora cracked, obviously finding the sense of humor she'd misplaced during her moment of frustration.

"Yeah, yeah," Addy said, trudging down the hall. She wished she hadn't said anything to her aunt about the stupid laundry. Should have let her pass without calling out and reminding her of the curse her aunt now bore.

Aunt Flora had always been Addy's soul mate. Growing up in a large family in a too-small house in New Orleans East, Addy found Aunt Flora's rambling, quiet Uptown house a refuge. Anytime her mother came into the city to run errands, Addy begged to go to Aunt Flora's. Her mother's oldest sister had never married, electing to stay in the family house on Orchard Street, and run the floral shop she'd bought from the gentleman she'd trained under for many years, and who Addy always suspected her aunt had been in love with.

Addy had craved puttering in the garden with her aunt, learning the names of flowers, watching with interest as seeds sprouted, buds opened and pretty stems mixed with other pretty stems to become fabulous arrangements for which people paid money. Paired with butter cookies and sweet tea, gardening with Aunt Flora became Addy's sanctuary. Seemed only natural she follow in her mentor's footsteps.

After Addy had been attacked, she hadn't wanted to go away to college. She turned down the scholarships offered to her from schools out of state and elected to go to the University of New Orleans, commuting from her home. After years of therapy and after Aunt Flora had hired her to work part-time, Addy had moved into the city with Aunt Flora. Up until a year ago when Aunt Flora had officially retired and sold Fleur de Lis to Addy, their arrangement had been ideal.

Not that it still wasn't good.

But Addy worried about the ensuing years. Her mother refused to accept her older sister was slipping and that Alzheimer's increasingly progressed despite the prescriptive medicines, therapies and herbal supplements they researched. So Addy had no help in determining the future for the aunt she loved so.

As she stepped back into her office, a flash of color outside caught her eye. Pulling back the curtain, she saw Michael and Chris rolling around near her newly restored greenhouse beating the hell out of each other. Lucas was nowhere to be seen, and Michael decidedly had the upper hand…and he wasn't going easy on his younger brother.

"Oh, my Lord," Addy muttered before looking around for her gardening clogs. She found them beneath the desk, quickly slid them on and took off for the back door.

Seconds later she shouted at the boys, "Hey, cut it out!"

But either they didn't hear or didn't care they'd been discovered. They didn't stop grunting, punching and rolling around before popping up and tackling each other again.

Chris's lip bled and Michael's shirt was torn at the collar.

"Stop it," she yelled again, reaching toward the nearest boy and catching only air. "Chris. Michael. Stop now!"

She heard the heavy pounding of feet coming her way and knew it was Lucas.

The large man grabbed each kid by the upper arm, ripping them apart before giving them a shake. "What in the hell are you two doing?"

"I'm kicking his ass," Michael shouted, jabbing a finger toward his younger brother, who started crying.

"No, you're not," Lucas said, letting each of the boys go but keeping himself firmly between them.

"It's not my fault," Chris said, choking as he said it. The kid needed to go into acting. He could summon tears at the drop of a hat and his expressions…he had the wounded victim down pat. "He attacked me and I didn't do nothing."

"Yeah. Sure you didn't," Michael said, straightening the shirt bunched up around his skinny torso. Hair flopped into his eyes and a bruise formed on his cheekbone.

"Hush, Chris," Lucas said before looking over at her. "Thanks for coming to break this up."

"I didn't do much good. They're nearly as big as me."

She should go back home, but she didn't. Though she'd never before interfered in the lives of her neighbors, she felt she was needed here. Strike that. She knew she was needed here.

"Okay, Michael, what's going on?"

The thirteen-year-old gave his uncle a withering look, turned then stomped toward the front of the house, effectively telling them all to go to hell without even opening his mouth.

Lucas's mouth almost dropped open, but he locked it into a tight line, his eyes betraying disbelief over the lack of respect. He started toward the front of the house.

"Lucas," Addy said.

He turned his head.

"Let me go after Michael. You take care of Chris."

"Hell, no, I've have enough of his disrespect. He's acted like a turd since the moment I arrived and I'm done with him."

"Look, let me try first. Okay?"

The man stood for a moment, shoulders tense, before finally taking a deep breath and nodding. "Okay."

Addy walked around to the front of the house and found Michael sitting on the porch steps. Obviously, the shady location was the go-to spot for calming down. Except Michael didn't look calm. With his forearms propped on his knees and his jaw firmly set against the emotion he obviously battled, he looked anything but calm. He looked more like a kid about to lose it.

"Hey," she said, hoping he wouldn't bolt…or turn his anger on her.

"Hey," he said, staring out into the last fingers of sunlight stretching toward the darkening sky.

"You okay?"

"Sure. Fine. In fact, you can call me dandy."

Addy climbed the steps and sat down beside him. "I know you don't know me well, but is there some way I can help?"

"Help what? Help me undo the shit storm Chris just caused on Instagram? Or maybe you can call my mom and tell her to stop treating me like a baby? Or maybe you can heal my father, bring him home? Turn back time so everything is like it was months ago?"

"You know about your father?"

Michael looked at her. "Do I look totally stupid? You think I don't know this has something to do with his getting injured overseas? I heard my mom talk to my dad weeks ago. She wanted to fly into Germany and he wouldn't let her. He wanted her to stay with us. So what happened to make her leave?"

"I don't know."

He shook his head. "My mother's bullshit gag order on everyone means it's pretty bad. She left us with an uncle we've never met before. I get As in math so I'm pretty sure I can add all that up."

Addy could add, too, though minutes before reconciling her bank statement might have proved differently. "Lucas hasn't told you anything."

"Par for the course."

"I'm sorry."

He didn't say anything, and Addy knew she wasn't helping any. She had no clue why Courtney hadn't told her kids anything about their father's condition. Seemed wrong not to reveal the situation…to leave them with an estranged relation.

"Why did she leave us with *him?*" Michael's voice trembled with unshed tears. "We don't even know him. We've only seen his picture at Grammy's house."

"I don't know, but I do know he's trying to do his best."

"Yeah, well, it sucks. I want my mom to come home. We can deal with everything if she'll come home and tell us what's going on."

"Sometimes people do things we don't understand. It's not fair."

Michael snorted. "That's an understatement."

"I've spent my life accepting I can't control everything. It's hard to swallow being powerless, but once you accept it, it's easier to face the world around you. You can't control things with your father…even if you knew what was going on with him. You also can't control the fact your mother left you with your uncle. So what can you control?"

For a moment, Michael was silent. If she could see into his mind, she guessed she'd see the cogwheels turning, pulling in her questions and churning them to make sense of it.

"Nothing," he said with a shrug. "I guess I can't control anything. Dumb-ass Chris just posted on my Instagram a pic of me looking at that orchid and put something stupid about how I wanna give flowers to Hannah Leachman. Now everyone is going to think I like her."

"Oh." Addy paused thinking about that one. "Do you like her?"

Michael shrugged. "She's kind of cool, but now I'm going to get ragged about it, and I didn't even post it. Chris did it to make himself look funny."

"All brothers and sisters cause us trouble. Trust me. I have four of them. My older sister still tries to set me up with guys. The last one she set me up with lived with his mother and played in Boogle tournaments. He also walked around with a parrot on his shoulder all the time."

A semismile twitched at the boy's lips. "Yeah, sometimes it sucks having siblings. Lottie spilled hot chocolate on my math homework last week and Chris used up all my body spray. He got sent home because no one in the class could breathe and one kid was allergic and swelled up."

Addy smiled. "Yours are definitely interesting."

"You like Lucas, huh?"

"What?"

"My uncle. I can see you like him."

Addy blinked. Well, she hadn't thought it was that obvious. "I suppose so. I have to give him credit for showing up. He's a bachelor, you know? Not use to kids and animals and noise. This is a shock to his system, yet he's still here. He stepped up when no one else did."

"Why, though? He and my dad have been mad at each other for a long time."

"Not sure. Maybe because your mother asked him. Maybe he needed a reason to connect with you and your family. I don't know, because I don't know the background between Lucas and your parents. But that doesn't change the fact he's here."

"Yeah, he's here, telling me how to live and think. He doesn't have the right to tell me anything."

"Have you talked to him about the way you feel? Not just complained?"

He didn't respond.

"Because Lucas can't change something he doesn't know about."

Michael slid his gaze to her and in those chocolate depths she saw a tiny crack, a sort of "maybe she's not totally stupid" fissure in his wall of mistrust. It was about as much of a thank-you as she'd get from the kid.

Addy rose and stretched. "Why don't we go inside and get a bag of frozen veggies for your cheek? You might turn a shiner out of this one."

"'Kay. In a minute."

Addy left him, sending up a silent prayer of thanks for the words she'd managed. All those hours of sitting in therapy group noshing on doughnuts and sipping weak coffee had paid off. Of course, she hadn't fixed anything between Michael and his uncle, but she had given the kid something to chew on. An old proverb her aunt Flora used to say sprang to mind—"Wish in one hand and spit in the other and see which one fills up the fastest."

Addy had held plenty of spit in life and she knew more than most that complaining about how life deals you a shitty hand doesn't take the spit away.

CHAPTER EIGHT

Monday morning came with unsigned school papers and a glass of spilled milk, but otherwise, Lucas made it. After navigating New Orleans traffic and hitting two different schools for drop-off, he needed something stronger than PJ's coffee but he took a large cup anyhow. Then he would head back to the blissfully silent house. He was nearly giddy with the thought of being alone, even if it was in a house that needed three maids to give it a good scrub down.

He'd never been good at dealing with clutter. His ranch house back in Texas was remarkably well organized. In Lucas's world every item had its place. In his brother's world, Lucas had concluded every item had to be handy, which meant things were rarely in their places.

It drove Lucas crazy.

But he had only a few more days to live within chaos.

Courtney had said she'd make other arrangements for the kids, and then he'd be free to head back to West Texas and his open spaces. He thought about Addy and something that felt like regret pinged within his chest. But that was likely for the best. Wasn't like he had a future here in New Orleans. Everything was messy here and he no longer fit in this world of crooked streets, tropical plants and ornate architecture. He needed clean lines and open space. He took a deep breath, angled his truck toward Orchard Street just as his cell phone trilled.

His sister-in-law.

"Morning," he said.

"Hey," she said, sounding even more tired than she had the day before. "How are the kids?"

"Still alive."

"Don't joke about that."

"Sorry. They're fine. Just dropped Charlotte by preschool and I managed to not offend any clergy this morning."

"God, I don't know what I would have done if you hadn't said yes."

He hooked a U-turn and made a right onto Claiborne and said, "You keep saying that, but you would have figured something out. You're resourceful and tough."

"I don't feel that way. I feel defeated, like God is punishing me for all my past mistakes."

He couldn't respond to that comment so silence pulsed between them for a good ten seconds or so. Finally he asked the inevitable. "So, how is Ben?"

"Not good. His body stopped responding to the antibiotics. New drugs today and he'll undergo some tests so they'll know more about what course to try next. I don't know why he's doing so poorly—everything went well during the surgeries in Germany. He was fine, so I don't understand this." She sighed and he could hear her swallowing. "Luke, his body is starting to shut down."

He couldn't respond to that, either. Something grabbed him by the throat, sunk its teeth in him.

"I'm so scared."

"I know you are, but have faith. Ben's a fighter."

"I hope so," she said, tears in her voice choking her. Again regret or sympathy or some emotion he hadn't felt in a while moved in his chest. "I hate putting you out like this."

"No worries," he said, immediately wondering why he'd said that. Hadn't he wanted to escape since he drove past that New Orleans city limit sign a week ago? "I'm able to work from your house and I have a manager for the ranch so there's no rush."

"I'm getting you out and back to your life."

"Look, I can't say I'm good at this, but it's not a war zone. You don't have to medevac me out. I have help."

"Who?"

"Flora made gumbo for us and Addy paid the boys to wash her car yesterday while I took Charlotte to the Spring Fling. By the way, I let Charlotte have two snoballs and we were up until ten o'clock. Lesson learned."

He could hear Courtney's smile. "Thank you for taking her to the fling. She'd been looking forward to it."

"You're welcome." And he meant it. He'd actually enjoyed seeing the joy Charlotte took in playing "Fishin' with Barney" and walking on the cakewalk. Strange, but true.

"Hey, Luke, why did you say yes?"

He pulled into the driveway and killed the engine. "To going to the fling or coming here?"

"Watching the kids. I never expected you to accept."

He hadn't expected to say yes either, but the desperation in her voice paired with the sharp jab of learning his brother was on the brink of death urged him to agree to the madcap adventure. He still wasn't sure why he'd agreed... why he'd even answered a call from a woman he'd spent years hating. "I don't know."

"You don't know?"

"No."

"Well, I know you've got a ranch and a business that need you. My cousin DeeAnn should get there by Thursday afternoon. Took me a while to get in touch with her and agree to a fee, but she—"

"Agree to a fee?"

"Well, yeah. Dee's in cosmetology school on the West

Bank and will have to miss a few days of work in order to watch them."

He didn't like the sound of Dee. What kind of person charged a relative for helping out? "How old is she?"

"Twenty-eight."

"Is she married?"

Courtney sighed. "Why the tenth degree? She's available, of age and can come on Thursday. I'm sure the kids will be fine."

"I'm not."

"She's responsible," Courtney said, but she didn't sound convinced. That made him nervous.

"If you say so. They're your children."

"So I'll call later tonight to talk to the kids."

"Fine."

Lucas hung up, pulled into the driveway and climbed from his truck, wondering if he believed her when she said this DeeAnn character was trustworthy.

But he didn't have a say-so. Besides there was that getting back to normalcy thing he desired. He wanted to get back to Texas. Needed to brush his horse Cisco and eat chili and steaks and food that didn't have crawfish in it. Time to rewind and go back to being Lucas, photographer and part-time rancher. Not Lucas, poor substitute for Mr. Mom.

He hadn't seen Courtney in almost fourteen years, but the family pictures scattered throughout the house proved she was still pretty even with the smile lines around her eyes and rounder body. He'd once imagined himself standing next to her in those photographs…not his brother.

Lucas shook the sourness from his head.

No sense in crying over spilled love.

"Morning."

He turned to find Addy walking toward her car. He could barely see her through the waxy leaves of the camellia bushes, but he saw she carried coffee and wore a navy jumper-dress thing.

"Hey," he called back ducking between two bushes and coming out in her driveway. "On your way to work?"

She held up her travel mug in a mock toast. "Have to pay the bills."

"I'm about to pull out my laptop myself. Hey, I talked to Courtney and she's having her cousin come stay with the kids on Thursday. This DeeAnn woman will probably be more competent than I am, so..."

Something in Addy's face fell a little and hope fluttered in his gut...even if he told himself it shouldn't. "Oh, so you're leaving that soon?"

"I guess."

"You'll be happy to get back to Texas, back to normal," she said.

"I guess."

Addy licked her lips and he saw her grab hold of her emotions. "Well, then." She turned toward her car before spinning back around, a determined smile on her face. "By the way, Aunt Flora has bridge club this afternoon. They're making martinis so don't call the cops if it gets rowdy."

Addy paused, waiting for him to respond, as if at a loss...as if she didn't want him to go so soon.

"Hell, I'm so bored I might join them. Do they drink gin?"

"Oh, heavens, maybe I should stay home and supervise."

"Maybe you should," he said, giving her a wink. "I'll let you wear the lamp shade." Flirting again—something he rarely did. But something about her sadness made him want to flip her. He was someone different with Addy, that was for sure.

"I look terrible in hats. Just promise me you won't strip

for them. The last guy who took off his clothes at one of their bridge games needed therapy afterward."

Lucas laughed. Which hardly ever happened. "Ah, Addy girl, you do make me smile."

She stilled, her brown eyes growing sad. "Another time, another place, huh?"

"Yeah. It's too bad I'm leaving." He wanted to walk to her and take her in his arms. He wanted to kiss her, let her feel how much he wanted her. And, God help him, he wanted to stay a little bit longer.

"'Bye," she said, pulling the car door open. She stood a moment as if she wanted to say something more before giving her head a little shake and sliding into the car. Her sleek brown hair fell into a silk curtain as she ducked inside, and Lucas immediately wondered how it would feel tangled in his hand. He would tug her head back gently so he could taste her throat, slide his mouth against the pulse there, taste her, inhale her.

Addy lifted her hand to him in a small wave as she backed her VW out. A regretful smile curved those pink lips, lips he longed to cover with his, and for a moment he almost called out to her to stay.

Maybe invite her to spend the morning in bed with him.

But that was insanity.

He'd already decided not to venture into those waters. Wouldn't be fair to a woman who'd endured as much as Addy had…but that didn't change the fact he wanted her with a strange hunger he'd never felt before.

The car paused and the window lowered. Addy tilted her head toward him. "I meant to tell you I'd take Charlotte to her gymnastics class at five o'clock so you can take Chris to karate."

"Thanks. If you can drop her, I'll pick her up. Michael is riding home with the lacrosse instructor who lives a few streets over. His is the last class."

"Sure," Addy said, before pressing the accelerator and shooting out of the drive.

Lucas lowered his hand. This was it—all there was between him and Addy. Business only.

Shit.

He climbed the back steps and pulled out the key to the back door, not quite so happy to be alone in the rambling house. Somehow the thought of Addy being out of his reach was depressing.

ADDY PLACED a tiger lily in the bouquet before plucking it out again. The bold yellow distracted from the soft pink of the orchids. She tossed it down with a sigh.

"Ain't nothing satisfying you today." Shelia tsked, shaking her head, making her large hoop earrings dance. "That man got you wound up?"

"What man?"

Shelia looked at her with flat black eyes. "The one you had plans with on Saturday."

"Oh, well, dinner never happened. Charlotte threw up in the irises and ended any thoughts of more than work with the uncle. Probably for the best, though. He's leaving in a few days."

"Mmm," was all her friend said.

"He's not anything to me. I've been helping out with the kids. Being neighborly is all."

"That's too bad. I could tell you liked him, and usually it takes you a while to warm up to a man especially after the flower on your windshield."

True on all accounts. "You can tell that from one conversation about him?"

"I read body language. That's our thing, right?"

Yeah, it was their thing. Women who'd been victims of violence learned to anticipate a fist, sense a harmful presence. Reading body language saved lives and allowed women to live in a world they felt was against them. Addy learned how to recognize a threat and protect herself. Actually, she felt better prepared than the average person— she recognized evil because she'd met it. "Yeah, it's our thing. Lucas is a good man, but that doesn't mean he's the right man."

"Maybe it don't but you're too young to give up on love. Me? I'm past my prime and happy doing what I'm doing. What Alfred did to me didn't defeat me, but it made me awfully content to be alone. But you is just a child."

"Tell that to gravity," Addy quipped, grabbing a blue freesia to nestle into the arrangement. She affixed some moss to the base and added some small toadstools. Whimsical and fairylike. Perfect for the Sweet Sixteen dance.

"I'm serious. I know things didn't work out with that Stephen, but I couldn't have told you right up front he was too much of a weenie."

Addy laughed at Shelia's description of the last guy Addy had been serious about. "He screamed when that spider jumped on him and tried to climb in my arms. It was funny but telling. Not to mention he was so small I could easily cradle him."

"That's why this big one's such a departure. You usually like them manageable."

"That's not true. Stephen wasn't *that* small. And he made really good waffles."

"Baby, if you can bench-press them…"

"I don't choose guys based on…" Addy trailed off because in thinking about her last few relationships, she realized Shelia was right. The last three guys she'd dated were slight, nerdy and about as threatening as a puppy.

Shelia guffawed. "Yeah. You know what I mean."

"Okay. Fine. I've chosen guys who are a little less masculine than the Incredible Hulk living at the Finlay house. So what? Makes sense in a weird way. My subconscious probably overrode my brain, making me think on some level I could better fight them off if there was a threat."

"That psychology degree comes in handy sometimes, don't it?"

Addy shook her head and lifted the arrangement, placing it in the cooler sitting across from her workspace. The Mortillaros were coming in later that afternoon to look at Addy's design for the Fairies and Moonlight Sweet Sixteen Extravaganza centerpieces. The mock-up looked good, but who knew what sixteen-year-old girls liked these days.

Teenage girls—she'd been one of those. Cocksure, swaggering, glossed and moussed. She'd worn her hair permed, her makeup thick and her skirts short. She'd been on top of the world—a good girl who craved a little bad in her life.

Her seventeen-year-old self could not see what her thirty-two-year-old self could now see plain as day—Robbie Guidry was a stereotypical stalker type.

But to Addy, Robbie had been danger and desire.

Everything her parents would refuse her.

So many girls like her out there. She touched the charm of the Patron Saint Raphael at her wrist and made a mental note to call the archdiocese. She wanted her advocacy group to talk to the health classes at parish schools about recognizing dangerous relationships.

She turned to start on another order when the shop phone rang. Addy scooped the old-fashioned corded phone from its cradle. "Fleur de Lis."

"Why didn't you answer your cell phone?"

"Hey, Dad."

"I've been calling you all morning, and now you're forcing me to use your business line. If you're going to carry a cell, shouldn't you answer it?" Don Toussant's temperament was almost as bristly as his graying mustache.

Addy glanced at the locked cabinet housing her purse. "Yeah, I forgot to pull it out this morning."

Her father's silence was answer enough. Addy never forgot her phone. She kept it in a pocket or sitting nearby at all times…part of her process.

"Hate to tell you this, baby, but on top of what went down last week, the parole hearing for Robbie is next Monday."

Addy felt her stomach drop to the floor. The escalated threats now made sense. Robbie thought he was getting out and wanted her to remember he'd not forgotten her. "Oh."

"Yeah. Not good, but I wanted you to know I talked to Andre and he talked to someone down at the parole board and he thinks they'll grant parole this go around. Too much overcrowding and Robbie has been a good boy." There was anger in her father's voice, maybe a little of it leftover for her. He'd never gotten over the fact his good Catholic girl had conducted a secret affair with a creep.

"I knew this day would come, Dad," Addy said, her heart pounding at the thought Robbie would be out, able to contact her, able to cause trouble. She'd hoped after all the years he'd spent behind bars he would reform and want to move on, but the occasional reminders he sent to her told her differently. "I'm going to keep living my life. I refuse to live scared."

If she kept saying it, it would be true.

"Yeah, but after the crap he pulled last week, I wish you'd reconsider the gated community idea. I'd feel better if you weren't in that old house with your crazy aunt."

"Dad, don't call Aunt Flora crazy."

"She was crazy before Alzheimer's. I've always called her crazy…to her face. Not changing now."

Addy knew her father loved Flora so she let it slide. "I can't leave Aunt Flora and she won't move. We have sturdy locks and nosy neighbors. I feel good about where I live, Dad—it's safe."

"Call a security system company. At least get an alarm, baby."

"I'll think about it. But remember I know how to protect myself. I live smart and I listen to my intuition. I have a plan for dealing with whatever Robbie throws my way."

"Which is?"

"Ignore him but remain vigilant. Any attention I give him is fuel for the fire." Addy had spent years in therapy studying people like Robbie. She understood him better, and that gave her added protection. Understanding the threat was half the battle.

She could get lucky and not have to deal with him at all. Maybe freedom and no response to his threats would work and Robbie would leave her alone.

Probably not.

But she could hope.

"If he gives you any trouble, I'll finish what I started with that baseball bat." Her father wasn't a big man... he just thought like one. "I'll be at the parole hearing on Monday. Let's see if my statement can sway the board."

"Glad you got my back, Dad. We'll hope Robbie doesn't get his freedom. That will solve everything."

"Hope for the best, plan for the worst."

Addy allowed a smile to curve her lips. "That's always been our family motto."

"Yep. I'll call you after the hearing. Be safe, my darling. And keep the dang phone close."

"Always, Dad."

Addy hung up. The last parole hearing had been a year ago and Robbie had been denied early release, but some jittery feeling in her belly told her this time would be different...or maybe she was hungry.

"Want some pirogues today, Shelia?" Addy asked, unlocking the cabinet and withdrawing her purse. She slid the cell phone into her smock pocket and grabbed her wallet. "My treat if you'll walk over."

"Like I'm turning down red beans and rice?"

"Only good thing about Monday." Addy smiled thinking about the steaming mound of red beans and andouille sausage. In New Orleans, red beans and rice was a traditional dish served on wash day—Monday. "I'll call ahead."

Shelia grabbed the twenty dollar bill and hugged her. "I overheard your conversation with your dad."

Addy hugged her friend back. "I'm not scared."

"Of course you're not," Shelia said, chucking Addy playfully on the chin.

But they both knew a lie sat between them.

CHAPTER NINE

"YOU GOTTA sign this permission form, Uncle Lucas, and I need ten dollars for concessions." Chris waggled a crumpled piece of paper at Lucas's head as he tried to figure out the complicated satellite television box. Charlotte sat on the couch crying because something had happened to the TV in the middle of *Ms. Calico and Creampie,* whatever that was.

"Okay, get it out of my face." Lucas pushed Chris's hand downward and glared at the stupid black box. "Wait, ten dollars for concession?"

"I eat a lot."

Chris didn't move the paper. Lucas jerked it out of his hand. "I'll give you five dollars."

"Awww," Chris whined.

"But if you go get Michael, I'll make it ten."

"Woot!" Chris fist-pumped and galloped up the stairs shouting "Michael!" at the top of his lungs.

"Dear God. I need whiskey and a pair of noise-cancelling headphones. That's my fee for this gig. Booze and silence," Lucas muttered to himself as he punched the input button. He glanced back at the television but found the same blue screen.

Mother Fricker.

"Creampie was gonna win a medal in the pet show," Charlotte moaned between sniffles. The child sounded as weary as Lucas felt. Maybe she hadn't gotten a nap at pre-school. Lucas sure the hell hadn't. The dog had pissed on the floor again, and he had to take him into the vet. His afternoon had been chopped in half. By the time he'd shoved the pills down Kermit's throat and finished a conference call with his business manager, it was time for carpool.

And Lucas was certain carpool was the devil's afternoon recruiting ground. He probably claimed a dozen souls that very afternoon when someone had blocked the K-2 loop. Who knew soccer moms had such creative curse-word combinations?

A rumble down the stairs along with shouting announced the arrival of the two boys.

"You're such a moron, Chris," Michael said before slinking into the family room and casting Lucas a withering look. It was always a withering look, as opposed to, say, a helpful look. "What?"

Lucas tried really, really hard to be patient, but the day had been crappy and he was tired of being Mr. Nice Guy. Okay, he hadn't been exactly Mr. Nice Guy, but he'd attempted to keep up the good-sport veneer he'd painted on before walking into his brother's house last week. That veneer had cracked and worn thin and the bill had come due.

"How about you lose the attitude?" Lucas said, rising and stretching to his full height of six foot four. He glowered at the kid, but the effect was lost on Michael because as usual he'd shifted his gaze away. "Your whole moody teen thing is on my last nerve."

Michael gave him a blank stare. "Like I care? I'm controlling what I can control and I'm leaving you alone. You're the one who wanted me down here, and I'm here." The kid straightened his spine but still looked vulnerable as he tossed his hair out of his face with a practiced flip of his head.

Lucas reigned in his aggravation and took Michael's advice—control what you can control. He needed the damn TV fixed so Charlotte would stop whining. "Something happened in the middle of your sister's video—I think she sat on the control—and I can't get it back on."

Michael sighed and took the control from Lucas. "First you have to make sure it's on this channel. Then you go to Input, then make sure—"

Performing a complicated series of button-pushing, Michael nodded in satisfaction as a cartoon tabby appeared wearing a huge pink bow.

"Creampie!" Charlotte shouted, pointing at the screen.

"There, squirt," Michael said, rubbing his sister's hair and moving toward the foyer and stairs.

"Thanks," Lucas called, impressed, but afraid he'd never be able to mimic what the kid had done with the remote.

"No problem," Michael called back.

It was the most civil conversation Lucas had had with the kid since arriving last week…if one could call that a conversation.

"Pay up," Chris said, shoving a grungy palm Lucas's way.

"You really need to wash your hands, dude." Lucas reached for his wallet right as the doorbell sounded. He glanced at his watch. Six o'clock. Dinnertime. But he hadn't ordered pizza.

Maybe Addy would be standing on the porch with something Flora had cooked that day. He'd hated the way it had felt that morning. The vibe had been wrong, and he'd spent the day thinking about her, about how he could change things. But he had come up with no solution. Pursuing anything other than temporary friendship was selfish of him.

Besides he wasn't a man to lose his head over a woman…to daydream about her soulful eyes and long dark hair. The kids and lack of sleep were pecking at him, making him weak, making him poetic.

Ugh. He hated poetry…unless it showed in his photographs.

The doorbell sounded again, and Lucas took his boots to the front door. Two seconds later he was looking at Tara Lindsay, aka Sheldon's mom.

"Hey," she said smiling with overglossed lips. "Thought I'd be a good neighbor and bring you guys some supper."

For a second, he just stared. She wore tight jeans, high heels and a shirt that dipped dangerously low between her breasts. Her perfume wrapped around him, making him want to turn his head for a good deep breath of night air.

"Lucas?"

"Oh, sorry. Been a rough day. Come on in." He stepped back and she sauntered in…without Sheldon. Maybe the kid was afraid of Charlotte exacting revenge. Or maybe Tara wanted to concentrate on other things like exploring what she thought to be an invitation. He shouldn't have put his arm around her. Dumb-ass move.

He closed the door as Tara turned toward him. "You want this in the kitchen?"

"Yeah." He gestured toward the back right corner, wondering if the "this" was the foil-wrapped pan in her hands…or something else she wanted to give him. Uh, seemed determined to give him.

She strolled back to the kitchen, each click of a heel preceded by a little hip wiggle.

Here was an obvious woman.

Even the ten-year-old standing in the open entrance of the foyer got that. He turned to his uncle and wiggled his eyebrows.

Cheeky kid.

Lucas shrugged and followed behind the sexy kitten in eff-me heels because there was really no other recourse. The woman had brought a casserole…and the kids needed to eat.

Tara tossed her hair over her shoulder as Lucas entered the kitchen. "I brought some lettuce and tomatoes. I'll toss the salad together real quick if you'll grab me a bowl."

"Awfully nice of you to do this, Tara."

Her answering smile made him nervous. "I love the way you say things. *Awfully*. So deliciously cowboy."

Cowboy. Ah…now he understood. Some women had fantasies about men in worn jeans and boots—a romantic notion of cracked leather, hard abs and a soft heart. It was almost laughable. Most cowboys Lucas knew were about as romantic as cow crap. They were surly, out of shape and a dentist's dream. Lucas wasn't a cowboy, though he liked his comfortable jeans and boots fine. He was a photographer who dabbled in ranching. Big difference. "You know I'm not a cowboy."

Her laugh was soft. "Well, to a city girl like me, you're close enough. Do you know where Courtney keeps the cheese grater?"

Lucas spent the next several minutes opening and slamming drawers but couldn't find the grater. The whump-whump of Tara slicing small cherry tomatoes echoed in the kitchen, along with the off-key song she sang under her breath. Somehow it seemed too intimate and made Lucas feel itchy in his skin.

"I brought ranch dressing because that's what men always seem to like, and I pride myself on knowing what men like," she said, casting blue eyes on him.

"Do you?" Shit. What could he say to that? He shouldn't have put an arm around her when her husband acted like an ass. This is what being nice got him. Another problem…and Lucas Finlay was full up on problems in his life.

"Yeah," she said, setting the paring knife on the cutting board and moving closer to him. Lucas tried to step back but he hit the cabinet. Totally cornered.

"Makes you quite the catch." He braced his hands on

either side of the granite and tried to figure a way to slide out of the corner without being offensive.

"Mmm," Tara purred, reaching out and straightening the collar on his shirt. "I'm a talented woman. Be glad to prove it to you."

"Uh, here's the thing, Tara. I'm leaving in a few days—"

"I don't want to marry you, Lucas," she said with a drawl, her blue eyes twinkling with something he recognized as turned-on woman. "I want to fu—"

"Yoo hoo!" someone called at the back door.

Tara snapped her mouth closed and looked at the back door slowly opening. Lucas almost sighed in relief as Flora popped her head in.

"Hey, there, tall drink of water," the older woman said, elbowing the back door open while balancing a huge Dutch oven in her hands. The smell of something spicy wafted in with the night air. "Brought you some jambalaya, but it looks like someone beat me to the punch. Do I need to arm wrestle her?"

Addy followed behind with a gallon of tea and a couple of sacks with French loaves peeking over the edge. Her brown eyes widened when she saw Tara standing beside him…close beside him.

Lucas moved past Tara to help the older woman with the dish. "I'm not sure Tara here can get much traction in those heels so you'd have the advantage," he joked.

Tara flipped her hair. "Don't be so sure, honey. Women can do more in these things than you think."

Addy didn't seem to find it funny. She lifted her dark eyebrows and sat the tea on the counter.

Tara's gaze darted to Addy and he saw something fire in her eyes. "And don't you just have women jumping to help you? Those dimples work magic."

Lucas hated his dimples.

"I'm Tara," the blonde said, stretching out an arm jingling with bangles toward Addy. The light caught the glowy flecks in her nail polish, and when Addy reached out with her own small hands tipped with short unpolished nails the difference was marked.

"I'm Addy and this is my aunt Flora. We live next door," Addy said, keeping her gaze from him. Somehow he knew her feelings were hurt, though he doubted anyone else in that kitchen caught on. Somehow, some way, he could read her.

"This jambalaya will keep," Flora said, lifting the lid. The smell made Lucas's stomach growl.

"I made chicken spaghetti," Tara said, lifting the foil off her pan revealing golden cheesy goodness.

All three women stared at him, silently asking him to choose.

"I hit the jackpot, huh? Lucky for me I'm hungry enough to eat both," he said as the door leading to the innards of the house swung open. In trooped Michael and Chris.

"We smelled something good," Chris said, rushing toward the stove. Michael hung back, but grabbed a stack of paper plates sitting beside the fridge and eyed the two dishes sitting on the stove hungrily.

Addy pushed some school papers to the side and sat the bread on the counter. "I'll leave this here."

"Oh, don't be silly," Aunt Flora said, brushing her hands together. "We need to slice it. It will be perfect with that salad Ms. Tara made. The kids can choose whichever they want to eat, and we'll put up the rest. I'm going back to my kitchen and grabbing some of those plastic disposable storage containers."

For an older lady, Flora moved fast. She was out before Chris had dropped his first spoonful of spaghetti on the floor. Luckily Kermit had come in with the kids and went right to work on cleanup.

"Where's Charlotte?" Lucas asked Michael.

The older boy shrugged. "Where you left her?"

Lucas made a move toward the door, but Addy beat him to it. "I'll get Charlotte. You have a guest."

The way she said "guest" made him cringe. He felt guilty, too, though he didn't know why. He and Addy weren't anything to each other. It was silly to feel guilty for being caught with a woman he didn't want by a woman he did want...but couldn't have.

Lucas wanted to bang his head against something to shake the befuddlement out. Unfortunately, he didn't have time because Kermit reared up on the stove.

Tara shrieked.

"Get down," Lucas said, pulling Kermit by his collar. "Stupid dog."

"He's not stupid," Michael said, grabbing the bread and pulling a hunk from the loaf. "You forgot to feed him."

"That's Chris's job," Lucas said, toeing the dog away from the stove and eyeballing the kid who had already wolfed down half his plate.

"Mff?" the boy said, looking up with a greasy look of innocence.

"When you finish eating, you need to feed your dog and cat. Where is the Wicked Cat of the West?" Lucas asked, wiping up a spill on the stove.

"Curled up in your cowboy hat," Michael said, with a gleeful voice.

Great. Cat hair on his Stetson.

Tara grabbed a serrated knife and started slicing the bread, piling the slices onto a paper plate. The door swung open and Addy entered, holding a sleeping Charlotte. "She's down for the count. You want me to put her to bed?"

Lucas shook his head. "I'll take her. I know where everything is, and I need to put out fresh water for Pickles and Fancy Nancy."

"Who?" Addy whispered.

"The hamsters." Lucas reached for Charlotte, sliding his hand between the child and the woman who haunted his thoughts. Addy had changed after work into a pair of jeans and a soft Beatles T-shirt and his hand brushed beneath her breasts. Inhaling her scent, he plucked the child from her grasp, wishing he could find a reason to touch her again. Her gaze flicked up to meet his, and in that brief glance he tried to convey how much he wanted her.

She looked away and he resettled the child against his shoulder, glanced around the near-surreal scene unfolding in his brother's kitchen and pushed out the swinging door.

Five minutes later after tucking Charlotte into bed in her clothes, feeding the noisy hamsters and ignoring the toothbrush Courtney had demanded he use every night, he made his way back into the kitchen where Addy sat chatting with Chris, Tara washed dishes and Flora lifted pieces of pie from the depths of a tin pie plate.

"One down, two to go," Lucas said.

"Poor little tuckered-out angel," Flora said, grabbing a fork from a drawer and taking Michael and Chris a slice of lemon meringue pie. "She's about as cute as they come."

The domestic scene should have been comforting to Lucas—three women taking care of the Finlay children, coming to the aid of a helpless man—but he didn't feel comforted. In fact, the glances Addy and Tara kept trading made him decidedly jumpy, so he grabbed a plate and heaped a spoonful of jambalaya and chicken spaghetti on the plate. Ignoring the salad, he grabbed some bread and settled in at the kitchen island, near where Flora served the pie. The older woman looked up at him, a smile hovering at her lips as if she understood he was a chicken.

"Guess I better scoot," Tara said without enthusiasm, after drying her hands on a clean dish towel. "Sheldon's at my mother's and she goes to the casino on Monday nights with her gentleman friend. Walk me out, Lucas?"

He paused, fork halfway to his mouth. "Uh, sure."

Proud that he resisted glancing at Addy, he slid from the stool and waited on Tara to pass. The blonde tossed a small wave over her shoulder. "'Bye, everyone. Nice to meet you."

The women murmured polite responses while the boys, mouths full, waved.

Lucas followed Tara out. Once they reached the front porch, she turned and pressed her hands against Lucas's chest. "I'm sorry we got interrupted."

Lucas removed her hands, ignoring the narrowing of her eyes at his move. "I'm not. Look, Tara, I'm leaving in a few days and I don't think it's such a good idea to proceed with what you were about to suggest."

"Why not? I'm not asking you for anything but a good time. I'm too old and too busy to beat around the bush, Lucas. I want you…with no strings attached."

He curled his hands around hers, trying for friendly and not encouraging. "I appreciate your bluntness, but it's not that easy."

She cocked her head. "Is this about that woman in there?"

"In where?"

"Don't play dumb with me. That Abby. I saw you looking at her."

"Addy?"

"Yeah, whatever. Addy. Surely you're not into her?" Her voice sounded incredulous.

"I'm not into anyone right now." Now he out-and-out lied. He was "into" Addy…even if nothing would happen.

At that Tara smiled. "Are you gay?"

"No."

"Then why would a healthy, single male turn down a little afternoon delight with a woman who wants nothing more than a ride on a cowboy? Unless you don't find me attractive?" Her voice faded with the last question…as if she feared the answer.

"You're a beautiful woman and I'm sure most men would punch me in the face for being so stupid as to not take you up on your very appealing offer, but…" He tried to finish the sentence, but couldn't come up with a reason that didn't sound, well, stupid. Maybe he should take her up on her offer. No-strings-attached sex with a hungry woman. It was most men's dream. Hell, a week ago, he'd already have her on her back, knees around his hips. But something inside him balked, and he listened to his gut on this one.

"Look, I'm not begging," Tara said, pushing back from him. "Enjoy the spaghetti."

"I'm sorry," he began.

Tara turned, grabbed the front of his shirt and tugged his head down to hers. "You should be."

It was a good kiss, soft then intense with a little tongue. Tara knew how to kiss and his mouth softened beneath hers, his body tightened in response.

She broke the kiss and smiled, satisfaction gleaming in her blue eyes. "Thought you should know what you're missing, cowboy. 'Bye."

Tara turned and tripped down the porch steps, her heels ratta-tatting a cadence of regret.

Lucas swiped a hand over his mouth, opened the door and walked back to the woman he wanted to kiss. Kissing Addy was something he didn't want to miss.

A simple kiss and then he'd stop, but he couldn't leave New Orleans without kissing Addy.

No regrets.

CHAPTER TEN

ADDY LAY THE BOOK across her chest and sighed. Sheriff Cade McGarrity was in the process of seducing uptight spinster Sophie, and Addy couldn't stop picturing Lucas's face on the tough facade of the fictional lawman.

Insanity felt very real at that moment.

She picked the book up, determined to put the man next door out of her mind, determined to enjoy the new story. Reading spicy romance was her secret addiction. Some women hid chocolate in their desk drawers, some wore lacy lingerie beneath their power suits, but Addy read about brooding knights, race-car drivers and steamboat captains with wicked smiles and big packages to satisfy the trembling young heroine. Something about passion on the page allowed the naughtiness, the wildness inside her to find a safe home. She had stacks of steamy romance in her bedside table and hundreds more in her Nook library.

Her eyes refocused on the story of the injured sheriff, taking refuge in the schoolmarm's clapboard house, who was about to slip Miss Sophie out of her nightgown, but she couldn't focus. Why did she keep imagining her and Lucas in place of Sophie and Cade? The past two nights it had been the same. She should have stuck with the damn sheikh. No way the world of harems and forbidden love could evoke images of the big man stomping around in cowboy boots feeding hamsters and cradling three-year-olds. Sheikh Omar Asseff was dark and cunning, a veritable satyr with smooth words and a big manhood.

So why had she traded swarthy and horny for a man in boots?

Oh, she knew why.

She was stupid.

And if she were honest, she'd admit she wanted to unbutton her own nightgown, shuck it off and show Lucas how much she wanted to act out all those scenes in the books she'd been reading. But she wouldn't admit it. She didn't want it to be real. It had been well over a year since she'd ended her last relationship. Wasn't as if she didn't want another, but not with a guy so wrong for her, a guy leaving in a few days' time. She wasn't the kind of girl to hook up with somebody for a booty call. She had never wanted to be that girl, even if a little piece inside her wished she were. So maybe reading any erotic romance wasn't a good idea with Lucas next door, distracting her from what was about to go down in her life.

Stupid, Addy. You can't afford to be distracted with a threat looming on the horizon. Get a grip, sister.

Addy snapped the cover closed.

Setting the book on the nightstand, she slid out of bed, not bothering to shove her bare feet into the fuzzy slippers sitting by the rocking chair. Maybe some chamomile tea would help her nod off.

Silently, she tiptoed past Aunt Flora's room, where the flicker of the TV cast shadows on the wood floor, and down the stairway to the kitchen. Five minutes later the kettle chirped, and then with a steaming cup of tea in hand, Addy tucked her toes beneath her nightgown hem at the kitchen table. Moonlight streamed through the café curtains above the breakfast nook, casting a quiet glow. Silence, offset by the creaking of the settling house, blanketed Addy in calmness.

Just what she needed—a moment of peace.

She sighed.

Then heard *whap, whap, whish* coming from the side yard.

Rising, she peered over the curtains but couldn't see. Climbing on the chair, she could just peek over the black smudge of bushes to see Michael standing in his driveway, tossing the basketball at the hoop affixed to the detached garage.

She should ignore him. Even if it was near midnight on a school night.

None of her business. Never before had she seen about the kids next door, so why was she sliding the dead bolt and slipping out the back door?

Without her pepper spray.

The night was crisp and the stars winked at her above. She crossed her arms, tucking her hands over her breasts so they didn't pucker against the thin cotton nightgown. She glanced around, surveying the perimeter, but the night was calm and nonthreatening. Her inner safety alarm was silent.

"Michael?"

The boy turned, wiping tears from his cheeks. "Yeah?"

"What are you doing out here so late?" she shifted on her bare feet because the concrete pavers were ice-cold.

"Shooting hoops." He turned and bounced the ball once, twice and then sent it arcing in the air. The accommodating swish had her lifting her brows. He might not be good at football, but he could hit a basket.

"It's almost midnight."

"So."

She didn't know what else to say. Pretty obvious he wasn't getting the message. "It's too late for basketball. People are trying to sleep."

Two bounces and a swish later, he turned to her, taking in her long-sleeved gown and her chattering teeth. "Did I keep you awake?"

No, images of your uncle naked kept me awake.

"Uh, not really, but you have school tomorrow, and you shouldn't be out here unsupervised."

Michael tucked the ball under his arm and looked disgusted. "Yeah, because I'm a baby, right? I needed a nanny. A babysitter. Gotta make sure I don't shit my diaper and spill my milk."

"That's not what I meant and you know it."

His answer was to turn and resume his relentless bounce-and-shoot rhythm, blocking her out. Pretending she wasn't there.

"Michael."

He missed the shot. Lurching toward the bouncing ball, he snagged it and turned to her with a sour frown. "What?"

"You need to go to bed." She used her pissed-off tone.

His eyes narrowed and she could tell he struggled with what to say. "No."

Addy frowned. Her feet were freezing, but no way would she let him get away with that. "I know you're upset, but you're being a brat."

He turned from her, bouncing the ball, ignoring her.

Now she was even more pissed. Uncrossing her arms she lunged toward him and snatched the ball.

"Hey!" He looked at her now, anger crackling in his eyes, before he tucked it away and stepped back. "Fine. Sorry, Addy."

Addy held the ball to her chest and raised her eyebrows. "You don't sound all that sorry and you're still carrying a huge grudge, kid. Don't you know crap happens? Don't you remember you can't control everything?"

"Yeah, but knowing and feeling are two different things. My life is complicated."

"Everyone's life is complicated, Michael."

"I know there are kids who have it worse than me, but I don't even know how bad life is for me. No one will tell me anything. Don't you understand? It's hard to deal when you don't even know what you're dealing with." He propped his hands on his hips, his breath puffing out into the cold.

Addy nodded. "I know how you feel."

"Do you? Really?" His voice was heavy with disbelief. "I feel like I'm about to explode inside, and being in that house makes me feel like I can't breathe."

"I don't know what to say, Michael. I don't know how to help you. I wish I did. I wish there was a magic button we could hit to make everything clear, but this is life, not a game show. There aren't good things behind secret curtains and there's no strategy. It just is what it is."

His shoulders sunk. "Yeah, it is what it is."

"Did you talk to your uncle?"

Michael dropped his chin and shook his head. "I don't want to talk to him. I want to talk to my dad." His voice trembled and Addy wanted to pull the boy into her arms, but knew it would be inappropriate…and that Michael wouldn't want her pity. Even at thirteen he seemed a rather proud boy.

"I know you do, Mike. I get it. Life sucks right now, but it won't always. When life ricochets out of my control and I can't get a grip, Aunt Flora tells me 'This, too, shall pass.' And it will. Things will get better."

"Sure. I guess. Thanks, Addy," he said, looking up and giving her a half smile, but she could see she hadn't helped. He turned and Addy bounced the basketball toward him, tucking her hands back over her breasts. She watched him go, saw Lucas step out and place a hand on the boy's shoulder.

She couldn't hear their words and it looked as if all was taken care of, but she didn't turn and leave. Instead she stood like a moron, craving Lucas, wanting to see him one more time before she slid into her lonely bed.

Pathetic.

She wasn't too far from being Tara.

The woman had watched Lucas like a vulture sitting on a fence post the entire time they had sat in the kitchen. When Lucas had come back from walking her out, Addy could tell something had gone on. The man had a swipe of shimmery lip gloss on his upper lip and he'd worn the sort of look a man wore when he'd been thoroughly kissed. Something had shriveled inside her when she'd seen him mussed and perhaps turned on. She suspected it was the small bit of hope she'd nurtured that Lucas wanted her.

At that thought she willed herself to turn around and go back to her house.

"Addy," Lucas called softly across the drive.

She turned her head. "Yes?"

He jogged toward her, wearing a worn pair of pajama bottoms, a white T-shirt that stretched deliciously across his broad chest and a pair of moccasin slippers. "Wait a sec."

She turned fully toward him, trying to control her chattering teeth. "It's cold. I don't have shoes."

"Yeah, a little chilly. Hey, I'm sorry Michael woke you."

Her eyes came level with his chest. She didn't lift them. She wasn't sure if it was because she couldn't look away from the muscled breadth or if she didn't want him to see the desire in her gaze. "He didn't. I had slipped down for some tea. Couldn't sleep."

"You, too, huh?"

She lifted her gaze, trying to control her chattering teeth.

"Jesus, you're freezing," he said, reaching out and rubbing her upper arms. "You need to get inside. Here, let me walk you."

"You don't have to." But his hands felt wonderful on her arms. She longed to step into him, have him wrap his arms around her, but she didn't want to look like she'd come out for a chance encounter with him. Didn't want to come across Tara-like, ready to sink her claws into a cowboy.

Maybe she shouldn't think so much. Maybe she shouldn't try to control every aspect of her life. Why not invite him inside? Maybe it would lead to a kiss. She'd really like to kiss him. Or maybe it would lead to a cup of tea. Period. "Would you like a cup of tea?"

"I'd love some."

She walked back to her aunt's house, trying to rationalize her being a good neighbor. Wasn't like inviting a man in his pajamas inside for tea was code for bend me over the breakfast table and do me. It was just tiny little leaves and scalding hot water. She needed to get a hold of herself…and her libido.

Damn book.

"I like the retro feel of your kitchen," he commented, sinking onto a kitchen chair. He looked so large sitting at the small table. So male. So beautifully male.

"Thanks," she said, turning the flame on under the kettle that still felt warm. She picked it up and poured water over the tea bag. The aroma bloomed up in a cloud of steam. "Sugar?"

He nodded so she scooped some into the cup, stirred and took it to him. Lucas took the cup, set it on the table and pulled Addy into his lap.

"Oh," she exclaimed, grabbing his shoulders so she didn't tumble onto the floor.

"You know, I didn't really come in for tea." His voice was low and very sexy.

Pleasure joined the conga line of hunger and desire dancing in her belly. "You didn't?"

She leaned a little closer, inhaling his scent. He smelled so good. Like woodsy cologne mixed with a wonderful maleness no one could bottle. Just a warm, clean yummy smell that made Addy want to nestle her head into his shoulder to draw in more of him.

He slid his hands up her sides, making goose bumps sprout on her arms. "Drinking tea was an excuse to come inside and warm you up. Just being neighborly and all."

"Just like you were being neighborly with Tara earlier? 'Cause I could have sworn you warmed her up, too." Damn it. She closed her eyes, admonishing herself for playing the jealous idiot. Who said stuff like that? Insecure little girls. That was who.

"Tara?"

She opened her eyes and saw his smile. He teased her. "I shouldn't have said anything. Not well done of me."

His arms closed around her, pulling her tighter to him, warming the cool flesh beneath the thin nightgown. "I'm not interested in Sheldon's mom, but I like you're jealous. Tells me what I want to know."

She arched an eyebrow, trying for cool but knowing she failed. She was a hot mess of insecurity and trembling horny woman. Not a good combination in a moonlit kitchen. After midnight. With a cowboy in pajama pants. The intimacy of hard male beneath the worn, thin flannel did funny things to her...dangerous things. "What's that?"

"You want me." He slid one arm between her shoulder blades and cupped the back of her head, bringing it down toward him.

Addy let him because he was right. She wanted him. Maybe she had some residual horniness from reading about Sophie and Cade getting it on. Or maybe it had been too long since she'd had a man hold her, care about warming her up. Or maybe ever since she'd laid eyes on Lucas Finlay she'd wanted to also lay her hands on him.

Didn't matter because at that moment she didn't care about why. She cared only that he touched her.

Resting her hands to his shoulders, she tilted her head and settled her lips against his, tasting him for the first time.

Wonderful liquid heat poured into her as he slid his free hand up her rib cage, grazing her breast, to cup her jaw and tangle his fingers in her loose hair as he coaxed her mouth open, sliding his tongue against hers, making her sink into him.

After several seconds, Lucas pulled back, breaking the kiss. He leaned his forehead against her chin and sighed. "Just as I imagined."

"What?" she whispered, inhaling the scent of masculine shampoo and something uniquely Lucas.

He tilted his head back so he could look her in the eye and his dark eyes twinkled. "You taste like mountain rain."

"How does that taste?"

He laughed low in his throat and pulled her lips back down to his. And then he kissed her again. And again. And again.

By the time the kettle whistled, Addy nearly straddled Lucas, her gown bunched around her thighs, her breathing out of control. The man devoured her, his hands roaming, hot against the thin cotton of her nightgown, cupping her bottom, teasingly brushing the side of her breast, and never leaving her body for a second.

His touch was more delicious than mountain rain, better than expensive chocolate…better than the first bloom of her great-grandmother's Peace rose.

"The kettle," she murmured, dropping her head back as he kissed his way down her neck to the eyelet trim lining the square neck of the gown.

"Hmm?" he murmured against her skin.

"Kettle."

He released her. "Go turn it off but come back. I want to taste you some more."

She'd never moved so fast. When she returned, she

plopped right down in his lap and drew his head to her, seeking his lips. For several seconds she reveled in the fuel spilling into her belly, revving her, making her forget every admonition about leaving Lucas Finlay alone. When she broke the kiss, it was only to drop her head back so he could slide his lips down her throat.

She groaned as he met her unstated request.

"Ah, that's my girl," he whispered, resuming his work at the sensitive base of her throat as his hands moved to cup her bottom before alternating with caressing her back and thighs.

Her answer was to rub against his erection. The delicious friction made the ache between her legs painful. He felt so big, so hard, so what she needed.

But…

"Lucas, we can't. I can't do this here." She tried to protest, but it was halfhearted. She wasn't sure if a pack of wild horses storming the kitchen could stop what was happening to her.

Okay, yes, wild horse could likely stop it.

But she didn't foresee a herd of mustangs breaking into her kitchen. Maybe Aunt Flora, but not horses.

Aunt Flora.

She stiffened beneath the heat of his mouth on her shoulder.

"Shh," he said, nipping her collarbone. "Just a few more seconds before I have to join Mittens, the meanest cat this side of the Mississippi, in bed."

She giggled. Couldn't help it because the image of Lucas sleeping with that mean tabby was ridiculous.

Her laughter made him laugh and he laid his head against her breast, wrapping his arms around her waist, holding her against his body…against a rigid erection.

Oh, passion still lingered, but both knew it was neither

the time nor the place for anything more than sweet kisses and a slice of something wonderful.

For several seconds neither of them said anything, just sank contently into the other, Addy's gown rucked up, Lucas's heart still racing against her belly. Finally she pulled back, pushing her hair from her eyes. "I asked you in for tea. Not this. Sorry."

"You're apologizing? For this? 'Cause that was the best damn tea I never drank," he said, his dark eyes moving over her face.

Addy felt her face grow hot. The sweet moment faded and she became aware she straddled him. She shimmied back and his arms fell away. "I can't believe I lost my head that way. It was—"

"Wonderful."

"With a side of embarrassing," she said, only partly comforted by his words. She'd lost her mind, straddling a man in her aunt's kitchen...a man she barely knew. They'd never even kissed before, for heaven's sake, and she'd mounted him like a sex-starved spinster.

"Why? I just told you it was the best tea I never had. Can I come over for tea every night?"

Addy slid her hand over her face and laughed. "Jeez, if I start offering tea like that every night, I'm going to have problems."

"I'm a good problem solver," he said, his teeth flashing in the moonlight.

"You're a flirt."

He shook his head and stood. "No way. I'm a mean, lone rancher."

She laughed again and her mortification fled. "You look mean, but you're really sweet."

"No way," he joked, drawing her back into the circle of his arms. "I'm nasty. I smack around kids and trip old ladies crossing the street."

"I saw you scoop an inch worm off the steps and put him on a bush so he wouldn't get squished by small feet," she murmured, looking up into his face. "You're a hoax of a mean man."

Lucas dropped a kiss on her nose. "When I have time, I'm going to show you what kind of man I am. But tonight I have three children I need to get back to."

"But that may never happen," Addy whispered, shaking her gown so it covered her legs and regarding the man who'd stood and adjusted himself within the pajama pants. "This was a weird moment...I never do anything like this."

"Shh." He pressed a finger against her lips. "If we never make it to a bed, then I have the sweetest memory to take with me."

Addy closed her eyes. "I can't believe that's how you'll remember me. Jumping your bones."

He squeezed her tight. "You're honest and sweet and pure, and this moonlit moment is the best thing that's happened to me since I came home."

She nodded, believing the conviction in his voice. "Okay."

"I'll see you tomorrow."

Addy looked up. "I owe you tea, Mr. Finlay."

A flash of teeth in the light of the moon. "I'll look forward to receiving that payment, Miss Toussant."

She figured he wasn't talking about the same kind of tea she was.

Lucas walked out, pajama pants tented, moccasins sloughing against the tile and cold night air blasting in as he closed the door, leaving Addy to wonder if the moment had actually occurred...leaving her to wonder about his statement about making it to a bed.

She had no answer.

So she dumped out his cold tea and went to bed.

CHAPTER ELEVEN

Lucas eyed the bathroom door before refocusing on the magazine sitting in his lap. *Modern Parenting* sucked as bathroom reading material, but he'd forgotten to grab one of his photography magazines before locking himself in. He wasn't actually using the bathroom so much as escaping from Charlotte and her bevy of tea-swilling dolls.

Jeez, you play dolls with a kid once and you're tied up for hours. Charlotte's preschool had parent-teacher meetings every afternoon for the rest of the week, which meant no afternoon care Tuesday through Friday, which meant no free afternoons for Lucas. He'd spent the past few hours making burnt grilled cheese, playing "house" and begging Charlotte to take a nap.

As a last resort, he'd locked himself inside the master bathroom for a moment of peace.

The door rattled and he glanced at it again. Sure enough four little fingers wiggled into the space between the bottom of the door and the carpet.

"Uncle Wucas, you have to come out," she said in a muffled singsong voice.

"Uncle Lucas is going potty," he said, shaking his head at using those words. Who had he turned into? Potty? Dear Lord, he was a changed man.

In more than just his language.

What he'd experienced the night before in the neighbor's kitchen had cemented what he already knew—he had a bad case of the hots for Addy Toussant. And it wasn't merely about how incredible she felt in his arms. It teetered on something bigger…something that scared the hell out of a solitary man such as he…a man who had planned to live out his life in blessed bachelorhood.

Not that he didn't like company of the female variety at times. He did. But the way he gravitated toward Addy had him worried. Like maybe he should dig in his heels a little and slow down. After all, he was going home in a few days' time. Maybe being around kids and a cluttered house had him reaching for something pleasurable, maybe it had him convinced he felt something he didn't.

"Uncle Wucas?"

"Charlotte, go feed Baby Carrie a bottle and put on a new pot of tea. I'll be out in a minute." He glanced at his watch. And then glanced at it again. Was it already three o'clock?

Oh, crap.

"A lady's here."

Lucas scrambled off the closed lid of the toilet, dropping the magazine—dog-eared on the page with advice dealing with troubled teenagers. "Who? Go find your shoes. We're late to pick up your brothers."

He slid the chain from the door and opened it slowly because Charlotte's fingers were still beneath it. He glanced down to find her lying on her stomach wearing a tutu. When she tilted her face to his, bright red lipstick was smeared all over it. Then he saw the lipstick smeared into the beige carpet.

"Holy sh—" he breathed, catching himself at the last minute. "Uh, where did you get that lipstick? Why did you—"

"It's Mommy's. I weared it for the tea party but it got on the rug. I clean it," the child said, hopping up, waving a hand towel smeared with more red makeup.

"Christ, Charlotte. Give me that," he said, grabbing

the guest towel and swiping at her face. She ducked and bobbed. "Okay, later. Give me your hand. We're late."

The little girl's lip wobbled but she did as bidden. Lucas had no idea how to clean up red lipstick. Sure, he'd had some on his collar once before, but the cleaners handled that. Maybe he'd better call a professional service and make an appointment. But first he had to pick up Michael and Chris.

Dear Lord, please let me be able to fasten the car seat in minimal time. And let there be no traffic. And all stop lights on green.

"What about the lady?" Charlotte asked.

"What lady? Is she one of the ones who came to our tea party?"

"Nooo."

"No? She's a real lady?"

"Yesss."

"Where is she?"

"Down there." Charlotte pointed toward the foyer below them. He reached the stairway and peered down into the first floor, but saw no one. Maybe the girl was confused between imaginary and real…and maybe he shouldn't have spent the past fifteen minutes locked in the bathroom.

Red lipstick on the carpet equaled lesson learned.

When Lucas reached the landing, no lady stood in the foyer. And his keys weren't on the table. He patted his pockets and looked back at the staircase. Had he left them upstairs? He was a man of habit. Keys by the front door. Always.

"Where's the lady?"

"I don't have time for games, Charlotte. I have to find my keys so we can go get Chris and Michael. Did you put them somewhere?"

"Hey, you the uncle?" a voice over his shoulder asked.

He spun to find a woman standing between the dining

room and kitchen. She wore a tight sweater that came to her knees, some legging or tight things and high-heeled boots. Her hair resembled something in the skunk family and her skin was the color of crunchy toast. Earrings brushed her shoulders and the skinny dude behind her looked like the caricature in the old Atlas Gym commercials…the before shot.

"Yeah, I'm the uncle. Who the hell are you?"

"That's cussin'," Charlotte observed as wryly as a near-four-year-old could.

Lucas ignored Charlotte and concentrated on the couple standing next to the table stacked with school books and a basket of crayons. He'd meant to clean it off, but such messiness didn't seem important at the moment.

"I'm DeeAnn. Courtney's cousin. This is Joe, my boyfriend."

"Fiancé," the guy said.

"Yeah, fiancé," she said, giving the man a look that made Lucas uncomfortable. "I almost forgot, baby."

Joe pinched DeeAnn on the ass, earning a little shriek, and then he grinned good-naturedly at Lucas. "Women."

Normally Lucas might have agreed with Joe. "You don't know how to use the doorbell?"

"We knocked," DeeAnn said, with a shrug. "Little… what's her name again?"

"Charlotte," Lucas said.

"Oh, yeah, Charlotte. She let us in."

"You're two days early."

DeeAnn broke away from Joe, turning to him with a smile. "Courtney sounded desperate, so I took the rest of the week off and got over here on the double."

Lucas didn't like the looks of DeeAnn, much less Joe, but he couldn't put his finger on why. They didn't look depraved. Maybe challenged in the fashion department, but not dangerous. "So Courtney's paying you by the day?"

"Look, I'm not doing this for the money, but I gotta have something to offset the fact I'm taking vacation from the tanning salon where I work."

He couldn't necessarily fault her that. He could work from here. A tanning salon? Not so much.

"Where are we sleeping?" She jerked her head toward the bags sitting in the doorway. Lucas had missed them earlier but that was because they sat behind a laundry basket full of towels.

Joe picked up the two duffel bags and cocked an eyebrow.

"We?" Lucas crossed his arms. "Don't you mean you?"

"Dude, I'm not leavin' her here with the kids by herself. Where she goes, I go," Joe said, winking at DeeAnn.

"Then you can follow her right back out that door." No way in hell would he leave his niece and nephews with a stranger. He knew Courtney didn't know about Joe, and in his mind, Joe had to go.

"Don't be ridiculous," DeeAnn said, sticking her hands on her hips and smiling at Lucas as if he were a blooming idiot. "Joe's practically family."

But not yet.

Something didn't feel right, but maybe Lucas threw up barriers because of something wriggling inside him he didn't want to admit—the fact he wasn't ready to go back to Texas. The fact he cared more about his brother's kids than he thought…even if he still had to clean red lipstick from the upstairs carpet.

Charlotte ducked behind his leg, giving him a small thrill of victory he acknowledged by reaching around and patting her shoulder. "That might be, but you aren't shacking up in the house with these kids."

"Who are you, head of the morality police?" Joe asked, dropping the bags at DeeAnn's feet. "It's the twenty-first century, dude."

"I'm not sitting in judgment of you, but it's not a good idea. Gut instinct. No offense."

"Well, I *am* offended. We're in a serious relationship." Joe puffed out his chest and mimicked DeeAnn's pose.

Lucas sighed. He had no right to undermine Courtney. DeeAnn was her cousin, and his sister-in-law obviously trusted her enough to supervise the kids. Besides this was what he wanted…to go back home, forget about New Orleans and sew himself back into the man he had always wanted to be.

"Joe's out." Lucas pointed toward the front door just as it opened. Michael and Chris trooped in, arguing about who had to feed the dog and cat. They dumped their backpacks and fell silent when they saw the adults assembled.

"He's not going anywhere," DeeAnn said, tossing her head and standing akimbo à la superhero. But without the cape. "We've already made plans to stay with the kids. So you get out."

"Who's she?" Chris asked as Michael kicked the front door closed.

"Who brought you home?" Lucas asked, flashing a glance at his watch. He should have left thirty minutes ago for pickup. He'd totally screwed the pooch on pickup today. Shit.

"David Peace's mom. I tried calling your cell." Michael stared him down, aggravation on his young face…and maybe disappointment. "What's DeeAnna doing here?"

"DeeAnn," the woman corrected, tucking her hands into her pockets and looking over the crew of kids populating the foyer. "Your mom wanted me to stay with y'all until she gets back from Virginia."

"Is that where she is?" Chris asked, cocking his head. "What's she doing there? We don't know nobody in Virginia."

Michael didn't flinch, but his eyes widened slightly. "You're joking."

"Nope," DeeAnn said with a fake smile. "She tried to call me last week but I was out of pocket. I'm here now, so your uncle can go back to his cave."

"Does your parole officer know you're here?" Michael asked, sliding behind Lucas and turning Charlotte toward him. He frowned when he saw the lipstick smeared all over her face but didn't say anything.

"I don't have a parole officer. You know that." Dee-Ann had dropped the sunny smile and looked aggravated.

"Wait a minute," Lucas said, pointing a finger at the woman. "You have a parole officer?"

"I don't have a parole officer. I got busted for pot years ago. No big deal, and Mikey knows that. He's trying to make me look bad is all."

Michael glanced at Lucas, his dark eyes unfathomable.

"Besides, I'm a woman and can take care of kids no problem. *You* forgot to pick Mikey and Chris up. Pot calling the kettle black." DeeAnn crossed her arms and gave a supercilious nod.

"I don't want to stay with her," Chris said.

"You don't have to," Lucas said.

For a moment they all stood looking at each other—a veritable standoff. He could hear the clock ticking in the hallway, measuring out the seconds of tenseness.

Lucas should have been relieved to have Courtney's cousin show up early. He wasn't cut out for taking care of three children and a menagerie of animals. Hadn't forgetting about Chris and Michael that afternoon, along with the lipstick debacle, proved as much? But the whole thing felt wrong.

"Let's just call Courtney," DeeAnn said, pulling a cell phone from her back pocket.

"You do that," Lucas responded, picking up Charlotte

and heading to the kitchen so he could clean her face. Chris followed.

"Why didn't you pick us up today?" Chris asked, heading to the fridge, pulling open the door and mulling over his choices.

Lucas sat Charlotte on the counter next to the sink. The child rubbed her eyes and yawned. He should have made her lie down for a nap. "I was on my way, but I couldn't find my keys. And then those two showed up."

Chris pulled out a pudding cup, ripped off the lid and licked it before tossing it onto the counter. "Oh. We thought we'd have to go to Mrs. Gruden's room. We hate that place. And why are they here anyway? You're doing okay…even if you forgot about us today."

"Put that in the trash," Lucas said, ripping off several paper towels, wetting them and then scrubbing at Charlotte's fat cheeks. "I didn't exactly forget you. So is Michael pis—uh, mad?"

"Ow!" Charlotte wiggled under the duress of the paper towel.

"He's always mad," Chris said, doing as Lucas suggested, but not before dropping the foil top on the tile, smearing it with chocolate. "I don't think he likes too many people. He used to have lots of friends, but now he don't play with no one."

"Doesn't play with anyone," Lucas corrected, refusing to give up on the mess covering Charlotte's face. He tried to be gentle but the blasted lipstick didn't want to come off. "Why is that?"

"Dunno," Chris said, slurping the pudding straight from the cup.

"Get a spoon," Lucas said as the cell phone attached to his belt vibrated. He pulled it out.

Courtney got right to it. "Why are you giving DeeAnn

a hard time? Do you know how difficult it was to get her to come and watch the kids?"

"Michael said she has a record," he replied.

"Just possession years ago. At a concert. She was twenty and stupid. She's cleaned up her act since."

"She brought her fiancé with her."

"Oh," Courtney said, obviously unaware of that particular. "She never said anything about bringing someone with her, but still, you want to leave and I need someone there."

Yes, he wanted to leave.

Didn't he?

Of course, he did. He had a life in West Texas. A business. A ranch. A free round of golf at Las Colinas Country Club that expired next week.

But why did that sound so…unappetizing? Mundane? Boring?

"But not at the expense of leaving the kids with a couple of whack jobs. If you could see your cousin and her fella, you'd know what I mean."

"She's always been a little colorful," Courtney's conviction faded a bit. "But she said you forgot to pick up Michael and Chris today."

Accusation in her voice.

"I was on my way out, but Charlotte found your lipstick, I couldn't find my keys and those two showed up. I didn't forget the boys. There is aftercare and I was on my way."

"Wait, what do you mean *found my lipstick?*"

That was what stood out to her in all that? "Uh, she found some red lipstick and tried to put it on. Don't worry, I'll call the carpet cleaners."

"Carpet cleaners? There's lipstick on my carpets?"

"A small spot, but we digress."

"I thought you wanted to leave."

"I do, but something doesn't feel right with these two. I'm not Mary Poppins, but so far your children are alive, healthy and fed on a regular basis." He couldn't believe he even offered her a choice. He should be packing. Ben and Courtney had sent a savior…even if she reminded him of Mittens who stared at him from the kitchen table.

"Get that cat off the table," he whispered at Chris.

"Luke, I don't know when I can come home."

"I can work from here," he said, wishing it were true but knowing that with Charlotte out of school every afternoon this week the chances were slim.

"DeeAnn's going to be pissed. I'll have to give her a little money for her trouble."

"Maybe that was her main motivation."

"She's not bad. I wouldn't ask her if she was," Courtney said, sounding defensive.

"Don't worry, I'll cover it. I'm the one being difficult."

"What's your motivation?"

He glanced over at Chris who held Mittens out with two hands while walking toward the back door, trying not to get scratched. And then back at Charlotte who had nearly fallen asleep against his chest, making smears of red on his clean white shirt. "I'm a glutton for punishment?"

Silence hung on the line. "Okay. Thank you."

"You're welcome." And he actually meant it.

He ended the call just as the back door slammed shut, and scooped a sleepy Charlotte into his arms. "Okay, kiddos. You're stuck with the mean old giant for a little bit longer."

Chris whipped his head around, withdrawing his hand from the candy jar, spilling jelly beans onto the kitchen floor. "Wait. You're really a giant?"

He gave the kid a flat stare.

"Oh, right." Chris stooped and started glomming jelly beans off the floor.

Lucas caught Kermit who heard food hit the floor, and hauled him out the back door. "Go play with Mittens."

Seconds later Lucas pushed back through the swinging kitchen door to find loud voices coming from the family room.

"I said get the hell outta my bag, kid," Joe said in a loud voice—a voice full of menace.

"This proves exactly what I was talking about. You're not staying here with my brother and sister. No freakin' way," Michael's voice sounded shrill...and panicky.

"Hey, just put it back, Mikey. It's not a big deal. Really." This from DeeAnn.

"I'm showing Lucas. I can't believe Mom would let you take care of us."

"Give me it, you little shit," Joe yelled, and Lucas heard the sound of heavy footfalls advance.

Lucas emerged right as Joe lunged toward Michael. The teen feinted to the left and spun right instead, but Joe still managed to grab him by the sleeve.

"Hey. Cut it out," Lucas said, setting Charlotte on the floor and striding toward where Joe and Michael struggled over a bag of...marijuana?

Jesus.

Michael pushed against Joe, struggling to hold the plastic bag away from the man who once again lunged toward it. Michael twisted away but Joe managed to shove the boy, making him clip the coffee table and tumble onto the floor. The fireplace tools sounded like a gunshot as they crashed to the marble hearth.

Lucas grabbed Joe by the collar of his shirt and spun him. "Hands off, bud."

The smaller man drew back his fist and let it fly, catching Lucas on the jaw, snapping his head back. Not bad for a flea.

Lucas didn't release his hold on the smaller man and ducked as the man threw another punch, which glanced off the back of his head.

If Lucas had less control, he'd have wiped the floor with Joe, but two impressionable children watched. So instead Lucas grabbed the smaller man by the collar and shook him hard before tossing him onto the sofa as easily as he tossed bags of feed on the ranch.

Joe hit hard enough to knock a picture frame off the table resting against the back of the sofa. He sputtered and scrambled to stand up once again. DeeAnn screamed and launched herself at Lucas, but Lucas had played quarterback in high school and still had pocket awareness. He scooped her to the side and dropped her next to Joe, knocking the man once again into the cushioned depths.

Lucas pointed a finger at both of them. "Don't get up, or I'll beat you like you stole something."

Chris sock-slid into the room. "Cool."

"You okay, Michael?" Lucas asked, not taking his eyes off Joe because he trusted him about as far as he could throw him…which was obviously about three feet. Maybe four.

"Yeah," the kid said, rising slowly and holding up the baggie of what looked to be weed. "And I held on to this. You want to call the cops?"

"No," DeeAnn said, shooting upright and casting Michael a pleading look. "I didn't know he had that. You can flush it."

"Flush it? Hell, no. That's grade-A shit." Joe didn't take his eyes off Lucas. Smart man.

DeeAnn punched Joe on the arm, making Lucas wonder if he'd been teleported to one of those crazy talk shows. "Shut up, Joe, and do what he says."

"You don't go to jail for a little weed, Dee."

She turned to Lucas. "Do whatever you want to with it."

"Both of you get out," Lucas said.

"But I—" DeeAnn started.

"Now." Lucas stepped toward the two sprawled on the couch and they both shrank from him. Good.

"Fine," DeeAnn huffed, struggled to her feet. "I didn't want to watch the little bastards anyhow."

Lucas tsked. "Apologize."

She rolled her eyes but looked over at Michael. "Sorry."

"Hey, can I have my stuff back, dude?" Joe asked.

Lucas lifted the baggie and cocked an eyebrow. "What do you think?"

"Frick!"

Except Joe didn't say "frick." Pretty well established the man had a mouth like a sailor and Lucas's gut instinct had been spot-on. No way he left the kids to these two morons.

Lucas tucked the marijuana in his back pocket and glanced back at Michael. Chris had moved to stand beside his brother. Charlotte stood behind Michael. They looked scared and that pissed Lucas off all over again.

Joe and DeeAnn tromped from the room and Lucas followed. He didn't want any more trouble. Before he left the room he turned back to the kids. "Stay here."

All three nodded, somber and still wary.

Lucas oversaw the two as they gathered their bags and slunk from the house. No tender goodbyes. In fact, he got the finger from both of them as they drove away in a clown car badly in need of paint. He wanted to return the salute but decided to be a high-road kind of guy.

He glanced briefly over at Addy's house and saw she still hadn't arrived home. A funny little plink echoed around his ticker. Which was plain dumb. Wanting Addy had nothing to do with anything above his belt.

Or so he vowed to think.

Turning, he went back in the house and found the kids still huddled silent in the living room. He walked over to the sofa and nudged it back into place, resetting the picture frame. Michael silently separated from his siblings and walked to the fireplace. Stooping, he righted the fireplace tools. When he'd finished, he glanced over at Lucas. "You were gonna kick his ass, weren't you?"

"If I needed to."

Michael nodded. "But you didn't…because we're here."

"That's part of it, but I didn't need to hurt Joe to make my point. He's a coward at heart. I could see that."

"He kinda scared me," Chris said, wrapping an arm around his sister who for once didn't cry. Charlotte stood beside her brother, blue eyes full of fear.

"But not me." Lucas moved around and sat on the sofa. "As long as I'm here, I'll protect you. That's why your mother asked me to come."

"So why did she send DeeAnn, then?" Michael asked, still crouched by the fireplace.

"I needed to go home so your mother tried to come up with a replacement."

"You don't need to go home anymore?" Michael asked.

Lucas didn't want to lie to them. Hell, their mother was already keeping secrets from them. "Not more than I need to take care of you. I miss my horse Cisco and I miss the miles and miles of pasture, but I'm coping in the clutter."

"So how long you staying with us?" Chris narrowed his eyes, the normal confused look back again.

"Until your mother and father come home."

"And when is that?" Michael asked.

"I don't know." Lucas spread his hands toward Charlotte. "You okay, Miss Charlotte?"

The little girl didn't say anything. Just moved toward him, arms raised. He scooped her up and she laid her head on his shoulder, clutching him tightly. This time there wasn't a ping around his heart so much as it was a swelling with something he'd rarely felt. He rubbed the child's back and looked at the two boys. "I'm tired of eating take-out pizza, and I'm not in the mood for leftovers. Wanna go out for dinner?"

They both nodded.

Charlotte lifted her head. "Can we go to Chuck E. Cheese's?"

Michael and Chris glanced at one another, some unspoken message transmitted between them.

"What's Chucky Cheese?" Lucas asked.

"It's a pizza place."

"I'm kind of tired of pizza, guys," Lucas said, setting Charlotte down between his knees and inspecting her face again. Who knew lipstick soaked into the skin like that? "How about tacos?"

"I wanna go to Chuck E. Cheese's. I wanna ride the horsie."

Lucas sighed. "Fine. We'll do homework when we get back."

"Yay!" Chris yelled, pumping his fist into the air.

Michael gave Lucas an indecipherable look. "You might want to see if Addy wants to go with us…or maybe grab a flask of whiskey or something."

Lucas stood, warming at the thought of inviting Addy. He almost liked the kid for suggesting it. Okay, he liked the kid anyway in spite of his bad attitude. "Whiskey? Why would I need whiskey?"

Michael grinned. "Dude, have you ever been to Chuck E. Cheese's?"

Lucas slowly shook his head.

Michael's response was laughter…evil laughter.

And Lucas knew he'd been had.

CHAPTER TWELVE

ADDY STEPPED ONTO the porch, glad for the night air cooling her heated cheeks. She hadn't seen Lucas since the night before and still felt weird about what had gone down in the kitchen. But here he was on her back porch…much earlier than midnight. In fact it was barely eight o'clock. Post Chuck E. Cheese's. Poor man, maybe she should have shrugged off her Survivors of Violence meeting. No, she needed them after the threats last week. Talking through her fears always centered her.

"Jeez, why didn't you tell me?" Lucas said before she could even say good evening.

"What?" She couldn't meet his eyes. Why did she feel so embarrassed about the night before? She was a warm-blooded woman, a warm-blooded modern woman. Just because she straddled a man she'd known less than a week didn't mean she was a hootchie mama. Much.

"Chuck E. Cheese's." His disgust drew her gaze up to his eyes.

"Oh, not exactly an adult's favorite place."

"Understatement of the year. They don't even have beer. It was an exercise in weathering the torments of hell. Two birthday parties were held there tonight. Two."

"You want a beer?"

"Is that code for the same thing as tea?"

Addy stiffened. "No."

"Damn."

And that made her smile. "Last night just sorta happened."

"Hell, I planned on coming over for tea every night," he said, his grin awfully sexy in the weak porch light.

"You're down to two nights. You're leaving in, what, a few days." She averted her gaze because a low hum had started in her belly. Thoughts of his hands on her invaded, pricking at her reserves, urging her to let the passion bubble to the surface again. Last night had whetted her appetite for Lucas.

"Nope. That's what we were celebrating with the giant stuffed mouse. DeeAnn didn't work out."

"The cousin?"

"She came with herbal supplement." He unfurled a bag of what looked to be...

"Is that weed?"

"Yep. Courtesy of DeeAnn's boyfriend."

"You didn't come over here to—"

"Get high with you?" He laughed before shaking his head. "I don't smoke this stuff. You?"

"Never." Addy took the bag and held it up before looking around as if a policeman might jump out from the bushes and take her down. "What're you going to do with it?"

"Don't know. Put it in your compost heap?"

Addy laughed. "Maybe it will make my plants happier."

"Or more relaxed." Lucas smiled and again funny stuff happened in her belly. "But how are you going to explain your secret ingredient for prize-winning flowers?"

"Better flush it." She handed the baggie to him.

Moving closer, Lucas tucked a strand of hair behind her ear. "So me staying awhile longer, that's a good thing?"

Something else trickled into her stomach—a sort of pleasure not stirred because of what this man could do to her body...but of what he could do to her soul. Lucas was staying longer. What did that mean for her and him? Was there even a her and him? "I'm not exactly sure what's going on between us…except me jumping your bones like some deprived—"

"Nah. Don't diminish last night, Addy. You're like an addiction. I want more of last night," he said, lowering his gaze to her lips.

She reigned in her inner Catholic schoolgirl. Okay, so she liked to be a little naughty. Did she *have* to feel guilty about it? Was it coded in her DNA? "Me, too."

"Good girl," he breathed low, tracing her lower lip with his finger. Her body began to hum and she leaned toward him.

Then she heard a car crank.

Right. She stood on her back porch where her other neighbor or the kids could see them. She edged back on the stoop. "I'm glad you're staying. It's better for the kids."

Lucas perceived the situation and tucked his hands into his jean pockets. "Not sure they agree but after I voluntarily took them for pizza and skee ball, they're being a little nicer. Only had to ask three times for them to do their homework and Charlotte didn't throw a fit when I made her brush her teeth."

"So what brings you to my door…besides the potent fertilizer?" Maybe he wanted a repeat of last night. Maybe she should invite him in for "tea."

"I wanted to ask you out this weekend."

She jerked her gaze to his. "A date? How?"

"Well, the kids have to come along, but I think it will still be fun."

She lifted one eyebrow. "Define fun."

"So today when I locked myself into the bathroom—"

Her befuddlement gave him pause.

"Long story. But anyway, *Modern Parenting* had an article on dealing with troubled teens and ways to connect them to their family."

"Modern Parenting?"

"I forgot my *Photography Today* magazine. But anyway, one of the suggestions was to root the child into the parents' past, sharing favorite reminiscences of their own formative years with the teen. So that got me to thinking about my own past in New Orleans. I thought I might share some of mine and Ben's favorite places when we were kids."

"And you want me to go with you?"

His normally stoic expression melted into pure charm. "Pretty please?"

"I work on Saturday."

He frowned. "Maybe when you get off? And we can always hit a few places on Sunday."

Spending the weekend with Lucas sounded…scary. But in a good way. If there was a good way to be scared. Maybe it was more like guarded anticipation.

She wanted to get closer to him, but doing so felt like placing a big target on her back. Cupid already swooped dangerously close to her. Did she want to get shot by love's arrow when she knew the man, though staying longer than anticipated, would pack his big truck and ramble off into the sunset?

But another voice rudely interrupted the voice of doubt. Addy was fairly certain this voice was the one who had urged her to throw her legs around Lucas in the kitchen last night. And that voice said to stop thinking and take some chances.

But that voice was also the same voice that had urged her to sneak out with Robbie Guidry…to allow her present-day tormentor to be her first sexual partner. Bold, reckless and oblivious to consequences, that voice didn't represent the smartest of part of Addy. Most of the time, she ignored that part of herself, choosing to control it with safe activities, like reading spicy romances. No one could hurt her in those books, unlike the real world.

"Addy?"

"What?" She refocused on Lucas.

This man was not Robbie Guidry. Didn't mean he still couldn't hurt her emotionally, but physically he was quite the opposite of a threat. His touch awoke something beautiful inside her.

"Sorry. I'm not sure it's a good idea for me to get this involved with you."

He lifted his eyebrows. "I didn't expect you to trip over yourself running toward me, but I didn't expect you to slam the door neither."

"What *did* you expect?"

"I don't know. We enjoy each other's company. And though I want you in a not-so-friendly way, I'm a man of some control. I'm pretty sure I can handle an innocent outing chaperoned by three kids without humping your leg."

Addy couldn't stop the smile at that image. She read too much into the invitation and allowed the mixed-up emotions she felt for Lucas to shade her responses. He was right. What he asked was no different than what she'd been doing with him and the kids for the past few days. Hanging out. Last night hadn't changed that.

Okay, maybe a little.

"I'm not asking you to climb into bed with me…though that idea has merit," Lucas said, charming grin back in place.

She shoved her doubts to the back burner. "You have power in that grin."

He made a face.

Addy nodded. "I'll go. And if my delivery guy comes back this week, I'll take Saturday morning off."

"Good." Lucas nodded, glancing back at the Finlay house. "I should get back."

"Yeah, I promised to watch TV with Aunt Flora. She didn't have a good day today. Missed her turn for the library and ended up lost. She found her way back eventually, but it upset her more than normal."

"A kiss before I go?"

Addy stepped back and eyed him. Dear Gussie he was gorgeous. All hard planes, broad shoulders and hewn oak. Chocolate eyes, crooked nose and sensuous mouth. She wanted to kiss him till the cows came home—whatever that meant. But her voice of reason was being awfully forceful that night.

Lucas quirked an eyebrow.

"I'm thinking about it," she said.

"Ah, hell, Addy girl, if you gotta think that hard, I'll say good-night."

"You know my history. You know why I'm cautious."

"You told me I didn't scare you."

I lied.

Addy shook her head. "You don't. But I'm not sure we should repeat last night."

He stepped back, inching off the porch stoop, stepping down one, two, three steps. "Fine. I respect your decision. I didn't come to seduce you."

His words tore a little at her heart. She wanted him to want her…so why was she hiding behind fear? Again, her past clutched at her, preventing her from reacting as a normal woman would.

Damn it. She wasn't a victim and she wouldn't be controlled by fear.

Jogging down the steps so she was eye level with him, she leaned in, planting a kiss on his lips.

It was a soft kiss that turned hot in the blink of an eye.

Lucas cupped her head and made her kiss worth his

while. What felt like minutes later, he pulled back and studied her in the dim porch light. "Don't be afraid, Addy."

"I'm always afraid," she whispered.

"Ah, Addy, you break my heart," he said.

She tapped his chest. "Good to know you got one, tough guy."

He smiled. "It's in there somewhere."

Addy brushed his jaw with the back of her hand, liking the way the rasp of his emerging beard felt. "I fight fear every day, and I win. Just sometimes my rational voice overshadows the voice that had me straddling you last night."

His eyes grew softer. "I like the voice you listened to last night. I like the woman you are in my arms." He ducked and gave her a quick kiss before turning toward the house ablaze with lights.

"Me, too," she said quietly. Her admission wafted in the night air. "But she's the girl who gets me hurt. Been there. Done that."

He turned. "You chose the wrong guy, that's all."

And then he turned again, his footfalls soft on the winter-weary ground. Addy watched, a silent shadow, her mind wrapping around his words. She knew Robbie Guidry had been the wrong man for her. As a seventeen-year-old his only appeal was in how wrong he was for her. Having a secret affair with the older man down the street was forbidden…exciting…rebellious.

Until it was not.

But that didn't mean Lucas was the right man even if from the start she'd been attracted to him. That atypical response didn't mean anything. So it usually took weeks or months for her to feel comfortable around a guy? Just because it happened within a couple of days signified nothing.

But she knew it did…even if on paper Lucas was all

wrong for her. In the long run, he was inaccessible—didn't live in New Orleans, had a life elsewhere. New Orleans was a pit stop for him, and all she could ever be was a nice memory.

Was that enough to take a risk?

Especially when Robbie might be paroled in less than a week? Did she really want to let down her guard when danger lurked around the corner?

"Addy?" Aunt Flora's voice boomed from the innards of the house.

"Coming," she shouted, trotting up the porch steps, shutting the door and twisting the lock before setting the kettle on the stove.

"What's taking you so long?" Aunt Flora asked, schlepping into the kitchen with Bugs Bunny slippers and a wildly patterned caftan.

"Lucas stopped by," she said, grabbing two cups and the tin of chamomile. Both she and Flora needed something to calm their nerves.

"I tell you what, I wouldn't be talking with that man around. I'd be doing." Aunt Flora folded herself into a chair and watched Addy. "No tea for me tonight, dear. I'm having vodka."

"Vodka?"

"Diane found a wonderful cotton candy vodka. It's delish to sip."

Addy wrinkled her nose but slid her aunt's cup back into the cupboard. Aunt Flora wasn't supposed to mix alcohol with her medications, but Addy figured she shouldn't point that out tonight. Aunt Flora finally acted more like herself. The jittery shell of a woman who had met her when she had arrived home had scared her. A teary Aunt Flora was like eating week-old meat loaf…not fun to experience the blowback. "Fine, but I'm not going dancing with you later when the booze kicks in."

Flora laughed. "When is the last time you danced, Addy? You used to love it."

Addy stiffened. "I don't have time to dance."

Her aunt tsked and shook her head sadly. "Honey, you gotta start dancing."

"I'm assuming you're talking about more than actual footwork?"

Aunt Flora tilted her head, her silvery hair dropping against the bold red, yellow and orange silk, and gave her a bemused smile. "I used to dance with Millard every Saturday."

"Mr. O'Boyle? The guy you bought Fleur de Lis from?"

"Millard was a fine dancer, so light on his feet. He always hummed as we danced, holding me so close as we circled the potted plants and waltzed past the cut stems. Best end to a workweek ever."

"He was married with four children, Aunt Flora."

Her aunt narrowed her eyes. "I know, but what's the harm in a dance?"

The kettle whistled and Addy poured steaming water into her cup and swirled the tea ball, releasing the aroma. She inhaled deeply. "Were you in love with him?"

"Of course. There was much to love about Millard. He had a deep laugh that nearly shook his entire body and a neat mustache he liked to stroke when he contemplated his designs. And he was always so sweet to children, giving little girls flowers and young boys a sweet from his candy jar."

Addy contemplated Flora sitting in her kitchen, staring out into her past, a half smile on her face. After several seconds of silence, Flora glanced at Addy. "If only we'd met in another time and place. He was too good a man to hurt his wife. The only leave he gave himself to be another man was when we danced. Still today I can hardly stand the sound of the 'Tennessee Waltz.'"

Addy didn't know what to say. "I'm sorry." Her voice held sorrow and regret.

"Bah, years ago, but the heart does remember." Flora straightened and then pointed a finger at Addy. "My point is don't miss the dance, honey. Anyone with eyes in her head can see the man next door wants to be your partner. Don't deny yourself because there's no forever in it. Sometimes you have to settle for one dance a week to get you through a lifetime."

"I'm not avoiding the potential for something between us. Things just aren't ideal for romance."

"When are they ever ideal? There is no such thing. It's like saying you'll have kids when you can afford them. Or saying you'll do the things you dreamed of when you retire." Aunt Flora gave her a look that made Addy want to cry. "Look what that got me."

Silence reigned and Addy busied herself by putting away the tea and tossing the spoon into the sink. Mostly so she wouldn't cry in front of Flora.

"But I'll tell you what was worthwhile—dancing with Millard. I don't regret locking the door, pulling down the shade and losing myself in a man who was mine…if only for thirty minutes. Sometimes I wonder if I should have…" Aunt Flora's voice trailed off. "Know what? I wanna get out of here and sip some more of that vodka."

"Your wish is…" Addy turned off the kitchen light, and in the glow of the night-light sitting above the counter she extended a hand to her aunt, seeing she couldn't handle the memories of a love unfulfilled.

"My command," Aunt Flora finished, winding her arm around Addy pulling her into a hug. "Your father called earlier and wanted you to give him a ring."

Addy's heart sank.

Robbie Guidry. Her father had gone to talk to the assistant D.A. who had prosecuted Robbie, taking all the evidence tagged by Lieutenant Andre. But Addy didn't want to talk about parole boards and safety issues at the moment. Nor did she want to talk any further about taking risks with big, sexy men living temporarily next door.

She wanted to lose herself in a world somewhere far away, and maybe later find out what Sheriff Cade and Sophie were up to.

Ha! As if she didn't know.

THE PHONE WOKE LUCAS from where he dozed in the recliner. All the lights were still on and ESPN blared on the TV. One of the announcers mentioned a trade deal between Philly and the Texas Rangers for a pitcher, but the incessant ringing kept him from hearing what player it was.

"Hello," he said, trying to sound awake and read the closed-captioning at the same time.

"Lucas?" It was Courtney.

"Hey."

"Sorry I'm calling so late. I'd meant to call earlier but got tied up." She paused. "Luke, he's awake."

"Ben?"

Courtney laughed. "No, the Easter Bunny."

"Of course I know what you meant. How is he?"

"He's still weak and a little confused. He thought at first he was still in Germany and wanted to know how I got a passport so quickly. Oh, and your parents arrived this evening. It's been crazy."

Relief blanketed Lucas. Until that moment he hadn't realized how much he wanted his brother to pull through. The betrayal was still there, but somehow lessened.

He didn't know if he wanted it to lessen. He'd held on to his anger, his pride, for so long it had become like a favorite sweatshirt, easy to pull on.

"Lucas?"

"I'm here. Sorry, I had fallen asleep and was a bit disoriented. Still surprised to wake up somewhere other than my own bed. I'm glad to hear he's awake."

"Are you?"

He stiffened. "Why wouldn't I be?"

"You haven't cared in years." Her voice was solemn, not the least bit flippant. He figured she'd been thinking about him and their past. Being alone with fear gave a person plenty of time to examine and reexamine life.

"Did you think I wanted my brother to die? Jesus, Court. I've been angry a long time, but I never wished harm on either of you." Lucas stood, outrage coursing his blood. She thought him that sort of monster? Had she ever really known him?

"We haven't seen you since the night we told you we had fallen in love. You disappeared and blocked us out of existence. What do you think we were supposed to think?"

"That you broke my heart, that my brother betrayed me."

Silence reigned on the other end.

"You know, this is a bad time to bring up the past. Ben's awake. That's what matters. Be happy and don't jab old wounds," he said.

Courtney inhaled and exhaled. "Yes, that's the most important thing, but I've been thinking about you and about Ben. What happened to you both doesn't seem fair. That was my fault. I'm the one who ruined everything. I shouldn't have… I should have resisted him."

"And been untrue to your feelings for Ben? Pretended to love me when you didn't? How would that have been better? It wouldn't. What happened happened, Courtney. From the looks of things around here, I'd say it worked for the best."

"But not for you."

He couldn't deny that. Or maybe he could. If he hadn't left New Orleans, he never would have picked up a camera, he never would have taken the chance on a new career. Never would have seen the beauty of the Hill Country in Texas or tasted Angela Verra's tamales or climbed through the canyons of New Mexico. His life would have been lesser if he'd stayed in New Orleans with a woman who didn't love him. "I'm fine. I've made a life I'm proud of."

"Your pictures?"

"Yes, and I have a home, a place I find peace and acceptance."

"But no family."

He didn't have words for her. He had his parents, but rarely saw them. An occasional cousin passed through and an aunt and uncle who sent him cards on his birthday. But he'd never been lonely. Not really. "Get some rest, take care of Ben and call tomorrow. The kids will want to know their father is okay."

"Not yet. Ben's better tonight. The doctors are cautiously optimistic. It's the *cautiously* that scares me."

"But soon."

"Soon."

Lucus hung up and turned out the lights downstairs before trudging up to the bedroom his brother shared with Courtney. When he'd first arrived, he'd balked at sleeping in their bed. Didn't sit right with him. But there were no other beds to be had, and Lucas's frame didn't fit on the sofa. So he'd begrudgingly accepted he'd have to sleep in their bed.

He tried not to think about the irony of sleeping in the place where they'd made love, made the family that should have been his.

But he was a practical man. Mostly. So he sucked it up and laid his head on their pillows, trying not to think about how much it bothered him.

Of course, Lucas didn't love Courtney anymore. Maybe he never had. She'd been his shadow during his childhood, then suddenly she was beside him. It was a natural progression, almost comfortable, to concede spending the rest of his life with her.

As he tugged off his clothes, he looked hard at the room his brother and sister-in-law shared. A collection of photos of their children cluttered the simple oak dresser. Hand-painted pictures drawn with little fingers were framed on the wall. Worn quilts he recognized from his mother's house. The gun cabinet with the rifle his great-grandfather had used, locked and sitting in a corner. A rocking chair to nurse babies. All these things represented a life built between a husband and wife.

And then there was the photograph in a simple silver frame stretching across nearly an entire wall. *Sunset at Havasu Falls*. He'd taken it the year after he'd graduated from art school. Rich orange and sun-baked yellow stretched by the shadows of the canyon where the clear waters poured into blue depths. It was an original piece sold in his gallery in Manhattan. Probably cost at least ten grand. Not an easy sum for an insurance salesman who was a National Guardsman and a Realtor with three kids and a hefty mortgage.

Lucas snapped off the bedside lamp and slid beneath the sheets, determined to shut his mind off and not think about his brother and the resentment he still held against him nor the trembling in his gut when he thought about facing Ben again. Nor did he want to think about Addy and her silky hair and reticent smile and the fact that she skirted around something more with him.

He wanted to think about nothing.

Darkness and quiet.

And then he heard footsteps…and a horrible noise.

He'd heard the same noise days ago when Charlotte had tossed her cookies in Addy's flower bed.

Dear Lord, no.

CHAPTER THIRTEEN

WHEN FRIDAY MORNING ARRIVED, Lucas rolled over and blinked at the alarm clock. Six o'clock. He pressed the snooze and contemplated going back to sleep, but then thought better of it and struggled from the bed, marveling he'd actually been able to sleep the whole night through.

Tuesday night after Lucas had switched the lamp off, preparing to block his mind and catch some z's, Chris had thrown up all over the hall floor. And then he'd been up all night sick. When morning had come, Michael joined his brother, clinging to the porcelain throne between the boys' bedrooms.

The stomach virus had arrived for a spring visit.

Wednesday evening Charlotte started throwing up and the misery had lasted until Thursday night.

Lucas had never prepared for anything like three sick children, especially ones apt to launch their stomach contents all over carpet, bedding and, once, the cat. Mean Mittens probably deserved it, but Lucas hadn't deserved bathing a cat. Hadn't been pretty.

He'd found cleaning solution and had done his best to scrub the carpets. Washing quilts and comforters was a new challenge but he managed, and Addy was nice enough to get ginger ale and disinfectant spray, delivering them with a comforting pat.

"You want me to help with the kids?"

"No, I'm doing okay. No need for you to be exposed to the sickness."

"So what do you think about this weekend? I can take the whole day Saturday…"

A sweet piece of satisfaction sank into his bones. "They should be okay by then, but we'll play it by ear."

Dear God, please let the kids feel better by Saturday. He wanted to spend time with Addy. Who knew how much longer he'd be in New Orleans. He'd hate to miss even a minute with her. But barfing kids kinda put a lid on his plans for spending nights in Addy's kitchen, with or without "tea."

And he'd kicked DeeAnn out why?

Of course, he knew that answer was twofold—he wanted to stay close to Addy and he cared about his niece and nephews, even though two weeks ago they'd been strangers to him.

Lucas padded toward the shower, turned it on and went to wake Chris and Michael who had recovered enough to go to school.

"Wake up." He switched on Chris's bedside lamp.

Chris groaned, tossing the covers over his head. "I'm still sick."

"No, you're not. And you can't go on Uncle Lucas's Weekend Extravaganza if you don't get up and go to school."

The covers flipped back and a burr-headed Chris peeked out, blinking owlishly in the light. "Where are we going?"

"It's a surprise."

Chris's feet hit the floor. "I'm up."

Next was Michael's room.

"Wake up, buttercup," Lucas trilled in a falsetto voice.

Michael, wrapped like a burrito, didn't move. Lucas tapped his shoulder while turning on the lamp. "Come on, Mike. Up and at 'em."

"Go away."

"If you don't go to school, you won't be able to go on Uncle Lucas's Weekend Extravaganza."

"You promise?" Michael rolled over and grabbed at the lamp.

"Let me try this again. If you don't get up, I'll tell Chris your new phone pass code."

Michael sat up. "How do you know my pass code?"

Lucas picked up Michael's phone and wagged it. "I have my ways, 4-1-9-9."

Michael's mouth dropped open.

"Your birth date? You really need to think outside the box."

"Fine." Michael rubbed his messy hair and yawned. He'd slept in a too-tight T-shirt and a pair of plaid boxers. Lucas noted the kid had started growing hair on his legs. Michael was growing up and Lucas had never been there to see a sleepy sweet toddler in airplane jammies and dinosaur slippers. Regret flooded him.

He shouldn't have stayed away from his family. He'd allowed his anger to keep him from a blessing. Even after cleaning up vomit and spooning chicken broth into Ben's kids, he realized he'd made a mistake with Michael, Chris and Charlotte.

He bypassed Charlotte's door, allowing her to sleep in. The little girl had been sickest of all and had finally started feeling better last night. She wasn't going to preschool.

The boys were surprisingly cooperative at breakfast, having only one fight over who had drunk the last of the sports drinks. While they packed up their lunches and combed their hair, Lucas slipped over to Addy's. If Aunt Flora would keep an eye on Charlotte, he wouldn't have to wake her and load her into his truck in order to take the boys to school.

He'd only knocked once when the door swung open.

Addy stood in pink silk pajamas, tangled hair and sleepy eyes. "Everything okay?"

He couldn't help himself—he dropped his gaze and took in every inch of her. He loved the gap revealing her delicate collarbones and he could see the faintest outline of her nipples against the soft fabric. Oh, he hoped he got to glimpse those sweet breasts, hoped he got to taste the sweetness of Addy before he ambled back to West Texas.

"Lucas?" Addy said.

He jerked his attention back to her pretty brown eyes. "Huh?"

"Stop staring at my boobs and tell me why you're here so early. Is everything okay with the kids?" She crossed her arms over her bosom.

Damn.

"Yeah, they're all on the mend. About to take the boys to school and wondered if Aunt Flora might go over and stay with Charlotte. She's still sleeping and I didn't want to wake her up."

"Let me grab my robe and I'll go over. Flora's still in bed. She's been sneaking vodka every night before bed. Think she's been having some trouble sleeping. Give me a sec. Grab some coffee if you want."

Lucas shuffled into the kitchen as Addy padded out barefoot.

She had nice feet, something he'd failed to notice in the moonlight nights ago. But he'd been busy with other delightful parts.

Grabbing a mug from the cabinet, he poured himself a cup and stood sipping, enjoying the quiet of the house. No arguing, no screeching, and thankfully, no retching. Just brilliant silence.

"Okay, I'm ready," Addy said, entering the kitchen in a pair of yoga pants and sweatshirt. Her face was bare of makeup and her hair was in a low ponytail. She looked about as glamorous as a wet cat, but somehow it made her all the more desirable. He loved how comfortable she felt around him, loved how much more he wanted her when she was naturally Addy.

"Wait," he said, scooping an arm about her waist and spinning her toward him. "A kiss before I go."

He didn't wait for permission, just lowered his head and stole a kiss. She tasted warm and toothpasty. She relaxed against him and kissed him back.

He broke the kiss and looked down at her glistening lips. "You just made my morning, lady."

"Hope I don't get the stomach virus."

"If you get it, that means I have it. We can throw up together."

"How romantic."

He laughed. "I'm in the clear, which is good because I got plans for you this weekend, lady."

Addy lifted herself on her toes and kissed one of his dimples. "I've decided to embrace the opportunity, Lucas."

The horn honking next door was the only thing that could tear him away from her. "Can't wait. Guess I better get those monsters to school before Chris decides to try his hand at driving. Wouldn't put it past him."

"He's a daredevil."

"That's putting it mildly," Lucas said, holding the door for her so she could slide by and head to his brother's house. "Thanks for helping, Addy."

She saluted. "That's what neighbors are for."

ADDY RUSHED INTO the Fleur de Lis with a folder of bills that needed paying, a bag of bay leaves and the FedEx box of wire that had been mistakenly delivered to her home address. She dropped the box and exhaled. "Whew, that was heavy."

Shelia turned and grabbed the scissors, starting on the box. "Wondered where you were. You're never late."

"I volunteered to watch the little girl next door so Lucas could take the boys to school. There was a wreck on Earhart Expressway and he had to reroute. Then Charlotte pitched a fit because I had to leave. Man, kids are hard."

"I wish I'd had the pleasure of knowing," Shelia said, her voice soft in the quiet.

Addy squeezed her hand. "I know you do."

"So those kids are better?"

"Yeah, I think poor old Lucas got more than he bargained for when he sent Courtney's cousin away. Lucas isn't warm and fuzzy, but he's competent. You should have seen his procedure for dealing with the sick kids—gloves, mask, Lysol and a schedule of medicine and hydration. Plus he actually rocked Charlotte to sleep."

Shelia clasped her heart. "If you don't keep him, give me his phone number. There's nothing I'm a bigger sucker for than a man rocking a sleeping baby…except maybe a passel of kittens."

Today Shelia wore a wig with looping black curls down to her shoulders. Big fluorescent earrings matching her sweater dangled to her shoulders. Her stretch pants were denim and the turquoise ballet slippers looked somehow right with the flashy duds. Addy wished she had the balls to pull of the same look. For the first time in a long time, she wanted to pull out clothes with color.

Of course she didn't have balls anyhow, but dressing in something other than black and gray for a man who did was suddenly on her mind.

She shook her head.

Remember your rational voice, Addy. You can't change all of who you are because you have the hots for Lucas Finlay. It was enough she took this slice of a chance, going out with him, kissing him, pretending she was a regular girl and not one haunted by a madman.

Better to cling to her black pullovers and plain jeans.

Addy glanced around the workroom. "So what's on our schedule today? I think we have some deliveries to a couple of funerals, right? Better check the gladiolas and lilies. I don't know why everyone wants those waxy flowers."

"People like what they know. Traditional flowers and such. And that's not just with flowers if you know what I mean."

Addy rolled her eyes, ignoring the pointed comment, and instead focusing on the reason she hated the ho-hum in her work. In her designs, Addy saturated herself in wild color. She hated traditional, unimaginative bouquets taking up shelves in supermarkets. She preferred mixing flowers, grasses, mosses and unusual reeds to create emotion. And her visionary approach to creating floral designs had paid off—creativity rewarded by lucrative business. Sometimes she was too busy, which was a blessing.

The front doorbell jingled and Addy glanced up to find her parents pushing into the shop, arguing about her mother's parallel parking skills.

Addy glanced at Shelia who grinned. Shelia loved Don and Phylis Toussant because when they appeared the shop became a stage for a vaudeville act. Like the classic show *The Honeymooners,* Addy's parents' bickering was grounded in sincere affection, but their interactions were amusing…to everyone but their children. The bickering annoyed Addy, especially when it was over her mother's driving skills.

Phylis thought everyone was an idiot who was out to rear-end or sideswipe her. The strange irony was the woman had never been in an accident, much less received a traffic ticket.

"She's crazy," her father said, jabbing a finger toward his wife.

"Pfft!" Phylis huffed, crossing her arms. "This from a man who ran over the curb at the church last week and nearly hit poor Mr. Martin. The man almost had a heart attack."

"He should look where he's going. Blind as a damn bat and he was halfway in the road."

"It was a parking lot, Don."

Her father crossed his arms. Addy waited for the canned laughter. All she got was Shelia's titter so she stalked to the back of the store.

"Hey, where you going?" her dad called.

"I'm too busy today to play referee."

Addy swept the stems Shelia had cut that morning into the compost bin and sprayed a vinegar mix on the counter, rubbing out the residue and the irritation she felt over her parents constant sparring.

"Hey, sweetie," her mom said, rubbing her shoulders lightly before sinking onto a stool.

"What are y'all doing here, Mom?" Addy finally glanced at her mother.

Her mother had grown up in Gentilly, raised by a traditional Italian mother and an Irish father who drank too much. Passionate, stubborn, with a cute, curvy figure and shoulder-length dark hair she tinted the same color of brown as Addy's, she looked pretty much how Addy expected to look at age sixty-six, sans the childbearing hips. "Your father has an appointment with the urologist and then he's dead set on talking to Lieutenant. Andre Greer."

"Andre can't do anything about the hearing."

Phylis sighed. "How do you feel about the possibility Robbie gets out? Have you talked to your group?"

"I didn't go last night."

Her mother frowned. Addy had a lot of trouble before

she found Survivors of Violence. Once she'd spent several months with women like her, she'd begun to trust herself, to actually heal from the attack and learn how to control her fear. She rarely missed a meeting because it was through SOV that she remained grounded.

"You rarely miss anything at SOV."

"Lucas needed me to help him with his niece and nephews. I had to go to the store."

"And that was more important than preparing for the problems you could face when Robbie is out?" Her mother ran a hand down her back and Addy moved away. She didn't need her mother applying her pseudopsychology on her. The fact she watched *Dr. Phil* every afternoon did not make her qualified to cross-examine Addy's motives behind not attending the meeting. She'd gone Tuesday night, hadn't she?

"Maybe it's time I stop carrying Robbie around with me. I'm tired of him, tired of worry. I love my friends in SOV, but steeping myself in memories of being a victim holds me back. I'm no longer wounded. Cautious? Yes. Crippled? No."

"So you feel worse when you're with your group now?"

"No, but I don't feel like I have to be there twice a week. Maybe not even once a week."

"Since when?"

Addy shook her head. "Since two days ago when I decided to stop overthinking my life."

"Does this have anything to do with this Lucas fellow?" her mother asked, reaching out to touch Addy again but then catching herself and tucking her hand back into her lap.

Maybe it did. Addy wasn't sure. All she knew was that she felt as if she'd been walking through life with her eyes closed. Sure, she'd told herself a million times she was free of Robbie, but she'd been lying. The fear he'd given her was still there, despite SOV. She used that fear conveniently, driving away people who got close enough to hurt her. But with Lucas, she wanted to say to hell with being afraid, to hell with protecting her heart.

"No, it's not him as much as it is me, Mom. I need to let go before it's too late."

Addy's father had been chatting with Shelia, ranting about the Louisiana State University's baseball team's ranking in the top twenty, but now he ambled over to where Addy stood scrubbing the counters like a demon possessed. "Let go of what? And who's this guy you mentioned? Is he Catholic?"

"I don't know. I haven't asked."

Neither of her parents said anything.

"That's your biggest concern?" Addy gave a wry laugh. Jeez, her parents were a piece of work, but she did love them. "He's Ben Finlay's brother and he's taking care of their children while they deal with some personal issues. He's a bit overloaded with three kids, so Aunt Flora and I have been helping out a bit."

Her mother's shoulders sank. "So just friends, huh?"

"At the very least. He's a great guy, but he'll be going back to Texas soon."

"Texas?" Her dad snorted, with a disgusted expression. "Figures."

Addy bit her lip. Her father thought anyone north of Baton Rouge and west of Lake Charles not worthy of spit. Born in the Irish Channel, raised on shrimp boats in the swamp around Lake Pontchartrain, and having returned to New Orleans East to rebuild what Katrina had destroyed, her father was a proud Y'at. Louisiana born and bred, with a decidedly snobbish tendency to think the world existed only around New Orleans.

"Yeah, Texas is a big ol' state you hit if you get on I-10

and drive west. Eventually you'll run into a little town called Houston."

"Watch it, smarty-pants," her dad growled.

"I know you're here to check on me, but I'm doing fine. I can't control Robbie or what he does once he gets out, and I'm not spending my life—"

"Shoot us because we worry about you," her mother interrupted, standing and pressing her hands down her bright red skinny jeans. "We're only doing our job, which never stops no matter how old you are."

"I know, Mom. But you can't control the world any more than I can." Addy reached for the hand on her mother's lap and gave it a squeeze.

"I've decided we're paying for an alarm system for Flora's house," her father said.

"Dad, you can't just decide that."

"I can and it will be done. Your mother's already talked to Flora and we've scheduled the guy to come out on Monday. Flora's going to meet with him because I'm going to the hearing."

"Dad, you don't have to—"

"I know I don't, but you and a frail old woman are all alone in that big house. Hell, you just admitted your neighbors are preoccupied and that weasel weirdo on the other side is never home."

"Troy? He owns a bar and keeps odd hours is all. And he's a nice guy. Tattoos don't make you a weasel weirdo, Dad."

"All the same."

Addy crossed her arms. "I don't like to be managed."

"I know you don't, sugar," her mother said, "and that's not what we're doing. Your father won't sleep once that man is out, and if, God grant our wish, he's not, it's not a bad idea to have added security. Should have been done long ago."

"It's too much money for y'all. Let me cover it."

Her father wagged his graying head and crossed his arms over his barrel chest. "I ain't rich, but I got enough to cover it, cher. Now no more arguments or I'll turn you over my knee."

Addy opened her mouth, but her father's soft "I need to do this, darlin'," stopped her.

"Fine. Put in an alarm system if it makes you feel any better."

"It does. If you had a husband like Ginnie and Caro, I wouldn't worry as much, but what can Flora do? Scare a robber off with her crazy-looking clothes? Do some—" He glanced at her mother. "What's that crap she does called?"

"Zumba."

"Yeah, zumber. Latin dancing for exercise? Jeez, what will they think of next? Polka golf or two-step boxing? I saw a show on how women are doing Roller Derby for exercise. And one woman took up pole dancing like a hootchie girl just to lose weight. I tell ya, what's wrong with the world?"

"Now, now, Don. Let that kind of thing go. Flora has always liked different things."

Her father leveled his eyes at her mother and gave her the look. He always gave Phylis the look when they talked about Flora being different. Her father was convinced Flora was a lesbian, which both amused and aggravated Addy. Like choosing not to marry and have kids automatically put you playing for the other team. He'd never understand Flora's tragic love for Mr. Millard O'Boyle—thought the whole thing was a beard for liking other women.

"Flora's not gay, Dad. And if she were, what would that matter?"

"Hrumph, I'm Catholic," Don said, glancing away and refusing to discuss the issue.

"Okay, honey, we need to be off to the doctor's office."

Phylis knew how to head off an argument. "The parking is horrible at that place, and your father refuses to park the Cadillac in the sun so we go round and round that parking garage."

"Like I want the sun to fade the paint? I paid over fifty thousand dollars for that thing and it's gotta last till I'm in the grave."

Phylis rolled her eyes and gave Addy a quick hug, patting her on the bottom like a four-year-old. "Be good, sweet girl, and don't mess around with that Texas man too much. You need you a good New Orleans boy. I want some grandchildren from you."

…and the clock ticked.

Yeah, that was mentioned every time she saw her mother. What was with mothers? They all wanted babies to bounce on their knees. And Phylis already had seven grandchildren. Besides, Phylis should have figured out warning her away from Lucas only made her want to run toward him.

Same ol' Addy. Rebellious streak a mile wide and doubly deep.

Her dad engulfed her with a hug and kiss on each cheek. "Don't forget to remind Flora about Monday. East Jefferson Security. Ten o'clock. On second thought maybe I better make it for the afternoon."

"Whatever you want, Dad." Addy sighed.

Her parents finally made their way to the door, but only after they had hugged Shelia and her dad had sneaked three pieces of candy from the candy jar that still sat by the register, just the way Millard O'Boyle had left it thirty-six years ago when he'd sold the store to Flora.

"Whew," Addy said, breathing a deep sigh. "My parents wear me out."

"They love you."

"Well, yeah, but they're always trying to manage me the way they've done all my life."

"So tell the security guy to get lost…though, I do believe your father is right. It would be comforting to press that button every night and know you have one more layer of protection. I know mine gives me comfort."

"If you say so, but we both know from our experiences a determined man can get around security systems, gated neighborhoods and even safe houses. How many tales have we heard of failed security?"

"Too many to name, but I'll stick by feeling a little bit easier when I put my head on my pillow."

Addy didn't say anything else, just moved to her bench and focused on losing herself in her work for the next few hours. She didn't want to think about Robbie and the way the thought of him roaming the streets, hers in particular, made her stomach curdle. Fear was a powerful motivator and it was damn near impossible to subdue when allowed to rear its head within her.

"I won't be a victim," she said out loud after several minutes of dwelling on alarms and events outside her control.

What had she said to Michael?

Control what you can control.

So what could she control?

Not her feelings for her Texas cowboy.

At that moment, her inner rebel ripped through the barrier she'd erected long ago and capriciously claimed Addy. Lucas wasn't forever, but he might give her something she needed in her life—an opportunity to feel normal with a man who turned her on and flipped everything sideways.

Addy needed Lucas…if only for a weekend.

Excitement and happiness over the upcoming "date" welled up in the empty places fear wanted to inhabit. This weekend was hers to laugh, smile and feel good about being desirable. Monday would come with alarms, parole hearings and the possibility of Lucas leaving, but tonight, tomorrow and Sunday belonged to her.

She was in control of that at the very least.

So why not go for it with a man she trusted? Time to stop second-guessing every emotion and action and…let go.

"Know what?" she asked, glancing at Shelia who held a roll of floral tape between her lips and glared at an arrangement that obviously wouldn't behave.

"Huh?" she mumbled.

"I'm going shopping."

"For what?"

"Something sexy to wear this weekend."

The tape dropped to the worktable and rolled off onto the floor. "Sexy, huh? I thought y'all was taking the kids with you."

"I'm not planning on looking like a hooker…but maybe not so much like a spinster librarian."

"I know some kinky librarians."

Addy laughed and it felt so freeing.

"I do love when you get sassy," Shelia said, with a twinkle in her dark eyes. "I'm about sick to death of looking at a walkin' funeral."

"I could wear gladiolas in my hair?"

Shelia snorted.

"I'm taking an early lunch and walking over to that cute boutique a few doors down."

"Good girl."

Addy grabbed her purse, double-checking she had her phone and key ring with the pepper spray.

She might feel bold, but she wasn't stupid.

She might take a chance, but she couldn't deny her past.

Addy would always be Addy.

That wouldn't change.

CHAPTER FOURTEEN

SATURDAY DAWNED PARTLY CLOUDY and warm. Lucas couldn't have dialed it up any better.

Finally, something was going right for him. He and the kids had been cooped up in the sick house for so long, he felt like a shaky colt emerging from the barn for his first romp in the yard. The sun felt almost too bright when it peeked out from behind fluffy clouds and the breeze was fresh.

"I'm going to get Addy," Chris yelled, running toward the camellia bushes and ducking between.

"Sure," Lucas muttered, tugging the bow he'd tried to attach to Charlotte's ponytail. It had taken him a good thirty minutes to wash and comb the snarls from the tight curls. He'd done the best he could and once it dried, he'd pulled it up with a weird-looking clear plastic rubber-band thing. Michael had taken the matching bow off a ribbon hanging in the girl's closet and clipped it in, but it looked crooked to Lucas.

Charlotte was dressed in a bright pink dress and something called tights that had little hearts on them. Little-girl clothing confused the hell out of him.

Grabbing his cameras, he escorted a finally happy Charlotte to the truck. Michael lagged behind, tapping on his phone. The boy had been eerily helpful over the past few days. Maybe Lucas saving him from Joe the Toad and seeing him barf his guts up had a way of mellowing the fury within the boy at the uncle who'd ignored him…or Lucas could hope.

"Hey, sport," he said over his shoulder as he settled Charlotte in her car seat. "How about we leave the phones at home?"

"Why?" Michael didn't look up.

"Because we're going to interact with the world around us…not the world on our phone," he said.

"What if we get separated? It's a safety precaution."

"We won't get separated." He looked for the stupid plastic piece that snapped between Charlotte's legs. Where was the stupid thing? "Tell you what. If you leave the phone, I'll let you use my Canon."

"Your what?"

"It's a camera."

"I have a camera on my iPhone."

Lucas found the fastener and clicked Charlotte in, handing her both a sippy cup and a book about that Creampie kitten. "Seriously? I'm talking about a real camera. The kind I use for my work."

Michael held up his phone. "How about I turn this off, but keep it in my back pocket, and then you show me this camera of yours."

Lucas nodded. "Deal."

"'Morning," Addy called from the other side of the truck.

Chris hustled by Lucas in order to move the scooter he'd left in the drive from behind the truck. "Wait till you see Addy."

Lucas walked to the other side to get the door for Addy and nearly tripped when he saw her.

"Wow," he breathed, stifling a wolf whistle.

"What?" She blushed, giving a somewhat breathless laugh.

She wore a soft-looking peach sweater with a square neckline that showed those delicious collarbones. It fit her like a second skin, covering almost every inch of skin but somehow looking incredibly sexy. Her hair was in a soft braid that reminded him of Meg Ryan in *Sleepless in Seattle,* one of his favorite movies—not that he'd admit to it. And her jeans were trim all the way down to supple gold ballet flats. Small pearl earrings dangled in her ears and she wore just enough makeup to look ravishing, but not enough to be overt. Shiny peach lips were his lighthouse.

Oh, sweet gravy, guide him home.

He couldn't help himself. He lowered his head and gave her a soft, quick kiss.

"Ooooh," Chris said, rubbing his fingers together in that ancient naughty-naughty signal. "Shame, shame."

"Oh, hush. You'd kiss her too if you were tall enough," Lucas said.

Chris waggled his eyebrows. "You know it, brother."

Addy laughed, ducking down toward Chris making kissing sounds. "Come on then, Chris."

Chris ran.

Both he and Addy laughed until Michael stepped around holding Lucas's camera bag on his shoulder. "Are y'all gonna stand around all day?"

Lucas stared into Addy's eyes. "If I could stare at her, I would."

Her smile was the invitation he'd been waiting for. This was an Addy determined to live…and perhaps love…if only for the weekend.

"I'd let you, but I'm pretty sure the kids would get bored. And you know what happens when kids get bored," she said.

He gave an exaggerated sigh, but started back around the front of the truck.

"Saddle up," Lucas yelled, loving Addy's giggle at his response.

He sent a glance heavenward and whispered. "Thank you."

ADDY HAD NO CLUE where Lucas was taking them, but it was definitely away from the heart of the city. She'd expected to go to the French Quarter or maybe City Park. "Where the devil are you taking us?"

His look was a little too lustful for a man with a truck full of kids. "You'll see."

"You said we were visiting your favorite places as a kid in New Orleans. This is Metairie," Michael said.

"Well, not every favorite place is in the Quarter, though I do love the history there. I wanted to take you to some of the favorite spots your dad and I enjoyed when we were your age. I hope some of them are still around."

"Oh," the boy said.

She caught sight of Michael in the mirror on the visor. He studied the camera. "Do you like to take pictures, too?"

The boy looked up, lowering the camera. "I've never used a camera like this. My iPhone works pretty good."

Lucas nodded. "It's crazy how good some of those phones can be, but it's not the sort you build a career with. The one you're holding is the first good camera I ever bought. A Canon EOS 1V, loaded with Fuji Velvia film that will still take damn good pictures. I still use it sometimes because I like the feel of the click, the sound of the camera rewinding and waiting on the images in the darkroom. Nothing wrong with a little old-school photography."

"How did you learn?" Addy asked.

"By doing. I dropped out of law school when, well, I decided it wasn't something I wanted to do—it was more like an expectation. Suddenly my world shifted and I didn't know what I wanted. I packed up my Chevy Blazer and headed west where I figured adventure lay. As I drove through countryside so different from what surrounds New Orleans, I felt a tug. I'd always loved drawing as a kid, and I used my grandmother's Polaroid one summer when we rented a house on the lake. But it wasn't some divine revelation out of the blue."

"So you just decided to become a photographer?"

"No, I became a waiter. In Phoenix."

Addy smiled. "That's a way different career choice from being an attorney."

"Wasn't a waiter for long. I saved up and took a photography class at a local community college because someone told me I could get a gig taking school photos for some company."

"We just had some weird guy take our spring pictures last week. I forgot to tell you and I wore my Saints T-shirt with the hole on the sleeve. Mrs. Creech made a face when she saw me," Chris said, lowering his iPod touch.

"Hey, you were supposed to leave that at home." Lucas stretched an arm back and opened his palm. "Give it."

"Come on, Uncle Lucas. It's boring in the car."

"Count license plates," he said, palm up. Emphatically up.

"I don't even know what that is," Chris complained, laying the device in Lucas's hand. "And Charlotte is picking her nose again."

Addy turned around and tugged Charlotte's elbow down. The little girl frowned but thankfully stopped. Addy turned back to Lucas. "So how did you end up in Texas?"

"After I got sucked into photography, I got into the San Francisco Art Institute. Suddenly this strange world I'd never imagined opened for me, and for the first time maybe ever I knew I was doing what I was supposed to do—climbing mountains, fording streams and lying on my stomach in the desert capturing the world in its splendor."

"Do you make a lot of money taking pictures?" Michael asked, dubious expression reflecting in Addy's mirror.

"Enough to live on. Being successful in photography is just like any other career. I work hard and pray for luck. My ship came in when a couple of New York socialites and their decorators found my stuff. Then I sold to several celebrities."

"Like who?"

Lucas laughed. "People you listen to on your iPod."

"We have one of your pictures," Chris said, interrupting. "But it's of a waterfall and red dirt. You could of at least stuck a dog in there or something."

Addy giggled and decided it felt pretty good. She hadn't used that particular response in a while. Maybe her giggler was rusty. "Wait a sec, we're in River Ridge."

"You know your geography," Lucas teased, maneuvering down Jefferson Highway toward Kenner.

Everyone fell silent for the next several miles. Soon Lucas maneuvered the truck into the quaint Rivertown district, tucked in between the city of Kenner and the Mississippi River.

"Why are we here?" Michael asked, his face squashed into disapproval.

"This area opened when your dad and I were kids. They had some cool museums, including a train museum I think."

Chris and Michael groaned.

"We're not four years old, Uncle Lucas," Chris said, slapping a hand against his forehead.

"Well, Charlotte nearly is and there is a story time with puppets." Lucas parked the car near the quaint district and turned to Addy with an alarmed look.

That was when she realized he had no clue what kids liked to do, but the fact he tried so hard warmed her heart. She gave him an encouraging smile and looked over her seat at the kids in the back. "My nephew said there's a cool science museum here…something about the Hubble and a space station? And there's a planetarium and an IMAX movie theater. Have you been in one of those?"

"Once," Michael said, nodding and looking somewhat interested. "It made me a little sick, but it was pretty cool."

Lucas grabbed the cowboy hat on the dash, opened his door and climbed out. "I remember liking this area when I was younger because it was like a small town. I think there's a park and they had this cool village with a black-smith shop."

"What's a blacksmith?" Chris asked sliding to the pavement below.

"We're going to find out," Addy said, grabbing her purse and glancing up at the rain cloud that moved steadily toward them.

Thirty minutes later her cowboy and his nephews were off to explore space, leaving her and Charlotte to wait for story time in Heritage Park. She sat on a bench, pulling Charlotte up next to her. There weren't too many other people present, but it was a nice day to be outside. Trees were starting to sprout new sticky growth and the dormant grass clothed itself in green clover. A few daffodils had arrived early, huddling at the base of small trees. The rain cloud seemed to have moved on, but other gray flannel clouds dotted the perimeter, and Addy knew a New Orleans shower could come at any moment.

A couple of little girls eyed Charlotte, and she eyed them back but made no move to slip off the bench.

"Do you want to play with those little girls?" Addy asked, giving one girl who looked about Charlotte's age a friendly wave. The adorable pixie ducked her head but didn't run away. She seemed interested in coaxing Charlotte to come hop about with her.

"I don't know that girl," Charlotte said.

"Well, that's how we make new friends." Addy had already checked out the area for any dangers. No skulking old pervs, no red-flag warnings popping in her mind…just a nice day at the park.

"Your little girl's welcome to play with Sarah," said a woman who sat cross-legged about ten feet away next to another woman who tapped furiously on her iPad.

Addy didn't bother to correct the woman about her role in Charlotte's life, but she did give Charlotte a little shove. "Sarah wants to play. Go have fun."

"No," Charlotte said shaking her head. A few pieces of her ponytail came down and the bow lurched sideways.

"You don't want to play?" Addy gave Sarah's mom a strained smile. "It's fun to make new friends."

Charlotte shook her head.

Addy turned to the mother. "Sorry. She's just getting over the stomach virus and hasn't—"

"Never mind," the woman interrupted, hopping up with a graceful leap and dragging Sarah back to where she sat. "We don't need that with our vacation coming up."

Addy snapped her mouth closed and looked down at Charlotte. "Well, guess you don't have to bother making new friends."

Charlotte scooted closer to her and rested her head against Addy's side. Addy curled an arm around the little girl, feeling her heart swell…and maybe something else move inside her.

She suspected it might be the tick of her biological clock.

Addy had never really given having children much thought, mainly because she hadn't had a successful relationship of late. Sure, she spent time with nieces and nephews she adored, but she'd never truly thought about what it would be like to spend her Saturdays in the park with little Addys and little—she refused to imagine Lucases—frolicking about her.

Did she even want to procreate?

Kids were messy. They got things like stomach viruses, they crashed into greenhouses and sulked, fought and made ungodly messes. But they also snuggled up to you and made your heart feel full and your throat a little scratchy with emotion.

What would her and Lucas's children look like?

Oh, dear Lord, Addy, don't go there. Don't you dare go there.

Thankfully a woman in a black dress carrying a rolling trunk appeared. Behind her came the rest of what should be the puppet show. Addy said a silent thank you for being saved from her dangerous thoughts. "Look, Charlotte. Here comes the puppet show."

The little girl straightened, her eyes growing big.

An hour later, Addy met Lucas in front of the science center. The boys each had changed into a new T-shirt with the space center logo, and Lucas waved a stuffed frog with a pink bow around its neck at Charlotte. "Look what Uncle Lucas found hopping inside."

Charlotte held little hands up to him. "Froggie."

Lucas gave her the stuffed animal, looking pleased with himself. Just as Charlotte took the frog, a raindrop splashed onto Addy's cheek.

"Uh-oh," Chris said as several more big droplets landed on her shoulder and head.

And then the bottom of the cloud fell out. The boys took off running for the overhang of the shopping area, hooting as they ran. Lucas scooped up Charlotte who screeched and wrapped her chubby arms around his neck. Addy calmly pulled her compact umbrella from her purse and opened it.

"Prepared, are you?" Lucas said, his brown eyes happy

and his broad shoulder speckled with dark spots of rain. He looked incredibly good in that straw cowboy hat.

Addy positioned the umbrella over both their heads, unintentionally bringing them closer together. She could smell the sultry cologne he wore and the clean smell of baby shampoo. His eyes crinkled as they looked down at her. "I try."

The moment crackled…even with Charlotte clinging to his side like a monkey and with a silly green frog crushed between them.

And there under her green umbrella in front of God and everybody, Lucas kissed her.

And it was such a tender kiss of possibility that Addy felt it down to her toes…which were sort of getting wet. But who really cared about wet feet when a gorgeous man wrapped you in his arms and took your breath away?

Not Addy.

But apparently Charlotte did.

Addy felt a little hand against her cheek and broke the kiss. Rain created timpani around them as Charlotte's blue eyes met hers.

"Uncle Wucas wants to kiss me now," the little girl said, turning her face to Lucas.

A small smile tipped the corners of his mouth. "I thought you were afraid I would eat you."

Charlotte shook her head and the hair bow nearly fell to the ground. "You won't."

Lucas unwound his arm from Addy, cupped the child's head and dropped a quick kiss upon Charlotte's cheek before dropping another one on Addy's. "Come on, girls. We better go find the boys."

The boys waited by the theater, clamoring to see the movie that would start in ten minutes. Well, Chris clamored. Michael just nodded his head in begrudging agreement, but Addy could tell the teen was having a decent time.

"I want popcorn," Chris demanded as Lucas purchased the tickets.

"They don't serve popcorn," Michael said, pointing to the no-food-or-drink-allowed sign.

"Man, I'm starving," Chris groaned.

Lucas dug a granola bar out of his back pocket, tearing it open and handing Chris half and holding out the other. "Who wants the other half?"

Both Charlotte and Michael grabbed at it, but Michael pulled back and allowed his little sister to have it. Lucas set her down on her feet.

"We'll eat after the movie, okay?"

All kids agreed and then sped off to look at the various machines offering to stamp their pennies into souvenirs.

Lucas turned to her. "Chris is always starving so I, too, came prepared…just didn't think about an umbrella. Am I doing okay so far?"

"On being a good uncle? Or being a good date?"

"Both?" he asked, tucking his hands into the front pockets of his Wranglers, looking atypical. This was a man who was rarely uncertain. A man who likely never worried about a performance report. That he cared so much made her like him all the more.

He wasn't merely some cowboy in a dark blue shirt offsetting his tanned skin, a hunk of manhood in a pair of tight jeans and boots. She flicked her gaze over him and was struck again at his sheer masculinity. Warmth bloomed inside her, a feeling that had a little something to do with cute kids and his success at being an uncle, and a lot to do with wrapping her legs around him.

Damn biological clock.

Nope, more like damn libido.

"I'd say you're shooting a thousand."

"You mean batting, right?" He stepped closer, his voice low, intimate, with just the right about of sexiness.

"Whatever," she whispered, studying his mouth. He had such nice lips. They probably needed to be kissed.

"Uncle Lucas!" Chris shouted.

"You know how in movies parents can never get it on because the kids are always knocking on the door or yelling about spiders in the kitchen?"

"What movies do you watch?" she joked.

"I know how they feel. And the really crappy part is neither one of us has kids. We should be pulling the covers over our heads right now and pretending the world away."

The image popping into her head made her body hum. Oh, to be under a set of soft sheets with him.

Woo.

Addy fanned herself and demanded her body take a chill pill. Pointing to where Chris and Michael stood, looking as if they might trade blows, she murmured, "One day. Maybe."

"Oh, you can bank on my getting you alone, Addy girl. We got unfinished business." And then he turned and strode toward his brother's children, who had emoted into a couple of wild dogs snarling next to an oblivious hopping bunny whose bow had finally fallen out.

Addy scooped up the bow and glanced over at Lucas. "Fine. I'm making you keep that promise."

Lucas's smile could have melted the ice caps. "Like I said, bank on it."

Lucas carried a sleeping Charlotte out of the theater and watched as his nephews excitedly discussed the movie with Addy. Those three had been here during Hurricane Katrina, though Chris had been a toddler, and they had tales to accompany the educational movie that depicted life on the bayou and the catastrophic results of the storm on the coastline and wetlands. But to Addy and the boys, the effects were much more personal.

Hours before Lucas had spent quality time with Michael and Chris, talking to them about their father's once-upon-a-time dream of being an astronaut and sharing funny stories about their days of growing up in New Orleans.

Funny how being home made the relationship with his estranged brother seem less tenuous. When he remembered the boys they'd been, nearly the same age difference between them as Chris and Michael, he didn't remember the squabbling and resentment between them, he remembered dressing up as their favorite WWF wrestlers and re-enacting matches on the trampoline or sun-streaked days of baseball in the empty lot across the street from their parents' house. He remembered gelatos at Angelo Brocato's and eating Tastee Donuts at the Mardi Gras parades. Plum Street Snoballs and swimming at the Metairie Country Club. Late nights playing Tetris and Christmas mornings eating King Cake and playing football in the yard in their jammies.

All those memories soaked in bitterness for years…but yet the good ones still came to him with a golden haze, sweetened like sugary jam.

He and Ben had loved one another, faced off against neighborhood bullies together, and grown up with love bestowed by a mother and father who both adored their boys.

How had it come to the present state?

Why had that betrayal seeped so deep inside him, especially when he could see fate had given them both what they needed in the long run? It was as if a boulder sat between them, and he had no clue how to move it.

Maybe he couldn't move it…maybe he needed to climb over it.

"I'm starving," Chris said for the umpteenth time.

"Okay, let's load up and head for lunch," Lucas said,

balancing Charlotte on his shoulder so he could fetch Addy's green umbrella and hand it to Michael. The skies had cleared and the sun made an appearance as they walked back to the truck. Lucas wound his free arm around Addy's shoulders.

"Are y'all like going out now?" Michael asked shaking the umbrella and casting a glance at them.

"Maybe," Lucas responded, sliding his eyes to her. She could see he had no better explanation. Neither did she. She didn't really know what they were, but that was okay.

"That's cool," Michael said, taking longer steps so he could catch up with his brother. He wrapped a congenial arm around Chris's shoulders. Chris looked up and said something to Michael with a grin.

"Aww, look," Addy said, pointing at the boys. "They're actually being—"

But then Chris pulled out from under his brother's arm as Michael threw a right jab at him. Chris immediately jumped on Michael's back and tried put him in a headlock.

Lucas snorted before jogging up to catch the back of Chris's shirt and pulling him off. "Enough."

"He said I liked Addy and you was snakin' me. He's the one who likes Addy," Chris said.

"I don't like Addy. I have a girlfriend," Michael said.

"Hey, you two," Lucas released Chris. "Wait, you have a girlfriend?"

His oldest nephew actually blushed. "Hannah Leachman."

Chris made a face. "Ooh, Michael and Hannah sitting in a tree—"

Lucas snapped his fingers in front of Chris's face. "Do you want lunch?"

Chris turned stricken eyes on Lucas. "I'm starving to death."

"Then declare a truce and don't touch each other for the rest of the day. Good behavior means you get fed."

Both boys muttered, "Fine."

"Bet they never used starvation as a method in any of those parenting magazines," Addy said with a laugh.

Lucas smiled. "Whatever it takes."

CHAPTER FIFTEEN

AFTER A DAY of remembering the past, Lucas felt like look-ing toward his future.

His future of a few more days…or a week…or maybe longer. Didn't matter as long as it had Addy in it.

When had he started to crave her with a hunger like no other?

When she'd told him about that dirtbag who'd tried to hurt her? When she'd first kissed him? When she'd brought chilled ginger ale for his sick nephews? Or maybe it was her face framed in against that green umbrella?

He wasn't sure. All he knew was his life would seem far emptier without her in it. He had to make the days he had with her count.

But would that be enough?

The sun sank over the thick oaks off Carrollton as they polished off their gelatos and spumoni at Angelo Brocato's Italian Ice Cream Parlor. Lazy fans whirled overhead and Charlotte's head drooped like a wilted daisy very near her cup of frozen custard.

"Today was fun, Uncle Lucas," Chris said, still work-ing on the huge cone he'd demanded. "I like knowing stuff about my dad when he was little."

"He was a lot like you," Lucas commented, shoving the last bite of spumoni into his mouth. He'd waited too long to come home. Too long for some sugary piece of yesterday.

"Who am I like?" Michael asked, not bothering to look up. He'd long ago finished his cookie and cocoa.

"A little like me, and a little like your mother."

"You and my mom were boyfriend and girlfriend for a long time," Michael said lifting dark eyes up to gaze at him. It was a question, not a statement.

Addy frowned. "You dated Courtney? One of the kids said something like that, but I…" She didn't finish her question and he understood why. It was a strange situation.

"I grew up with Courtney. She's a bit younger than I but she was in my grade because she started school in another state. We were best of friends. She was the pea to my carrot," Lucas said, not wanting to talk about Courtney and the past. It seemed so long ago…almost like a dream at times. "You're a lot like her, Michael. You hold things in and think you can handle everything life throws at you on your own."

"And you don't?" Addy asked.

He tried not to squirm, but it happened anyway. The day had been light, full of laughter and excitement. They'd gone to City Park and played Wiffle ball and then gone on to the Mardi Gras Museum downtown…even though there had been one in Kenner. And that was after they'd stuffed themselves on Deanie's Seafood in Bucktown a stone's throw from Lake Pontchartrain. He didn't want to trip back into the hurt of the past. "Sure. I'm a dude. We hold on to stuff, and in my case, I have things I've held on to for longer than I should have."

"Like hating my dad?" Chris asked.

"I don't—" Lucas snapped his mouth shut and shook his head. "I don't hate your father. He's my brother and brothers always love each other. That's something you two should think about."

"But Dad stole Mom from you. I hear things and I know you left New Orleans because of them getting together." Michael's eyes glinted with something Lucas couldn't define. Maybe he also knew Courtney getting pregnant with him also played a role.

"Is that why you left law school?" Addy asked softly.

"You know what? I don't want to have this conversation right now," he said, scooting back the old-fashioned iron parlor chair, dragging it across the floor with a loud squeak. "Charlotte's worn-out and I am, too."

Three pair of eyes stared at him, but they didn't move.

"Do you hate us, too?" Michael asked, his eyes now fearless, almost accusing. Obviously the kid wanted the truth.

Lucas paused. "Do you think I hate you?"

The boy shook his head. "No, if you did you would have left us with that crackhead DeeAnn."

Lucas sucked in air, feeling like the world pressed in on him. "Right. I don't hate anyone, but that doesn't mean there aren't some things between your father and I. Things you wouldn't understand."

"Michael says Dad is dead," Chris said, his brown eyes welling with tears. "That's not true, is it? We're kind of scared."

Michael's spoon clattered on the table but he didn't say anything.

"Your father isn't dead. And he's not going to die."

"His leg got blown off," Michael said, his voice quiet in the chattering cacophony of the busy restaurant. "I heard Mom tell Grammy and Grampy weeks ago. She was crying and said he was in Germany and then told them about the operations he would have."

Chris turned terror-stricken eyes on his brother. "His leg got blowed up?"

"Wait a sec, guys," Lucas said, holding up his hands and waving them before scooting his chair back toward the table. He glanced over at Addy who cradled her cappuccino in both hands, her deep eyes brimming with concern. "Let's take a deep breath and I'll explain some things to you, okay?"

Both Chris and Michael swallowed, their eyes glued to him, as they nodded simultaneously.

Lucas glanced over at Addy. "I'm about to piss Courtney off with this, so you vouch for me when she tries to shank me."

Addy bit her lower lip before saying, "I don't know what Courtney's intentions are, but I think easing your nephews' fears trumps any promises made, and for what it's worth, as a senior counselor in my victim's therapy group, I can say honesty is a good policy when facing fear."

Lucas nodded and looked back at his nephews. "Your mother is a good woman, and when she was in high school her parents were killed."

"We already know that," Michael said.

"Yes, but I was there with her when it happened, and a lot of false hope and promises were given to her by doctors and nurses…and none of those promises came true. They told your mother that her mother would live and get better. She didn't. Having hope yanked away really hurt your mother, so she truly thinks she's doing the right thing by protecting of you."

"Our dad…is he?" Chris started, his lower lip trembling with emotion. "I don't want my daddy to die."

"He's not," Lucas said, stretching out a hand and patting Chris's. "They thought your father was fine and moved him from Germany back to the U.S., but he grew sick when he got to Virginia. An infection developed from some wounds he received in his stomach and he didn't respond to the doctor's treatments. For a while, it looked bad."

"But now it doesn't?" Michael asked.

Lucas shook his head. "He's doing much better and they found the right combination of medicines to fight the infection. He's growing stronger every day and your mother thinks that after he's fitted with a prosthetic, they will clear him to come home to finish his recovery."

"What's a prosetic?"

"Prosthetic," Michael corrected, tapping on the glass tabletop. "It's a fake leg. You've seen runners with them. Remember?"

"That cool spring robot-looking leg?" Chris knitted his eyes together. "That's what Dad will have?"

"Or something like that," Lucas said, glancing again at Addy. Her face had assumed an ethereal quality, reminding him of Rubenesque paintings gracing cathedrals. Her soft eyes smiled at him and suddenly all inside him wasn't about wanting Addy beneath him. A piece of him was satisfied at that moment to be near her, to be able to reach out and draw warmth from her. "But I want you to take your frustration at your mother for not telling you and put it up on a shelf to be forgotten. She is what she is. This wasn't about not trusting you…it was about loving you so much she didn't want to hurt you."

"Wow," Addy breathed, turning a smile onto the two boys who looked oddly lighter than they had in the entire time he'd been with them.

"So are we good?"

Michael pushed his hair back and leveled his gaze at him. "Thank you for telling us, but you didn't tell us about what happened between you and Dad a long time ago."

At that moment, Lucas knew he couldn't put his brother or sister-in-law in a bad light…and explaining the cheating and betrayal would tarnish their images, which felt like the wrong thing to do. "You know, your mother and father were meant to be together. Sometimes we think we know what we want, but God has a better plan for us. He had a better plan for your parents and put them together. And thank goodness He did. He made you a family."

Chris nodded his head. "So what you're saying is that you're glad Mom and Dad got together because now you can marry Addy."

Addy choked on her cappuccino.

"That's not exactly what I was saying, but it's kind of right," Lucas said, popping her on the back and trying not to laugh. "So are we good here?"

Michael smiled. "Yeah, we're good."

And at that very moment, Lucas felt things shift between him and Michael. It was subtle, but present all the same. Maybe his words hadn't merely brought Michael some relief but had strengthened the fragile bonds they'd started forming over the past two weeks. Maybe he and Michael moved toward forgiveness.

On many levels.

"Ready to go?" Addy asked, reaching out for Charlotte and scooping her into her arms. Lucas paused a moment and watched how gently Addy moved her, how right she looked with the little girl cradled against her body.

He'd taken pictures throughout the day and itched for the camera in the truck to preserve the sheer beauty of Addy and the child.

"Yep, I'm ready to play 'Battlefield 3,'" Chris said, banging the chair against the table, waking Charlotte who started whimpering.

Addy nuzzled her and smiled at Lucas, and in her face he saw exactly what he looked for...understanding.

No need to rehash all that had occurred between him and Courtney because somehow or another, Addy got him.

And it had felt that way since he'd first met her.

Meant to be.

And just as Michael had looked lighter, Lucas felt lighter. Something about sharing that burden had given more knockabout room inside him. His heart beat strong against his ribs and his mind seemed to almost sigh with relief. Didn't make sense but he felt it just the same.

And as they walked to his truck, Charlotte asleep on Addy's shoulder, the two boys for once not arguing, Lucas slid his hand into Addy's and felt contentment make a home in him.

"YOU'RE HOME," Flora said when Addy unlocked the back door and entered the kitchen.

"I am, but only for a minute. Thought I'd come see if you wanted to watch a movie with us. Sanitized version of *Forrest Gump*." Addy opened the pantry and rifled through the snack basket for a package of microwave popcorn.

"No, I'm working on piecing that pattern for the dress I'm making for the Natchez Pilgrimage. These old fingers ain't what they used to be and neither are these eyes." Flora wiggled her fingers and eyed Addy as she retreated from the depths of the pantry. "You sure look pretty, my darling. So glad to see you wearing some color."

"Thanks. You sure you don't want to come? The kids are behaving and Lucas is baking brownies. Who knew the man could bake all along? We could have saved ourselves some work."

"You need a proper date with that man. Not one with kids around," Flora said, putting her hands on her hips. Addy's aunt wore a pair of pink Juicy Couture sweatpants and a tight long-sleeved T-shirt that said Cutie Pie. She looked like a teenager except with bifocals, age spots and gray hair.

"It's going to be hard to do since he's all they have," Addy said.

"Y'all have me," her aunt said, cocking her head. "Unless you don't trust me anymore?"

Addy would never admit her doubts about Flora's progressing disease to her aunt, but she wasn't sure Flora could handle three unruly, precocious kids for an evening. "Of course I trust you, Auntie. I just don't think it's fair to ask—"

"Why the heck not? Shit, I can handle a few kids," Aunt Flora cracked, waving a hand.

"Flora."

Her aunt smiled. "I'm getting too old to mince words."

"You look and sound like a rap video," Addy joked, ransacking the candy jar for Reese's Peanut Butter Cups.

"How about tomorrow afternoon, I take the kids to the movies? Or maybe down to Audubon to the zoo?"

"Alone?"

"I'll call Patti and she can bring her grandson Tristan. She has season passes and it's not hard to handle kids at the zoo…they can't touch any animals or break anything."

"I'll ask Lucas," Addy said, hoping she used good sense and hadn't let her desire to have Lucas alone skew her judgment.

Heck, her judgment had been skewed when she'd decided to not worry about forever, but to embrace the now. So un-Addy-like. Or at least unlike the Addy she'd become. But she wanted this weekend more than she wanted to be sensible.

Walking back into the darkening shadows, Addy's lizard brain kicked in.

Nothing but shadows. No movement but the wind. No sounds but the swish of nearby traffic and the leaves brushing against their neighbors. The dark wasn't scary…it was the evil in the bright light of day that scared the bejesus out of Addy.

She walked across the back porch of the Finlay house and Kermit brushed against her knees.

"Agh!" she stepped back and nearly fell off the step. Lucas poked his head out and she smelled the brownies baking.

"You okay?"

"Yeah, I didn't see the dog," she said, looking down at a smiling Kermit. His tongue lolled out and he lifted a paw and scraped it down her leg. She gave him a pat. Pavlov. Humans were ruled by it just as much as their canine friends.

Lucas stepped out and swept her into his arms. He didn't kiss her, just settled her into his chest, tucking her head beneath his chin. "Thank you for today, Addy."

"Mmm," she said, wrapping her arms about him, leaning into him, enjoying the hard warmth of his body against the softness of hers. She inhaled his scent, trailed her fingers up and down the ridges of his back. She wanted to memorize him so when he was gone and she lay in her bed alone, she could recall the way he felt. "Today was surprisingly fun. Never thought I'd say that about a date with kids along for the ride."

"You're good at Frisbee Golf."

"My nephew Connor taught me," she said allowing her hands to slide into the back of his waistband, massaging his lower back.

"You fit me, Addy," he said, dropping little kisses atop her head, brushing a hand through the tendrils falling from her braid. His head lowered and he kissed the spot beneath her ear, that oh-so-sensitive place on her neck.

A small shudder rent through her.

"Uncle Wucas! Chris woke me up," Charlotte said from the open doorway.

Addy peered over at the tot who rubbed her eyes and blinked sleepily at them. "We're coming."

Lucas growled, nipping her ear. "I told you. This isn't fair."

"Hey." She swatted him, smiling up at him as she stepped from his arms. "By the way, Aunt Flora wants to take the kids to the zoo tomorrow. Her friend has passes."

Lucas's eyebrows raised and she'd never seen such a satisfied smile before. "Really?"

"If you don't have anything to do…" she drawled, walking her fingers up his arm. "Tara wants you to go mow her yard."

He made a face.

She poked a finger at his chest. "Just kidding. I want you to mow my yard."

His eyes narrowed.

"And by yard, I mean mow—" she blew into his ear "—my—" she trailed a finger down his chest "—yard." She brushed her hand against his fly, feeling his arousal.

She smiled that smile given by all femme fatales throughout history and sashayed, yes, sashayed to the back door.

"I'll sharpen my blade," Lucas said.

Addy laughed.

SUNDAY DAWNED RAINY and gray, and Lucas cursed the clouds when he took Kermit out for a short run. Michael was reading, Chris was clicking that stupid control and making machines fight each other and Charlotte was glued to the Creampie kitten movie. He had about fifteen minutes to stretch his legs, gather his thoughts and expend the frustration at the damn weather. The drizzle spat at him, and Kermit took extra long to do his business.

Ben and Courtney's neighborhood was nice, sitting not far off Carrollton in a nice area of midsize, tasteful houses that clustered around the grand dames lining St. Charles, which ran perpendicular with the busy street. Not far away were the arches of Tulane and the graceful solidarity of Ursuline Academy. He hooked a left onto St. Charles and then huffed it back up State Street and then across to Nashville.

By the time he reached the gray-blue house on Orchard, the misty rain had stopped and the sun peeked out.

Hallelujah.

By the time he'd dressed the kids, fed them lunch, given them money and then warned them to behave or risk the loss of a limb…or at least phone privileges, he was a giant ball of horny need.

Not good.

Addy didn't need him jumping her bones the minute he walked through her door.

Flora showed up on the porch at a quarter of noon wearing jeans and a shirt that she'd likely stolen out of a teenager's closet. The woman took dressing young to extremes, but her smile was open and her friend had a four-year-old boy with her.

Lucas bent down and eyeballed Charlotte. "Be nice to Tristan. Remember what happened with Sheldon?"

She nodded. "He hitted me."

"Yes, so use good manners just like your teacher taught you, okay?"

"Okay."

He rose and gave Michael and Chris the look his father had often given to him and Ben. "Keep your hands off each other and be nice to your sister."

Chris saluted. "Aye, aye, Uncle."

And off they went, leaving Lucas to shower, shave and run out for a bottle of wine. He grabbed a small clutch of flowers as he checked out at the grocery and then booked it back to Orchard Street. He wanted every second of every minute with Addy to count.

When he pulled into the driveway, he groaned.

A car sat in the drive.

A car with a nun in it.

CHAPTER SIXTEEN

SISTER REGINA MARIA wasn't bigger than a popcorn fart, but she covered every inch of ground she trod.

And she trod toward him.

Glowering.

"Mr. Finlay?"

"You drive a car?" As opposed to flying on a broom?

She glanced back at the silver Toyota Highlander before piercing him with flinty eyes. "Why wouldn't I?"

He didn't have an answer. "What can I help you with, Sister?"

"First, I think it would be appropriate for you to ask me to step inside. I'm a human being, not an animal who conducts business in a driveway."

Something sank inside him and he shifted the grocery bag and gestured to the house before casting a desperate glance at Addy's place.

So much for every second of every minute.

"Come inside, Sister." He pulled out the key and unlocked the door, praying the living room was halfway cleared of toys, clothing and the load of towels he hadn't gotten around to folding.

Nope. Same ol' messy living room. Clothes-folding fairies had not descended upon the laundry basket.

Sister Regina Maria's eyes widened, but she was polite enough to keep her mouth pressed into a disapproving line. She refused to sit...of course, he didn't blame her. Chris had left his socks on the cushion. He sat the bag on the coffee table and turned to her. "So what brings you here on a most holy day?"

"The Lord's work, of course."

"No telephones at the nunnery?"

"Nunnery? We don't call our home a nunnery. Does this look like eighteenth-century Europe to you?" she snapped, crossing her whip-thin arms.

"Sorry. Can I get you a coffee? Tea? Beer?"

She shook her head. "I like cold beer but not on Sunday. My grandmother was Baptist."

He wasn't sure what that meant, but whatever. He wanted her to spit out the reason she'd invaded his quality time with Addy…and then get the heck out of Dodge. "Okay. How may I help you?"

"I understand the situation. You're taking care of your niece while Mrs. Finlay is away, but Charlotte is having some difficulties as I'm certain you've noticed."

He arched a brow. "Well, they're going through an adjustment having me taking care of them. I'm sure she'll be fine."

"She's hitting other children and she keeps wetting her mat at nap time."

"Oh," he said, wondering why the teacher hadn't called. Didn't they just have parent-teacher conference? Oh, damn. He'd missed it because of the stomach virus epidemic.

"Charlotte was out the last part of the week and no one was present for her conference. I figured a home-site visit was in order, and as I am the principal of the lower school, I must address what is amiss with Charlotte." She glanced around.

"It's not as if Courtney is at a spa. Ben is near death, and I, an uncle she's never seen before, have been left to care for her and her brothers. Whatever could be amiss in her world?" he drawled with an extra helping of sarcasm.

"Oh, dear," Sister Regina Maria said, lifting a weathered hand to clasp the dangling crucifix lying against her charcoal sweater. "Her teacher told me Mrs. Finlay was out of town, but not that Mr. Finlay had been gravely ill."

Lucas relaxed a little. "Charlotte's adjusting to change. I can talk to her about the hitting, but I'm not sure about the mat wetting. Perhaps those pull-up things? In *Modern Parenting,* a psychologist suggested major changes can set potty-trained toddlers back. I'm certain it's a phase."

"You read *Modern Parenting?*"

"When there's nothing else around," he said, shaking his head. "Look, I'll talk to Courtney. Ben is tremendously better and he may be moved to New Orleans the latter part of next week. I'll make sure Courtney calls the school and sets up a conference with Charlotte's teacher."

Sister Regina Maria nodded, resembling a crow with beady eyes. From around the couch, Mittens strolled, curling about the woman's feet. The nun bent and stroked the cat. Yeah, seemed about right. Like recognized like.

"That would be acceptable. Next time you need to inform the school when there is something of this magnitude ongoing in a student's life. We do care, Mr. Finlay."

"Note taken. My sister-in-law feels this is a sensitive issue, and I hope you will keep this conversation confidential. I appreciate your coming by on your day off," he said, acknowledging the nun had her heart in the right place... even if she was unforgiving of taking up too much time in carpool line. It was the stupid harness in the car seat's fault.

"Oh, today is not my day off, Mr. Finlay. For a woman of God there is no day off."

"Right," he said, motioning toward the door, wanting

her to leave as soon as possible. But also concerned about Charlotte. He'd had no idea, though come to think of it, she'd worn different clothes home a few days in a row. He'd thought she'd spilled something on them and had to change into her play clothes packed in her pink Creampie backpack. Now he knew she was having a harder time than he'd thought...and he needed to check those plastic grocery bags he'd tossed in the laundry room.

Poor child. Her world had been rocked to such an extent...and she'd had no way to tell him...other than hitting and pulling a Kermit on the plastic mat he sent with her every day.

"I'll be in touch if there are any further problems," the nun said, with a curt nod.

"I'm sure you will," he murmured, sweeping a hand toward the door. "If there isn't anything else..."

"That will be all, Mr. Finlay," Sister Regina Maria said, giving Mittens a final pat, skirting the couch and marching toward the open doorway. "I have other problems to correct. Unless you need further instruction on carpool procedures?"

"I've gotten the hang of it." He made a face behind her back but smiled when she whirled back toward him. "Yes?"

"Might I recommend procuring some help? This place isn't fit for children. Healthy environments make healthy children."

Lucas looked around. "They're the ones who did this."

She gave him a wintery smile. "But are *they* in charge?"

Good question.

He was pretty certain they were, but perhaps a little spring cleaning was in order.

But he wasn't admitting that to the Wicked Nun of the West.

"Have a good day, Sister."

"You, too," she said, stepping outside and clipping most efficiently down the porch steps.

"Oh, I intend to," he said, grabbing the wine and flowers and relocking the front door.

ADDY HAD FLIP-FLOPPED a dozen times on what to wear for her date with Lucas. Jeans and a T-shirt? A flirty dress? Or just meet him at the door in a bustier and garter belt?

Considering she didn't have the third option, she went with the second—a flirty dress she'd bought last year, pulled from the back of the closet with the tags still on. A pretty green-striped cotton maxi dress with butterfly sleeves and a graceful neckline, the dress had been one she'd eyed for months before buying on a whim. The skin it showed and the brightness of the pattern made her feel too conspicuous. But today she wanted attention on her.

Lucas's attention. Along with his hands and any other parts he wanted to use.

It was still too chilly for sandals so she tugged on the pair of gold ballet slippers and a pair of dangling gold loops borrowed from her hip aunt Flora. Since she didn't have the sexy bustier and garters, she skipped the underwear. Thankfully, her thirty-three-year-old breasts were still somewhat perky. A dot of perfume at her neck, wrists and behind the knees and she was ready.

…and he was late.

She peeked out the office window to see a silver Toyota crossover parked in the drive.

Who was intruding on her Lucas time?

Her heart skipped a beat when she thought about Tara… and the other women Chris had mentioned who'd clamored after the big Texas man stomping around in boots and delicious Wranglers. Had Tara come with another casserole…and an offer?

Or was it some other lonely lady?

She moved to close the blinds when a flash of silver caught her eye. A nun?

The diminutive woman stomped to the car and climbed inside. Seconds later Lucas appeared on the Finlay front porch carrying flowers and a bottle of wine.

Addy squealed and flew toward the kitchen. She didn't want to seem too eager...or get caught spying on him. Eyeing the Caesar salad she'd thrown together with crunchy Creole fried chicken breast, she pulled out two crystal goblets and slipped off her ballet flats, kicking them to the side. She was warm enough...maybe even flushed with nervous energy. The doorbell rang.

Hmm...he hadn't come to the back door.

Totally official on this date.

"Coming," she called, putting the lid on the salad. "Or at least I hope I am soon."

Padding to the front of the house, she stifled a nervous giggle and opened the door to find no one there.

"Lucas?" she called, sticking her head out. A white truck pulled away from the curb and Addy looked down to find a small box. Her name had been typed on the label, but there was no return.

"Hey," Lucas said, his head showing over the spindly azaleas clustered around the front porch. He'd worn a cowboy hat...this time a gray flannel that made his cheeks look even more chiseled. Sweet buttercups, he looked like what she needed—big, hard, hot cowboy. "I went around back."

"Of course," she said, picking up the box. "Come on in."

He took the stairs two at a time, ducking his head to give her a firm kiss. Pulling back, he offered her the clutch of flowers. "I know they're not as nice as the ones you create. Shit, now I feel lame giving them to you. They're substandard. I should have thought out of the box, looked for something unique."

"At Super 1 Foods?" she asked, taking the spring bouquet and eyeing the wilting lilies. "These are sweet, Lucas. I haven't had anyone give me flowers in, well, a very long time."

She refused to count Robbie Guidry.

She shoved the small box she held in one hand onto the foyer table. Didn't know who it was from, but today, she gave herself a pass. No worries. No thinking about parole hearings, invoices that needed paying or the dry cleaning she'd forgotten. Today was about flowers, good wine and a hot man in her bed.

Well, eventually.

Maybe.

Didn't have to be about sex. Could be just a date. Innocent, sweet—

Lucas closed the door, twisted the lock and lifted her into his arms. Addy squeaked but wrapped her arms around his shoulders…and her legs around his waist. Well, as good as she could in the long, confining dress she wore. Thank God for stretchy cotton.

Lucas bent and nibbled her collarbone.

"Did I tell you how much I love this spot? So delicate." He kissed from one across to the other. "So delicious."

Addy dropped her head back, bringing her bottom snug against Lucas's growing erection. "I had no idea my collarbones were so erotic."

"They are," he said, lowering his head to the box neckline and the hardening nipples below. "Oh, sweet—"

He paused, his eyes landing on her breasts taut against the fabric. "You're not wearing a bra."

Addy lifted her head. "Nope."

Lucas set her down. "If I keep kissing you, we won't make it to lunch."

"I made a salad and fried chicken. It will keep."

Lucas smiled. "I brought wine."

"I'll grab two glasses. You take your clothes off." She spun and headed to the kitchen, spurred by his low sexy laugh.

"Want me to keep my boots on?"

"And that cowboy hat," she called back, loving the flirty way he made her feel.

The two goblets were where she'd left them. She picked them up, double-checked the back door was locked, and waltzed out to her dance with a man who would never be hers. Just like Aunt Flora, she'd have to settle for the memory.

But would that be enough for her?

She didn't know, but she knew she'd rather have a little of Lucas than none at all.

It would be like the time she'd gone on a cruise with her family. As soon as they hit the sea, she'd been violently seasick and it had lasted for days. Finally, with only one day left on the vacation, she was able to don her swimsuit and attack the all-you-can-eat buffet. It was one day of splendor, a day of sun-streaked goodness, three ice cream sundaes and a dance contest won by her rendition of ABBA's "Dancing Queen." She'd packed the entire vacation into one day.

So she'd pack loving Lucas into whatever they had left.

"Here we are," she said, holding the glasses aloft.

Lucas stood in the foyer bare-assed naked except for his boots and hat.

Addy froze, glasses still in the air. "Oh, my."

He was like a wet dream…not that she'd had those…but sweet mother of Zeus. His broad shoulders were tanned and muscular above a massive chest lightly covered in hair. His stomach was flat and she could see the outline of his abs. Nothing freakish, just gorgeous male flesh. Trim waist, narrow hips, and taut thighs and calves. And she hadn't missed the important piece of equipment, but it matched the man.

And that made her smile.

If she were going to toss out good sense, she might as well do it with a man who could make it worth her while.

And she could tell Lucas Finlay was a man worth the while.

Lowering the glasses, she said, "I was kidding when I told you to strip."

"I'm not kidding. I'm tired of missed chances with you. Remember that promise yesterday?" he asked, moving toward her, those boots clomping on the floor, ratcheting her anticipation.

"Yeah," she breathed.

He took the crystal from her. "Well, you're over-dressed."

Addy hooked her fingers on the stretchy elastic lining both shoulders and tugged the dress down. She allowed it to fall, the cotton fabric lightly grazing her body as it hit the floor.

She stood before him totally naked.

Lucas looked for a good long time.

Addy knew she wasn't a cover model, but she had a nice body thanks to daily runs and yoga. She'd shaved her legs and bikini area, rubbed her best soft shea butter all over her body and dusted herself with some glowing powder her sister had given her for Christmas last year.

"I knew you were beautiful," he said, reaching out to stroke the curve of her waist. "The first moment I saw you, you reminded me of a mountain lake, cool on the surface, reflecting the world around you, but beneath all that, oh, Addy girl, you are a wonder."

Addy wrapped her arms around herself. "Are we going upstairs? Did you lock the front door?"

Lucas removed his cowboy hat, setting it on her head

and swept her into his arms. "Door is locked. Dead-bolted. If Flora comes back, she better have a tank to get through that door."

"She has a key." Addy wrapped her arms around his neck, loving the feeling of his naked skin against hers, as Lucas climbed the stairs. He nuzzled her neck, even once managing to almost reach her breast, as he climbed.

"Which room?" he asked.

She pointed to the open doorway.

She'd lit candles and a soft musky fragrance greeted them as she entered. The shades had been pulled to create intimacy because Addy had been ready for Lucas.

She'd been beyond ready for him.

Kicking the door shut and locking it, he laid her on the bed with reverent tenderness then lowered himself, tipping the cowboy hat back before settling in for a kiss.

"Mmm," he breathed, against her lips. "You taste like sunshine. Like clean open spaces. Like a woman should taste."

His words moved in her soul, a liquid balm soothing any reservations she'd harbored about being with him. This man made her body hum and her heart feel suspiciously full.

Addy pulled him to her, feeling the cowboy hat fall from her head, as she hungrily kissed him.

His chest slid against hers, brushing against her nipples, his hardness sliding against her thigh. Hot desire uncurled inside her…and Addy felt the wildness unfurl, felt the part of her that reveled in the naughty sexy books take over. It had been a while since she'd allowed herself such pleasure.

Pushing against his shoulders, she rolled him over, taking control of the kiss. Lucas fell back like a good boy and allowed her to take the wheel.

His lips beneath hers, his body so unyielding, caused

the hum to turn into vibration. Addy slid her hands into his hair, relished the scruff of his whiskers against her chin.

He broke the kiss and looked up at her. "Addy?"

She caught her breath so she could respond—she'd seriously been on the edge of losing total control. "What?"

"Are you okay? I mean, you were attacked long ago, nearly raped. I don't want to do anything wrong." His finger brushed her scars and in his eyes she saw such tenderness.

A ribbon of warmth curled around her heart. He was worried about her, about scaring her or making a wrong move. "You haven't done anything wrong. I'm good."

"You sure? Because I took off my clothes before I really thought about it. That might have been too presumptuous."

"And, uh, I took off mine, too. That's called a confirmation that I want you."

He smiled. "I guess it's obvious I want you, too."

She looked down. "Why, yes, it is."

Lucas opened his mouth to say something, but she didn't give him the chance. Instead she pressed her lips to his, kissing him so thoroughly they both became breathless.

"Now, you be quiet and let Addy have some fun," she said, sliding a hand down his chest, tracing around one flat nipple before trailing over to the other.

Lucas cupped her cheek. "Yes, ma'am."

"Mmm, just like the sheriff," Addy murmured before sliding atop him.

"Ah," he sighed, clasping her hips and fitting her to him. "Who the hell are you talking about?"

Addy laughed. "Tell you later, cowboy."

Their lips met again and there was no more talking. Only touching, stroking, teasing and once a grunt as Lucas reached for the cowboy hat where he'd cleverly hidden a condom.

Addy forgot about everything she thought she was, and

in that moment, when Lucas slid inside her, she became the woman she wanted to be…the woman she'd denied for too many years.

Hot, desirable and naughty—a woman of passion.

A woman who let go of inhibitions.

A woman who existed for loving Lucas.

And it was fan-freaking-tastic.

Lucas seemed to know where to touch her, when to let her take over, how to take her breath away and how to push her over the edge. Like the push and pull of a storm, emotion built inside her, spilling over, washing her clean… giving her life again.

Never had she felt such satisfaction.

When it was over, she lay across him, replete. Seconds ticked by, measured in the flicker of the candle's flame. The dim room allowed for weak sunlight to spill inside, enough for Addy to see the utter gratification on Lucas's face when she finally lifted her head.

"Hey," she whispered.

He tilted his head down. "Hey."

She propped her arms across his chest and studied him. "That was nice."

Lifting his eyebrows, he made a face. "Nice? That was amazing."

Addy rested her chin on her forearms. "I didn't hurt you, did I?"

The rumble of laughter in his chest made her lurch to the side. "Ah, Addy girl, you do something to me I can't explain."

"Is that a good thing?"

He lifted a shoulder. "Maybe. All I know is I'd be hardpressed to find another time in my recent existence I've been this content to be with a woman."

"You're just saying that so I'll sleep with you again."

He wiggled his dark eyebrows, his eyes glinting with mischief. "Sleep? I don't think so...and is it working?"

She reproduced his earlier move and lifted a shoulder. "Maybe."

Lucas's expression turned serious and he lifted his head dropping a kiss on her chin. "In all seriousness, I've never felt this way so fast...and that's not a line."

And that made her smile because she couldn't have said it better herself.

"So are you hungry?"

"Starving."

"Why don't I go downstairs and grab the French bread and the wine?"

"Sounds like a plan—" he tucked his arms behind his head "—'cause I have more things I want to do to your delectable body, but I'll need sustenance first."

A delicious shiver ran through her. "In that case I'll be quick."

"And grab another condom from my jeans?"

"Oh, so you're just gonna lie here and let me wait on you hand and foot?" She lifted herself from him, sliding to the edge of the bed.

"I need rest. You wore me out." His smile was smooth as Belgian chocolate. She knew. Gourmet chocolate was another secret passion.

"A kiss before I go?" She leaned forward.

THIRTY MINUTES LATER she finally made it downstairs.

Lucas watched Addy's bare backside sway as she left the room and nearly applauded at the beauty of the woman. Seriously. That kind of wonder deserved accolades. Standing ovations. Encores.

Damn, who could have imagined his little florist had been brimming with such pent-up desire. He'd never seen a woman so consumed by passion. The revving of that engine had been heady to watch and made a man feel almost honored to hold a woman who poured every piece of herself into making love.

She'd been so beautiful, so absolutely primal. Raw and almost untouched, though he knew it wasn't true. But still, it had felt that way…like he'd awakened a long-slumbering sex goddess.

Pushing himself up, he looked about her bedroom. Simple, organic. Very Addy.

Heavy curtains with swirling velvet loops hung down to the polished wood floor. The bed was made of simple metal with clean lines and white and light blue bedding. Evocative prints hung on the wall and a cluster of fresh flowers sat in an antique-looking vase on the dresser. The nightstand held a weird-looking white-dotted lamp and a stack of books.

He rolled over and picked up a book.

Surrender To Me.

The cover bore a mussed-looking woman straddling a man wearing tight tan trousers, cowboy boots and a hat almost identical to his own. The man's shirt was open, baring his chest, and the pocket had a star pinned on it. The sheriff…

Lucas thumbed through the book.

Whoa.

He snapped the book closed with a snort.

No wonder she nearly came when he touched her. Her reading material might as well be a drum of propane…all Miss Addy needed was a match.

Or a willing man.

Addy came into the room, holding a tray on which two glasses clinked. She kicked the door shut with a bare foot, and thankfully she hadn't put on any clothes. Her jiggling breasts fired a hunger inside him.

Speaking of matches…

He held up the book. "Interesting reading."

Her entire body flushed pink. "Oh, I'd forgotten about those sitting out."

"So now I understand why you wanted the boots on." He beckoned her with a finger. "Now come on over here and show me how Sophie rode the sheriff."

Addy sat the tray on the dresser and propped her hands on her hips. The sight of her rounded breasts, flat stomach and sleek thighs had him giving her a salute of appreciation. "I'm not acting out scenes from that book, Lucas."

He gave her a devilish smile, lifting himself from the bed and pulling her into his arms. "So why did you call me Cade when I—"

"I did not!" She shrieked as he nipped her earlobe.

"Hmm, I don't remember. We better try again." He cupped her breasts and lay her on the bed.

"After we eat, of course," she said, crossing hands over her breasts, her eyes taking on the schoolmarm's glint. "And I've not given you leave to call me by my given name, sir."

Lucas played along, skipping over the delightful breasts she hid from him to her belly button. Ringing it with tiny kisses, he slid lower, brushing his mouth against her hip bone, before sliding his hands beneath her near-perfect ass. Her tiny gasp of pleasure was a ticket to paradise.

"If you say so, Sophie."

CHAPTER SEVENTEEN

SUNDAY AFTERNOON WAS USUALLY for laundry, cleaning the bathrooms and running three miles, but that particular Sunday afternoon turned into a gift—unexpected, out of the blue and wrapped in a satin bow of pleasure.

For the entire afternoon, Addy and Lucas lounged around, talking, touching and reveling in the small cocoon they'd created in her bedroom. They sipped wine, nibbled on delicious French bread and ate fried chicken right there on her bed…and she didn't even worry about the crumbs when Lucas had laid her back and made love to her a third time.

For a moment in time they were isolated from kids who spilled things, dogs that peed on rugs and the truth of the world in which they lived. Addy didn't think about her past or her future…just the sensuous, enjoyable present in Lucas's arms.

And she loved every precious second of lying beside him, discussing favorite TV shows, the best New Orleans restaurants and the places he'd traveled and photographed. She'd never had a better first date but then again, she'd never spent an entire first date naked, either.

But eventually they rose and tugged on clothes.

Lucas tossed *Surrender to Me* onto the bed. "No more Sophie, Sheriff Cade McGarrity and hot Texas sex."

"That had nothing to do with a book," she teased, running a brush through her hair.

"So why do you read this stuff? It's almost silly. No

man says that when he's coming," Lucas said, tapping the book as he reached for his shirt.

"It's not silly. It's about two people falling in love. And you may not yell what Cade yells when you come, but you did say some pretty sweet things in my ear." She smiled, pulling her hair into a low ponytail.

"You believe love like that is real?" His question was a crack of the gun. Heavy. Serious.

She jerked her head. "Don't you?"

"What's written between those pages is a woman's fantasy. The whole concept of romantic love is flawed and overrated. Those feelings Sophie and Cade have is a lust thing. Sex. Not love."

She snapped the elastic in place on her shoulders. "Is that what this is between us? Two people acting on lust?"

Lucas stilled and she could see on his face he didn't know what to say. A cornered dog didn't look as scared as Lucas did at the moment. "Uh, I'm sure whatever my answer is it won't be right."

"No, I want to know. I can't imagine someone not believing in love."

Lucas glanced away. "I believe in love, but the whole 'true love, one person for one person, meant to be' kind of crap doesn't exist in *my* book. Maybe at one time I thought so, but I forced that feeling."

"So your parents aren't in love? Ben and Courtney? Millions around the world? They're all duped?"

He glanced away. "I don't know. I'm not them."

She studied him in the fading light. He looked spooked.

He tugged on the cowboy boots he'd kicked into the corner. "Honestly, I haven't thought about this much. I haven't had to."

"I've thought about it." She tossed her brush on the dresser. "I've always believed one day love would find me…and I would just know. I've never pushed it, and if

I never found it, I suppose I would be okay, but I thought one day love would walk in."

His eyes met hers and something moved between them. Addy didn't know exactly what it was, but it was something. And it worried her because she'd never thought that once love found her, the feeling wouldn't be returned.

"We better get downstairs. I think I heard a car in the drive." He scooped up his hat and shot out her bedroom like a scalded cat.

"Chicken," she called, trying to find the lightness that had briefly fled. She shouldn't have pressed him. Wasn't any of her business what he believed.

"You know it." His boots thumped down the stairs.

He didn't believe in love. Or did he?

Cryptic answer from a forthright man. But should it matter to her?

No.

But it did because she'd started falling toward love with a man who said he'd never go there. Sure, he'd murmured he'd never felt the way he felt about her...but how did he feel? If it wasn't love and wasn't lust...then what the hell was it?

Addy picked up the dishes and followed Lucas down the stairs. She found him in the kitchen rinsing out the wineglasses. Silent, thoughtful and not so charming anymore. The sound of children laughing and doors slamming met her ears.

"They're home," he said.

"Yeah," she said, setting the tray on the counter.

Reality wasn't nearly as fun as hiding away with Lucas and making love beneath her percale sheets.

But reality was part of life.

And it had just knocked on an ending she hadn't wanted for the afternoon. Addy opened the door to the sound of

Chris jabbering about Charlotte making faces at the sea lions.

"Yeah, and you should have seen Chris's face when that elephant took a dump," Michael said, hauling Charlotte on his hip. "That was right before Miss Flora got lost."

"Lost?" Addy cast a glance at her aunt who looked thoroughly bushed after a day spent with the children. A flash of guilt hit Addy. She hadn't actually thought about the wear and tear on Flora…she'd been more concerned with playing sheriff and the buttoned-up schoolmarm with Lucas.

Aunt Flora waved Addy's concern away. "Not lost. I just forgot where the entrance was. No big deal."

"But she cried," Chris said, wiggling a rubber snake toward Charlotte who screamed as expected.

"I didn't cry. I just got mad at myself." Flora crossed her arms and gave Chris the look. Her aunt must have worked out a story with the kids, but Michael had squealed. "Nothing to worry about."

Addy wasn't so sure, but she was glad to see the kids home in one piece. "Where's your friend?"

"She dropped us off. Had to get her grandson home because they had a dinner to attend or something like that. We all had fun."

"And I was good," Charlotte said, looking up at Lucas. "I didn't call that kid weird or nothing."

"Good girl," Lucas said, giving her a high five before looking at the boys. "Well, what do you say to Mrs. Demarco?"

"Thank you!" came the chorus as the kids turned toward the door and clambered back outside.

Lucas turned to her. "Well, I'm off to fix dinner. Thanks for lunch. Best fried chicken I've ever had."

Addy tried not to blush but didn't quite succeed. "You're welcome. It was a nice afternoon."

"Just nice?" he mouthed where Flora couldn't see.

Addy's face grew warmer. "Very nice."

Lucas poked his head back inside. "Thanks for taking the kids, Flora. Very decent of you to give me and Addy some time to hang out. I know the kids were probably glad to get away from me, too."

Aunt Flora fawned like a schoolgirl under Lucas's compliment. "Oh, heck, I enjoyed it, and you'd be surprised how much they talked about you. You've won over some kids."

"Hmm, I'll try to remember that when Chris is arguing with me about what to have for dinner."

Turning to Addy, he asked, "A kiss before I go?"

She brushed a soft kiss against his lips, feeling conflicted about his love and lust comments, even as she was crystal clear on being glad about what had occurred between them. No take backs. "'Night."

"'Night, Addy girl."

As she closed the door, something inside her sank as the click of the lock finalized her return to the same Addy she'd been for the past fifteen years. Or sort of the same Addy.

"I didn't get lost," Flora said, petulance shading her voice. She crossed her arms and assumed a defensive face that would scare the New Orleans Saints offense. Addy could see Flora craved the expected battle over her fading memory. Usually Addy would comply, but not tonight. Not after saying goodbye to what she'd had with Lucas... something she may never get again.

"You know, everything went fine, Auntie dearest. Let's not overanalyze."

"You aren't going to start a fuss and try to talk me into going to the doctor and trying new medicine?"

"Nope. Not tonight. Maybe tomorrow."

"What the heck did that man do to you? I may need to

hire him for a weekly session for you." Aunt Flora sank onto a chair.

Addy ignored her aunt because she didn't want to acknowledge how much Lucas could change her. Today was an anomaly…making love with Lucas wouldn't happen again. And if it did, it couldn't change her because she and Lucas were temporary. Turning on the hot water, she filled the sink and started the dishes.

But Aunt Flora didn't get the memo about her wanting to be left alone with her thoughts.

"You're seriously not going to talk about my lapse today?"

"No, because I realize I can't control your world any more than I can control mine. I've talked to you about seeing your doctor again, and I've talked to Mom. I'm not hog-tying you. Ball is in your court."

"Your mother made an appointment for me next week."

Addy swiped the counter with a red towel. "Really?"

"Yeah, Phylis and I had a nice long talk yesterday while you were out. She's after me to move in with her and Don, and now I'm thinking she has a point."

"What do you mean move in with them?"

"I'm getting older…and so are you. For a while, you've been focusing on building your career. Sure, you've dated and have a few friends in that victim's group you go to, but this isn't a good life for you."

"Says who?"

"Says your mother. Says me."

"I like living with you. I don't have rent, we split utilities and we both have someone to depend on, to keep us company. How has that changed?"

"But you're stalled out, honey."

"I'm not stalled out. I just had a man upstairs imprisoned in my bed for five hours. How is my living here with you holding me back?"

"Woot! Way to take charge, girlfriend." Her aunt gave a fist pump.

"Jeez." Addy rolled her eyes and tried not to turn the color of the dish towel. "I got laid. Big deal."

"But that's my point. You're young, you should be living with a girlfriend…or a boyfriend. Not an old lady who can't remember her name some days."

"I'm pretty sure you haven't forgotten your name. And I don't want to live with anyone else. This works, and I don't want Mom guilting you into thinking it doesn't."

"She's not, but this is not about just you. It's about me, too. Maybe I want to move—not with Phylis and Don, but into Crescent Gardens. Maybe I want to move out of this big drafty house that's more work than it is pleasure. I'm in my seventies, honey. All my friends live in that community. It's safe and has great activities…and some hot older dudes. I've been thinking about this for a while now."

Addy looked down to see if the rug was still beneath her feet. "Why didn't you tell me?"

"Because you weren't ready to hear it." Flora gave a wry smile. "You have a sweet, mellow vibe, but underneath the Zen beats the heart of Attila the Hun."

"Aunt Flora." Addy tossed the red dish towel onto the counter. "I'm not inflexible. You could have talked to me about wanting to move to Crescent Gardens."

"Well, you're not flexible either despite all the yoga." Flora cracked a smile and her blue eyes softened. "Honey, you've built this tidy world—work, gym, eat, sleep—without much give."

"You make me sound like a robot."

"That's not what I meant. Today is a good example of what taking a leap of faith brings you. When you allow someone in—" Flora waved a hand at Addy "—you wear something pretty with your hair loose and your face flushed from having a good time."

"I'm not unopposed to breaking my habits or letting go of my ordered world a little bit. You're argument is backfiring."

"I'm part of your ordered world. A safety net you can always use to pull yourself back from something that makes you uncomfortable. And not only am I a crutch, but I'm also the pothole you step in. You shouldn't be taking care of an old woman."

"That's not true." Addy grabbed Aunt Flora's hand. Her skin was dry, spotted with age spots, and so thin her veins showed. When had Flora's hands aged so? "You're so much more to me than an aunt. You know that. We've always been soul mates."

Aunt Flora patted her hand. "Sure, we are, pumpkin. But I can feel change in the air, and I know it's time for me to move along. It's time for you, too."

"I don't want to. I can take care of you, and Dad is putting in an alarm system. The guy is coming tomorrow. Look around. This is our home."

"What are you going to do, Addy? Become me?"

"No. But what's wrong with being you?"

"I'm lonely. I should have fought for Millard. I shouldn't have let him walk away."

Addy pulled her hand from her aunt's. "This is about your regret. Not mine."

"So you're going to give up on love? On having a family? On—"

"Wait." Addy scooted her chair back as anger flooded her. "Who says having kids makes you happy? Or getting married for that matter? There are plenty of strong, successful single women living their lives on their own terms."

"Sure." Aunt Flora shrugged. "I'm one of them, but don't you think for one minute that if I could go back in time, I wouldn't throw Millard O'Boyle onto that worktable and make him mine. And I wouldn't have slunk away and allowed him to leave me. I didn't fight for the life I wanted, Addy. Don't be me."

"I'm not. I'm me. I don't need a man to make me happy."

"No, you don't, but I want you to think about who you are and what you want. Don't settle for what's easy…for what's safe."

Addy wanted to argue, but didn't want the sharp probe digging around in her psyche anymore. Why couldn't Flora have forgotten to be smart…instead of forgetting where she hid the Christmas gifts they still couldn't find?

"Well, love, I'm off to have a bath and put on my jammies. Those kids are fun, but, woo, they're a handful, especially that Chris. I think that kid has ADHD." Flora rose and cracked her back.

Addy tucked her hands into her lap. "Hey, I do appreciate your taking them and giving me and Lucas some time together."

"I hope it was worth my aching bunion."

Making a face, Addy also rose. "I'm not kissing and telling."

"I hope to hell it was more than kissing. I've got corns, too." Flora swooshed out of the kitchen leaving Addy to tidy up. She pushed the chairs in, double-checked the dead bolt on the back door and turned off the kitchen light— all the while mulling over Flora's words. Maybe she had a point. Then again maybe it wasn't a worthwhile one. Flora hadn't held her back from taking the life she wanted. Addy had held herself back.

As she walked to check the door, her eyes landed on the small box that had been delivered earlier.

Who made deliveries on Sunday?

Maybe it was a second order of floral wire that had been mistakenly delivered even though she'd called them and double-checked the correct address of her shop. Definitely wasn't from Amazon.

Sliding a nail beneath the clear tape, she ripped the box open. Inside was bubble wrap. A creepy feeling slithered up her spine as she lifted the plastic.

Lying on the bottom of the box were several photographs. Addy swallowed panic, scrabbling with the ideas rolling in, and lifted the color prints into the light of the foyer sconces.

The first one was a picture of her climbing from her car, taken in broad daylight outside her shop. She wore the gray jumper she'd worn last week.

The second had been taken from inside her car. Whoever had taken it had slid behind the wheel and taken a picture of the shop rear door. But that was impossible—she always locked her car. Always.

Except one day last week it had been open when she had left work. She'd thought she'd left it unlocked. But she hadn't. Someone had jimmied the door…and she'd sat in the same spot he'd occupied.

The last picture chilled her to the bone. It had been taken last Monday night. She stood in her nightgown, arms crossed, framed against the darkness of the camellia bushes. Her face had been highlighted by the security lights outside the Finlay house and she could just make out the side of Michael and the basketball.

Addy's hands shook so hard she dropped one of the pictures. Then she dropped the other two.

Her legs gave out and she sank onto the floor, shaking so hard. The only sound in the house was Aunt Flora's television and the sound of her teeth chattering as she wrapped her arms around herself and squeezed her eyes shut.

She'd failed herself…she'd thought she could sense danger, but she hadn't. Terror overwhelmed her and she curled into a ball, tight as she could make herself. The photographs worked exactly as intended.

Robbie Guidry wasn't out of prison yet, but he could still get to her and the message was clear.

He would come.

ANOTHER MONDAY MORNING, but somehow this one didn't seem as bad. After surviving the stomach flu with his nephews and niece and spending a very nice weekend flirting, laughing and making love, Lucas felt as if the world was his oyster.

No, even better than an oyster.

And he wasn't going to let that weird conversation he'd had with Addy right before the kids and Flora came home ruin it for him.

After he'd successfully dropped off the kids, managing to navigate the carpool like a seasoned pro, he stopped off for coffee and headed to the Bywater District armed with his cameras. The light was perfect for some morning shots. Would have been better as the sun rose, but he'd take what he could get.

Humming a ZZ Top classic, he found a parking place and had just started surveying decent vantage points when his phone rang. Courtney.

"Hey, the kids are alive and well," he said, not without a good deal of cheer.

"That's the least of your problems," the voice said.

"Ben?"

"Who the hell do you think it is?" His brother's voice was guarded…and angry.

"Actually since this is Courtney's number, I thought it was her."

"I don't know what you think you're doing, but it stops now. Mom and Dad are headed back and we don't need you." More than anger. Suspicion.

Lucas slung a camera over his shoulder and walked to his truck. Several people sitting on their porches had turned to stare at him and he didn't want to have the delicate conversation with an audience.

"I have no motives, Ben. Your wife called me and I said I would help. It was past time for me to know your children."

A snort. "Yeah, past time. Well, we've gone this long without your presence, so…"

"Where's Courtney?"

"None of your goddamned business," Ben said, anger roaring into his voice, shaded by something uglier. "And you better keep your goddamn hands off her and my family. I don't know what you think you're doing, but you can forget about it. You are dead to me, you are dead to my family. You hear?"

In the background Lucas heard Courtney and then his father. Courtney yelled at Ben and the line clicked, losing the connection.

Lucas pressed the end button, feeling blindsided. What the hell? Ben should be grateful he'd come when Courtney called. His brother had been the one to screw up, and that he tried to paint Lucas as some kind of homewrecker pissed him off. Lucas wasn't sloppy seconds even if Ben had made him feel that way all those years ago.

So his brother could kiss his ass.

The phone rang, interrupting his thoughts. "Yeah?"

"Sorry about that," Courtney said, her voice steeped in aggravation. "I had to fill out paperwork and left my phone behind."

Lucas didn't respond.

"He's just dealing with a lot of anger right now. We both owe you, and I'm sorry he acted like an asshole."

Yeah, anger and jealously could eat a hole in a man—or it could find a home, knotting up, implanting in the lining of the soul. "He needs someone to blame for the shit life has handed him…and an older brother with questionable motives is handy."

"Are your motives questionable?" He couldn't read her voice, no longer knew her, so he couldn't tell the intent behind the question. Maybe she thought Lucas helped her in order to insinuate himself into her life. Maybe she wondered if Lucas still loved her.

But he didn't love Courtney any longer. "I don't have motives, but a man hurt by life imagines every shadow a threat."

Courtney didn't respond to him. Silence squatted on the line between them. Easier to change the subject. "I talked to Mom last night. She said they had him up and moving yesterday."

"Yeah, they'd started physical therapy before he got so sick with the infection and he's doing well. Physically, he tires easily, but considering how sick he was days ago, it's a miraculous recovery."

The doctors called it a miracle.

Lucas's mother called it merely Ben being Ben. Lucas's younger brother always had a flair for drama, even when at death's door. Sort of like Chris.

Though Lucas had been relieved to hear his brother had made such a quick recovery, the thought of facing Ben created a storm of emotion inside him. He still wasn't sure how he felt about the man who had stolen the life he'd built in his head and lived it out with the woman Lucas had loved. And he wasn't sure how he felt about leaving Addy.

Never had he contemplated a life anywhere but Texas. The open, rambling life had suited him, so why did it feel so empty to think about returning? What had changed him here in the place where he'd grown into a man? He had no answers.

"Any idea when you'll come home?"

"Unbelievably we're coming home on Saturday afternoon—a flight into the air station in Belle Chasse."

"Do I need to pick you up?"

"No, your parents are flying down Thursday or Friday, so they'll be there to help with the kids. You're pretty much off the hook."

Lucas leaned on the truck, nodding at an older gentleman walking by, his motley dog snuffing through the lanky weeds at the wall of a corner bar. "I'm inferring you don't want me around?"

"That's not what I meant. I assumed you needed to get back to your life."

He could tell it was indeed what she meant. Something hot and bitter flooded him. They no longer needed him. Both Courtney and Ben wanted him to slink away, fade into the horizon never to be seen or heard from again. Just like before.

But it wasn't just like before.

Courtney had changed everything when she'd called him and begged him to come to New Orleans and stay with the kids. Sending him back to his relegated place in their lives would be like putting toothpaste back inside a tube. Wasn't going to happen…and trying would make one hell of a mess.

Deep down Lucas knew he'd been changed by Michael, Chris and Charlotte. He'd wiped their tears, scrubbed their faces and caught their laughter in his hand, creating a place in his heart for them. He wasn't going to leave their lives and never come back. He wasn't going to resume invisible uncle status again.

Lucas wasn't going to be sidelined. "I'm not going home without talking to you and Ben about what happened between us."

Again silence sat heavy for a few seconds.

"What do you mean?"

"You know what I mean. It's time we dealt with what happened years ago, Courtney. Surely you didn't think I would come to your house, build a relationship with your children and then slip away like some stranger in the night. How fair is that to Michael or Chris? Even Charlotte likes me now."

"You intentionally forgot about us, Lucas, or had you forgotten the silence between us was your choice?" Courtney's voice rose in aggravation. "*You* wouldn't forgive us and you built that wall. Not us. But I don't think now is a good time to deal with what stands between us. Ben is going through a lot of emotional baggage with the loss of his leg. He's angry, grieving and still recuperating. Maybe later in the summer…when he's better."

Lucas understood her need to protect his brother, but every instinct in his gut told him now was the time. "No, I'm not waiting any longer to settle things between me and him. His injury has proved people can't continue to put off words that need to be spoken, thinking there will be a tomorrow. So, I will be here when Ben comes home…and then I'll go back to Texas. But things will be different."

Courtney took a deep breath. "Please, Lucas. Don't rock this boat. Not now."

"It's past time."

"We've waited over thirteen years. Surely, we can—"

"—stop being idiots," Lucas finished her sentence. Until that moment he didn't know what he wanted, but suddenly the windshield wipers to his soul kicked in, clearing off the gunk preventing him from seeing who he was. He didn't know if the change in him was because of what he'd faced with children who'd never seen him before or seeing how bravely Addy had stepped out of her own sheltered world to be with him…but something had changed. "Let Ben be angry. Let him hate me. But I'm choosing to let the past go."

"Fine. You do what you must, but please remember that he's fragile."

"But he's not broken and maybe if his anger burns out, if he and I can find a better place with each other, he can heal from the past and focus his energies on his future. I know I will feel a hell of a lot better saying what I need to say to you both."

"Shit," she breathed. "Closure is overrated, Lucas."

"I'd like to find out," he said.

"Fine. See you this weekend."

Lucas hung up, swung his camera forward and walked purposefully toward a small apostolic church across the street from Mabel's Jazz Club. The light streamed through the elaborate iron cross affixed to the top, making a long shadow along the street. The name of the street was written on chipped tiles at the top of the shot. It would make a nice print…and he knew what he'd call it. Redemption.

CHAPTER EIGHTEEN

ADDY WATCHED THE CLOCK on the wall of her shop tick and tried to remember how to breathe. Ten minutes until noon and her father still hadn't called.

"You're making me jump out of my skin," Shelia said, glancing at the clock Addy kept watching. "That hour hand isn't going to magically move."

Addy looked at her friend. "What?"

"I know it's a bad day, sugar, but you've got to work through this. You knew Robbie would get out. Think about what we talk about in group therapy. Handle what you can handle. Control what you can control. Be smart. Be aware. But live your life."

"I know, but saying it and feeling it are two different things. Robbie will come after me, Shelia, and I don't know when it will be. Maybe tonight or next week or next year. But he won't forget about me. Oh, my God." Addy sank onto a stool, trying to beat back the panic, but failing. She gasped, sucking in the smell of sphagnum moss and funeral parlor.

Shelia rushed over, wrapping an arm around Addy's shoulders. "Come on now, Addy. Deep breath, clear your mind, and remember you are stronger now than you were before."

Addy pushed against her friend. "You don't understand. All that crap I'd been convinced would save me—that inner awareness of danger—it isn't true. Listening to yourself doesn't work."

"Yes, it does, honey. Being aware and heeding your intuition is part of your natural protection."

"He sent someone to take pictures of me, and I never knew. I never felt unsafe or had any prickling of awareness. Don't you get it? I failed myself."

"What do you mean 'took pictures'?"

"I found several photos in a box on my porch. At first I thought the box was FedEx, so I didn't open it immediately because Lucas and I were having lunch together. But last night I remembered. No postage and no prints. I called Andre and he came over to procure the evidence. He's as frustrated as I am because we can't do anything with it. All circumstantial and we can't prove Robbie's behind this."

"Wait. Pictures of what?"

"Of me. Here at the shop, in my car…at home in my nightgown when I went out to check on Michael one night."

"How's he doing these things?"

"One of his friends on the outside?" Addy shrugged, tucking her trembling fingers into her pockets.

"You know he's just trying to get in your head."

"It's working."

"What did Lucas say?"

Addy turned away. "I haven't told him, and frankly it's none of his business."

"You haven't told him about Robbie?"

"I told him about the attack. Not about the gifts he sends. Or that Robbie might be granted parole today."

"You got a big hunky cowboy living next door, one who cares about you I might add, and you don't tell him about this scum trying to scare you? Are you plain stupid?" Shelia never minced words—it was something Addy loved and hated about her.

"No, but I didn't want to throw my issues at him when we first met. For one thing he was a stranger."

Shelia harrumphed.

"Okay, fine, I didn't want him to know I come with that kind of baggage. Acknowledging the sicko in my life who never really went away makes it too real. Not being able to stop Robbie from sending me this shit, for crippling me with fear, makes me feel weak. Makes me feel less than what I should be. I didn't want to be that woman to Lucas."

"And telling him would have sent Lucas running the other way?"

"Maybe." But even she wasn't convinced.

"Well, then, he ain't the man for you, is he?"

"You ask too many questions." Addy inhaled a deep breath and blew it out. "I'm tired of people seeing me as a victim. I didn't want Lucas to look at me that way. I wanted to be the woman who'd healed and grown stronger…even if I'm not."

"Now, that's a lie." Shelia tossed down the wire cutters. "You can handle anything. I did, didn't I?"

"But you don't have to worry anymore. Your cross to bear is rotting in the cemetery—"

"And good riddance." Shelia eased her girth onto a stool. She wore monochromatic red with jangling silver bracelets. Her curls had red woven within the ebony depths, a very edgy, hip look, but Shelia's eyes were those of an old soul. "Baby, tell your man."

"He's not my man. He's—" Addy snapped her mouth closed because she didn't know what in the hell to call Lucas. "Why mix him up in my misery?"

"Because you got a thang for him. Because he has a thang for you. What? You just gonna let him saddle his horse and ride away?"

"Yeah, I am. He lives twelve hours away. I've always known that whatever we shared—friendship, sex, whatever—was a blip on the radar of my life. Neither one of us can do forever. We each have our own lives to live, lives far away from one another."

"So love don't matter to you?" Shelia folded her arms and raised her painted-on eyebrows.

"Love?" Addy tried to snort like that word didn't make her knees weak. She couldn't go there with Lucas…or could she? They hadn't talked about a future, only a present. But what if… "I don't want to be in love with Lucas."

Shelia's crack of laughter made Addy jump. "Heh, you think you can control love? You can't. Love is a sneaky son of a bitch. He'll tap you on the shoulder and when you spin around, punch you right in the face. You can't run from it, sugar."

"I'm not in love with Lucas." Addy knew she lied like a dog…which really didn't make sense because dogs couldn't even speak much less lie.

Shelia's answering smile said it all—Addy's words weren't believed.

"Go over there and tell him tonight. Let him into your life, Addy. Stop running. Stand and fight."

"I'm not running. From him or Robbie." And as she said those words, she straightened. Last night she hadn't slept a wink. She'd woken this morning haggard and worn. After an afternoon basking in Lucas's arms, she should have faced Monday strong and content. Instead, she'd crawled into her existence, reverting into something she'd never wanted to be—a shadow, a scurrying bunny darting away, fearing the unknown. She'd become a victim all over again.

Addy lifted her chin. "I'm not running."

Shelia searched her face. "Good. I decided long ago I could be knocked down, but I'm gonna get up and fight for myself. That's what you have to do…on both accounts. Fight for love. And if the time comes you have to face your past, fight that no good piece of scum. He may come for you, but you'll be ready. 'Cause you ain't no victim, Addy Toussant. You remember that. We ain't rats, and we ain't hiding."

Addy smiled…the first one she'd tried on since she'd opened that damn box. "Hell, no, I'm not."

And then the phone rang.

"Fleur de Lis," Addy said into the receiver.

"He's out," her father said, disgust heavy in his voice.

Fear sneaked inside her resolve and sucker punched it. But Addy refused to give in and she choked it down, smothering it with determination. "Did you see him?"

"Of course. He came in and I said my piece. The jackass sneered at me the entire time, and when they announced he'd been rehabilitated and was paroled, he winked at me. Can you believe the nerve?"

"Good. He's feeling confident, isn't he?" Addy said, anger building inside her at the cocksure manner of the man who'd given her both physical and mental scars. "Well, I'm not a girl anymore. I'm a grown woman who understands better the sickness in his mind, and I'm a grown woman who knows how to defend herself. I'm not afraid of him anymore."

"Baby, you don't have to go all Rambo on me. I want you to be careful. Talk to Flora about her being on guard. The security guys will be there today, and I'll go out and meet with them. They'll finish by this afternoon, so tonight you will have an alarm. I also talked to Andre about having a few patrol cars drive by a couple times, especially at night."

"I'll be fine, Dad. At some point, he'll show up in my world so I'll be prepared. Hopefully, he'll see he doesn't scare me and all his crazy fantasies of me cowering in fear will pop like a balloon. He has delusions of power, and I won't let them persist."

"Baby, if he comes anywhere near you, you call 911 and find safety. You understand?" Her father's voice sounded near panic. She'd scared him by talking about facing her demons. She wouldn't provoke Robbie or try to fight him.

She wasn't stupid. But she also wouldn't let him think he had power over her. That was what Robbie craved…her fear. She wasn't hiding from him, for that would be giving him the gift of herself.

"I'm not dumb, Daddy. If I see him, I'm calling for backup. I have no delusions of being an ass-kicker. But I'm not giving him my fear."

"Good girl. I'll be there when you get home."

"I love you, Dad."

"You, too, angel face."

Addy placed the phone back on the receiver and turned to Shelia. "Robbie's out."

"Time to use all the tools you've prepared with over these past few years. I'm calling Sharon and Rochelle. We'll all be there for you."

Addy nodded. It was what Survivors of Violence did. Constant support system. They had each other's back and Addy had spent many a night worrying about her friends in her therapy group. She'd made casseroles, held hands and watched children all to alleviate her friends' minds. They were a sisterhood of survivors and had gotten Addy through some hard times.

"I'm a little scared," Addy admitted.

"Good. Being a little scared will aid you, honey. Being a lot scared will cripple you." Shelia wrapped her arms around Addy and squeezed tight.

"Thank you, Shelia."

"You don't have to thank me. If it wasn't for you, this job and all you've done for me, I don't know where I'd be."

"You know the offer you made a few months ago?"

Shelia lifted her eyebrows. "About buying into the business?"

"We should talk about it."

"I still wanna do it, but let's visit that topic when we're less emotional. Today is not the day."

"Okay," Addy said, stepping back toward her workstation and the arrangement she'd been trying to put together for a person having bypass surgery. She hadn't been able to concentrate well, but things looked a little clearer for her. Resolve was a funny beast. It settled in the bones and made her breathing steadier, her vision crisp and her intent sincere. Months ago she'd cringed when Shelia had approached her about buying into the floral shop. She hadn't wanted to let any piece of Fleur de Lis go. It was her identity, the world she clung to with tight fists. But at the moment she faced her demons, her life emerged from the fog, startling in its clarity.

She had to open her world so she could breathe.

After finding the photos, she'd been ready to pull the gates shut and man all stations to protect herself from every potential hurt…including Lucas.

Her initial reaction was to blame him for letting her guard down. He'd invaded her world and she'd let things slide—forgetting her cell phone and not feeling the presence of danger. Allowing the Finlay children in her house, leaving doors unlocked and distracting her from her vigilance had seemed a huge mistake. She should have kept her mouth—and her legs—shut.

But maybe Shelia was right. If she tossed away what she thought she had with Lucas because of Robbie, who would win?

Not her.

Perhaps a leap of faith was long overdue. Tonight she could tell Lucas about Robbie and the threats and show all her cards. No more shutting emotional doors with him. If they ended badly, it wouldn't be because she'd hidden her past from him on any level. Sharing her fears with Lucas, being honest about who she was and what she wanted could only be the right thing…unless Lucas didn't want

to bother with a woman who had a huge helping of crazy
on her plate.

Her stomach heaved as nerves latched hold. She reached
for an antacid and glanced out the window as if Robbie
might suddenly appear.

In the blink of an eye her life had changed.

MONDAY NIGHTS made Lucas want to drink. In fact, he now
held a tumbler of scotch and soda. He'd found some Glen-
livet in the pantry behind the saltines.

He'd intended to find some time to see Addy, but between massive amounts of homework, taking Charlotte to
dance class where she did nothing more than hop around
for fifty bucks, and picking Michael up from lacrosse, he
hadn't made it over and it was almost ten o'clock.

"Uncle Lucas!" Chris called, his high-pitched voice
slamming into Lucas from upstairs as he was finally sinking into the recliner.

"No more water. You'll wet the bed," he called up, not
moving even a toe. Damn, he was tired out.

"I forgot to tell you I have to go to Nola tomorrow and
I gotta have my bike."

"What's Nola?"

"It's my racing school," Chris called down, with the
slightest hint of "duh" in his voice.

"We'll talk in the morning," Lucas yelled, praying Charlotte didn't wake up. He'd read *Creampie and Calico Kitten*
three times before she'd finally closed her eyes.

"I gotta go. Mr. Pete wants to do my qualifying." Chris
was anything if not persistent.

"Okay. We'll get it set up."

"'Night," Chris called.

"'Night," Lucas returned, closing his eyes and pretending the messy living room away.

But it wouldn't be messy for long.

New beginnings.

After declaring he'd put the past behind him with Courtney and Ben, Lucas had decided he'd start in a literal manner. This morning he'd gone to the home improvement
store, matched the paint on the porches and started the
sanding process. He'd worked all day preparing to repaint
the porches, and he'd called a maid service to give the
house a good cleaning. He figured the last thing on his
sister-in-law's mind would be cleaning and repairing. If
Lucas wasn't going to get much of his work done, he might
as well get the house in better shape.

But the sanding, stripping and taking care of kids had
taken its toll. He needed a minute to sit.

The vision of a laughing Addy flitted across his mind.
She'd been such a sight, laid out naked on that bed, talking about how much she loved watching *The Big Bang
Theory* and how she'd once romanced the idea of being
a microbiologist. Her hair had fallen messily around her
pretty face and her warm whiskey eyes had glowed with
good humor. She'd been the sexiest thing he'd ever seen
and she'd filled up his heart.

Was this love?

He'd told Addy he didn't believe in romantic love…but
that wasn't necessarily true. Yesterday's conversation had
taken a strange turn and he'd panicked. Seeing the disappointment on her face told him all he needed to know—
he'd screwed up.

He'd always believed love wasn't something found as
easily as it seemed to be in movies or books. Commitment
was built on mutual respect, friendship and like goals.
Not a business arrangement per say, but more like two
like-minded people choosing to travel the hard road of
life together.

He'd always thought lasting love had to be intentional
and chosen by both parties involved…and that was why it

hadn't worked with him and Courtney—she'd turned her back on commitment to him.

But with Addy things felt different.

So had he been wrong all this time?

Lucas shifted deeper into the warmth of the recliner and sighed at the sweet silence. He'd seen Addy earlier, following some guy wearing a navy jumpsuit, nodding as he pointed out what looked to be a new security system.

He wanted to see her again, taste her again and find out about that security system. But he needed a few more minutes to decompress.

Shouldn't she have already had one installed? In fact, Courtney and Ben needed one, too. When he went over to Addy's to say good-night, he'd get the guy's card and see about adding one here.

He yawned and sighed again.

And fell asleep.

CHAPTER NINETEEN

ADDY POURED ANOTHER cup of coffee and tried not to look out toward the Finlay house.

Lucas hadn't come by last night like he'd said. Something about his easy dismissal of her stung. He'd struck her as a man of his word, so perhaps something had come up? But that was part of her issue—man of his word. What did she really know about Lucas? She'd known him for two weeks, hardly long enough to truly know what kind of man he was.

Logic told her it was a good enough reason to forget about their budding relationship and focus on her present. Just like the orchid she'd snipped weeks ago right before Chris had crashed into her world, his uncle trailing, she'd have to cull the weak part of herself to protect the whole. Her strong intentions of opening herself to Lucas and the potential for something more than a weekend together had dissipated as doubt grabbed her. Shelia had been wrong about going to Lucas.

Addy had needed Lucas…and he'd failed her.

She eyed the alarm system panel, its red light blinking, feeling comforted about the protection it brought and about how easy it was to use. After waiting up with a kettle of hot water and two cups of chamomile tea for her and Lucas, she'd armed the system and gone to bed, aggravated he'd baled on her when she needed him most. She'd expected not to sleep a wink, but she'd slept hard and dreamless.

"Morning, buttercup," Aunt Flora said, rubbing her eyes and looking around for the coffeepot.

"It hasn't moved," Addy said, pointing toward where the Bunn coffeemaker always sat.

"I know that," Aunt Flora said peevishly, schlepping over in her ratty old slippers. "I may be old, but I ain't stupid."

"Never said you were."

Flora sighed. "You're as grumpy as I am."

"Mmm-hmm," Addy conceded.

"Would you mind going over the alarm system with me again? I'm still foggy on it."

"Sure." Addy struggled to her feet and beckoned Flora over. After showing her repeatedly what to push, she decided it would be easier to make Flora a cheat sheet and put it by the phone near the door. After writing out the procedure and taping it to the counter, she turned to go get dressed for the day, but she saw a dark head appear in the back door window.

Her heart leaped into her throat.

She refocused. Not Robbie.

Lucas.

Flora opened the door and the alarm shrieked.

"Oh, dear," Flora screeched, her hands flapping as she lunged toward the security pad and started jabbing random numbers.

Addy covered her ears and hurried over. "Don't just push numbers," she yelled, tapping the card.

Flora read the instructions. Finally, the shrieking of the alarm stopped.

"Oh, Lord, I'm sorry. I panicked." Flora looked as if she might cry. "We never should have let your father put that thing in."

"It's not a big deal," Addy said, patting her aunt's back.

"It's new for both of us and there's a learning curve. We'll get the hang of it."

"This is the reason I need to get out of your hair. I'm a liability," Aunt Flora said.

"That's not true," Addy said, knowing it was indeed a little true. But she didn't want Aunt Flora moving out. She didn't want her world to change, but she guessed the good Lord wasn't listening because she'd been turned on her ear.

While Addy had dealt with the alarm, Lucas had stood patiently inside the door, strong, silent and looking a bit stressed.

Addy turned to him, lifting a questioning eyebrow.

"Sorry about last night. Sounds lame, but I fell asleep in the recliner," he said, giving her a sheepish shrug. "Guess between the busy weekend and all the kids' activities I wore out."

Logical reason, but still Addy felt out of sorts. She'd wanted to share her fears, her revelations…that having a partner in the floral shop freed her to travel to, say, West Texas upon occasion. But now in the light of the morning, the whole thing sounded asinine. She'd been naive to think she meant more to him than what she was—a friend and onetime lover.

"I've got to run—Michael has to make up a test early, but I wanted you to know why I couldn't come by for tea." He gave her a wicked smile, but instead of inflaming her, it made her uncomfortable.

Fine. Things happened. She understood. Still, she pulled away from him and all he represented.

Part of her protection?

Or maybe her inner alarm system told her it was time to shut that part of her life down for the time being. She'd thought she was ready to take what they had a step further, but now she wanted to do nothing more than draw her defenses around her.

"No big deal," she said, trying to sound casual and not like Aunt Flora when she forgot where the coffeemaker was. "Monday's exhausting for me, too."

He smiled. "Good. Thought I had screwed up. And speaking of screwing up, I wanted to talk to you about that last conversation we had Sunday."

"What conversation?"

"About—" The horn honked in the adjacent driveway.

"Better go," Addy said, feeling like her words held more meaning than the obvious.

He moved toward her as if he might steal a kiss, but Addy gave a slight shake of her head.

He frowned. "Later?"

"Maybe." She tried to smile but her face felt tight.

His eyes narrowed but the horn sounded again. "I'll come by tonight after I get home. I need to talk to you… Ben is coming home this weekend."

Addy's heart pinched as dread sank into the pit of her stomach. He was leaving. For good. Something about that finality, about the casual way he said it like it was no big deal to go back to Texas, made her feel so much more fragile than expected. Yesterday after talking to Shelia, she'd felt strong, but now she felt frayed around the edges, clinging to wholeness, knowing it was impossible to hold herself together.

Lucas leaving New Orleans, leaving her, festered like an open wound.

Hah.

She'd fallen in love with Lucas at the absolute worst time in her life and the bitter irony rubbed her like a new shoe.

The horn sounded again. Three sharp beeps and then a long drawn-out wail.

"Go," she said.

So he did.

Flora closed the door and shot Addy a puzzled look. "What's up with you this morning?"

"Besides the fact Robbie is out there on the streets and Lucas stood me up last night?" Addy said, dumping her cup into the sink.

"I see," Flora said, crossing the kitchen, half-full mug of coffee in hand.

Addy waited for her aunt to explain, but she said nothing else. "What do you see?"

"The same girl I've always seen. Pushing back, drawing in, closing ranks to protect herself."

Throwing her half-eaten bagel in the retro trash can, Addy put her hands on her hips. "What? I shouldn't do that? The man who nearly raped and killed me and who still stalks me is out there somewhere, and Lucas is leaving this weekend. No sense in pretending this will have a happy ending."

"Oh, my dear, if you expect to get shit on, you will." Flora finished filling her mug and walked out.

Frowning, Addy followed her aunt, but she didn't try to make her understand the reality of her situation. Aunt Flora had been in her shoes before, but hadn't even tried to change Mr. O'Boyle's mind. Even if she had made her feelings known, he likely wouldn't have left his wife, children or the life he'd created because of Flora's love. It was easy for her to spout off advice when she hadn't taken the risk herself.

Addy knew what needed to be done—she needed to end things with Lucas and focus on protecting herself against the immediate threat. After all, what good would it do to tell Lucas about Robbie and the threats over the years? He wouldn't be here to protect her.

So she'd protect herself. On all fronts.

And like her aunt, she would cling to the memory of what she'd had with Lucas. Two days of sun-filled, happy memories—a lifetime packed into a weekend.

Small comfort in her lonely life, but better than no comfort at all. She had no regrets about Sunday…but she wasn't about to leave herself open for more hurt in her future.

LUCAS HAD SPENT the day working on the front porch. He'd put a new coat of glossy black paint on the chairs and started painting the porch flooring while the rockers dried in the sunshine. The day had been gorgeous and it had felt good to have warmth on his shoulders and purpose in his stride. He was a walking John Denver song.

Tuesday afternoon had gone much more smoothly than the day before. Homework was light and Michael had no activities and thus could watch Charlotte while Lucas took Chris to his motocross practice. He'd never understood why his brother and sister-in-law had allowed Chris to participate in such a dangerous activity, but after seeing the boy on the bike, leaning into curves, looking like he'd been born on a motorbike, he understood. Chris had a passion for going fast…and perhaps channeling his reckless spirit into something he loved gave respite.

The kid's qualifying time seemed to please his coach and the Nola Springtime Classic was set for Friday night.

Maybe Addy would want to go with him. Could be fun watching the daredevil, who'd caused them to meet school some kids older than him on the course.

So once he got the kids in bed, he grabbed a bottle of chilled Riesling and walked over to Addy's.

She'd left the back porch light on and opened the door before he even stepped onto the concrete steps.

"Hey, beautiful." He hoped the gift of wine and his silver tongue would erase any lingering aggravation. He'd felt horrible about standing her up last night, but knew she'd understand. If anything, Addy got him, and that was what had him thinking about their future together. Surely, fate had handed him a gift when he'd agreed to come watch his niece and nephews, and he wasn't interested in returning this gift. He thought he might like to keep Addy forever.

"Hey." She stepped back so he could slip inside. She popped her head out and looked around before closing the door and sliding the dead bolt in place.

"Locking me in your lair?" he cracked as he sat the bottle on the counter and opened a cabinet door, looking for the crystal she'd brought out on Sunday. "Don't worry. I'm not running from you, babe."

"Don't." Addy dropped her head and shook it.

"You don't want wine?" he asked, reaching for her, sliding his hands around her waist.

"No, and please don't," she tugged at his hands, stepping back from him.

"What's wrong with you?"

She lifted her eyes and in the depths he saw something he didn't want to see—dismay.

"Addy?"

"Look, I don't want things to get weird, but this morning I realized the moment I dreaded was here—you said you were leaving and that got me thinking about what we've been doing."

"I've been thinking about what we've been doing all day long." He reached for her again, wanting to knock down the bricks of distrust she piled between them. He wanted his sweet, funny Addy back.

"Seriously." She pushed against him. "I need you to stop."

"What's wrong?" Lucas dropped his hands and crossed them over his chest. "You're shutting me out…because I'm leaving?"

Addy sucked in a deep breath and refused to make eye

contact. "Look, we both know this was a moment in time sort of thing. We live in two different worlds. Sunday was great, but I think since you've got things under control and since you're leaving in a few days, we should stop hanging out."

"Why?" He raked his eyes over her, trying to figure out why she'd grown so cold. There had been no indication on Sunday night she didn't want to continue what they had. What had happened to change her mind in such a short time?

"Because."

"Your answer is 'because'?"

She lifted her gaze to his. "I don't have regrets, but I don't want to—" she stopped and seemed to gather herself.

Lucas waited, giving her room.

"Truth?" she asked.

"It's usually the best policy."

She bit her lip. "You and the kids are distracting, and I need to go back to my world. These past few days have been a fun interlude, but reality is knocking, Lucas. For both of us. Time to get on with our lives."

Her words were cold water down his back. He'd never expected this from her. "So you're done with us? That's what this is?"

"There wasn't really an *us*. We both knew what this was between us."

"Are you afraid of getting hurt?"

"You can't have that power over me."

Sharp pain hit his chest. Damn. She made it sound no different than Tara's proposition. Big people. No strings. Walk away. "So you feel nothing for me? What we shared was about sex and that's all?"

"Isn't that what you thought?" She wrapped her arms about her waist, looking more little-girl lost than cold-hearted bitch. Still, her words had teeth, they shredded his hope.

"I didn't stop to put a definition on it. I just went with what felt right," he said.

"Well, I have a lot to deal with right now. It would be best for us to say our goodbyes. Why drag it out?"

He didn't know what to say. He turned and studied the way condensation rolled down the bottle of wine he'd chilled for them. Reality had stolen his glee, mocked his happiness and rocked his heart.

There was nothing good about not being wanted. He cleared his throat, and she looked away. Good Lord, she couldn't even look at him. "How can you be so cavalier about this?" he asked, trying not to sound pathetic.

"I'm not cavalier. It's just better for me this way."

He hooked an eyebrow.

"Did you think we had a future? Tell the truth." Her words fell like rocks on a stone floor.

"Yeah, I'd put off thinking about what would happen when I left, but I didn't think we'd be so abrupt about it. Haven't we grown into something more than 'fun'?"

Addy took several seconds to answer. "Robbie Guidry, the guy who tried to rape and kill me, got out of prison yesterday."

"So?"

"So?" Her face gathered into a thundercloud. "Don't you get it? My life has gotten infinitely more complicated. I can't be distracted, allow myself to be with you. I can't think when I'm with you. And what about the kids? I could put them in danger."

"Addy, that was, what, fifteen years ago? I doubt this guy's interested in repeating his last mistake. Don't you think you're overreacting?"

"No. You have no idea how I feel."

"Well, you shouldn't shut me out because you're scared of some phantom…possibility. That isn't logical."

"The hell it isn't logical. You're leaving, Lucas. I'm staying. I don't need to add nights of tears to my nights of terror. I need to declutter."

He felt like she'd punched him. "So I'm clutter?"

"No, I don't mean that. Ugh…you're taking what I feel and making it sound stupid."

"Maybe it is stupid." He shouldn't have said that, but it was too late to retract the words. Besides, she'd tossed him aside like he didn't matter…like she'd gotten what she'd wanted from him and was done.

Maybe all he'd been was a cowboy fantasy—her Sheriff Cade McGarrity stand-in, fulfilling her desires. No different than any other woman in his life. He'd been a fool to want more with her.

Her eyes crackled and she advanced on him. "You don't know what it is because you haven't lived my life. How dare you call me stupid?"

"I didn't call you stupid, only your motivations."

"My motivations aren't stupid. Robbie isn't going away. The mistake I made years ago still haunts me, and I can't make that same mistake with you."

"I'm nothing like that man." Anger poured into him at her unfounded accusation.

"But I don't know that, do I? Not really. And you invoke the same passion in me, the same need to ignore reality. I can't think when you're around, you invade every space, occupy every thought. And now that Robbie's out, I can't afford to be the girl I was Sunday. It's irresponsible."

Lucas stared hard at her, trying to peek beneath the illogical woman to understand what drove her to believe as she did. "He was the wrong guy to be that person with, Addy. But I'm not, and it's a shame you can't put aside your irrational fears to see that."

Addy's gaze sliced him like a cleaver. He almost looked to check if he bled. "I think you should go."

"Yeah." He grabbed the bottle. "I should. You're right. We don't have a future, and there's no sense in wasting any more time on what can't be."

He felt her hurt from across the room. It was as if she'd been waiting for him to say those words, as if his declaring them over, justified her.

This was what she wanted.

And evidently what he wanted too—he'd said the words, hadn't he?

As he closed the door and stepped into the night, he thought of the way he'd left her the last few times they'd parted.

A kiss before I go.

There would be no more kisses from Addy and something about that made him clutch his chest and wish things could be different for them.

ADDY SLUMPED AGAINST the sink, feeling as if all her energy had been sucked down the drain. An empty shell of a woman, doing what had to be done to survive another day. She'd made Lucas mad, had treated him as if he wasn't important to her. And he'd let her…even going as far to dismiss her fears as if she were a blooming idiot.

Oh, God, she'd broken things off with the man she loved. Wait. She loved him?

Yeah…love had finally walked in and Addy had shut the door and twisted the lock.

She'd seen his face—the hurt and disappointment—and still she had persisted in destroying any future they had because she was…

Refusing to acknowledge the word that popped into her mind, she covered her face with her hands.

No.

Being scared was healthy…it would keep her alive, keep her from being hurt literally and figuratively. Lucas would leave and she would stay. She knew what she faced with the nutso who'd been released from prison. She didn't need the distraction of Lucas…the distraction of love.

His words floated back *He was the wrong guy to be that person with, Addy. But I'm not.*

Her heart pulled her toward the back door, toward the man who'd just walked out… What had he meant? Maybe he did have stronger feelings for her than what she'd thought. Maybe…

No. She'd sacrifice love for life. Maybe that made her smart. Or maybe she was the stupidest woman on the planet. Either way she knew separation was the best way to protect everyone.

Trudging out of the kitchen, she steeled herself for a life without Lucas. She'd be okay, just like she'd always been. It wouldn't be bad, after all, she'd been happy without him, hadn't she?

Shaking her head she climbed the stairs, refusing to acknowledge what he'd brought her these past few days. Sunday seemed so far away, already a misty memory tucked inside the caverns of her heart, sure to arise to comfort her on lonely, cold nights.

No regrets.

Hope for the best, but expect the worst. That was her father's motto. Her motto.

She wouldn't dwell on how similar it sounded to Aunt Flora's declaration that morning. She didn't expect to get shit on, but she'd damn sure be prepared if any came her way.

No regrets. It was the only way to move forward.

CHAPTER TWENTY

DAYS LATER, Lucas was still pissed at Addy.

How dare she act as if she didn't have time for him? As if he was nothing more than a distraction? Hell, she'd insinuated he was halfway dangerous…like the guy who'd once hurt her.

His ego was bruised, but his heart felt battered. He'd never expected her to end things like she did—wintery with flinty resolve. He hadn't recognized the woman in that kitchen who'd tossed out what they had with little hesitation. No, that was wrong. He'd sensed sadness, perhaps even regret, but obviously neither was significant enough for her to take back her words. And he still couldn't figure out why she'd wanted him out of her life so soon. The whole "Robbie's out of prison" thing felt almost contrived. He couldn't see the dude coming after her in revenge for what had happened fifteen years ago—the idea sounded like something in a cable movie. Addy had looked spooked, but he suspected she feared commitment more than whoever had hurt her. The guy getting paroled was likely an excuse to keep Lucas back, to give a good reason for dumping him.

Maybe she needed time.

Or maybe it was truly over between them.

He'd tried to keep his hands occupied with getting his brother's house in order. He'd completed the painting of both porches, even calling in a roofer to fix a few shingles that looked damaged. The maid service had scrubbed every square inch of the house, and after one gave him the card of a professional organizer, he'd set up an appointment with her to organize the kitchen and the closets. The kids had been remarkably good for the past two days, as if sensing his hurt, not even mentioning Addy.

Well, except for Charlotte—she kept asking for chocolate chip cookies.

He'd glimpsed Addy only once, and she'd avoided eye contact. The sight of her made him ache so he'd turned his back and pretended she didn't exist.

It was for the best…he thought. His emotions were as tangled as the blind cords in the living room, and he'd spent a good thirty minutes trying to untangle them only to have to take the scissors and whack the cord.

"Time to go, Uncle Lucas," Chris said behind him.

Lucas turned to find Chris clad in a bright red racing suit. "Well, at least I'll be able to find you in the race."

"I'll be easy to find." Chris grinned, chest puffed out. "I'll be the kid out front."

Lucas chuckled as Michael came in…wearing *a lot* of cologne. "Dude, that's way too much Axe body spray."

Michael's face fell. "Really? How do I get it off?"

"You don't. And we don't have time for a shower. Rule of thumb is one, maybe two, squirts," Lucas said, glancing toward the stairway, placing the scissors high on the shelf of the nearby bookcase. "Don't worry, we'll put the windows down on the drive. Can you go get Charlotte? Grammy and Grampy should be here in the next few minutes."

Michael walked to the base of the stairs and hollered "Charlotte!" at the top of his lungs.

"Okay, I couldn't have done that," Lucas muttered looking for the Creampie backpack he'd filled for his niece's stay with his parents. Michael was attending his first school dance with Hannah, the chick he had a crush on, and Lucas hadn't wanted to take Charlotte to the moto-cross races…not with the way she climbed stuff. Luckily, his mother and father who'd gotten in last night had volunteered to watch her.

"We need to hurry," Chris said, glancing at the clock. "I don't want to be late."

Lucas's phone buzzed on the foyer table. He answered it as he picked up his keys. "Hey, Mom."

"Hey, honey, we're running late. There was an accident on I-10 and traffic is backed up everywhere. Rush hour late Friday, so it's going to be thirty minutes or so before we get there."

"I have to leave now, Mom. I'm dropping Michael off at his friend's house and Chris has to be at the race by six-thirty."

"Well, why don't we just meet you at the races?"

He glanced out the window, and in the darkening shadows, he could just make out both Addy's and Flora's cars in the driveway next door. "Let me talk to the neighbors. They might let Charlotte stay with them for a few minutes. Trust me that you don't want to go to the speedway or whatever they call it. Loud, noisy and lots of rails for Charlotte to climb."

"Call me back and let me know. If I don't hear from you, we'll go to the races and watch Chris."

Lucas pocketed his phone and looked at Michael. "Find Charlotte and her backpack and meet me by the truck. I'm running next door."

Michael nodded and Chris scampered toward the truck, where Lucas had loaded the repaired bike hours earlier, while Lucas crossed the familiar path to Addy's, feeling leery about facing her again after their bad goodbye.

He knocked several times, and saw the swish of the curtains before he heard the bolt in the lock slide. The door opened and Addy stood there in porch light, clad in sweats, looking tense.

"Hey, I know I said I wouldn't bother you anymore, but I'm in a bit of a fix."

Addy said nothing, lifting her eyebrows and peering out around him as if the bogeyman lurked in the bushes in the front of the house.

"I have to take Chris to his race over on the Westbank and my parents ran into traffic. Can Charlotte stay with you and Flora until they get here? Shouldn't be more than half an hour."

Lucas heard Charlotte behind him.

"Addy!" she screeched, running in a pair of pink high-heel slippers with crowns on them. She nearly fell and Lucas grabbed her before she cracked her head on the porch. "You have cookies?"

Addy smiled at Charlotte before looking at him. "You don't play fair, do you?"

Lucas shook his head. "She can go with me to the races, but—"

"No." Addy bent to take Charlotte's hand. "She'll be fine here until your parents arrive."

Charlotte beamed and held up her backpack. "Look what I got—the Creampie movie! You can watch it with me."

"Oh, goody, and I think Aunt Flora has some cookies." Addy tugged Charlotte's ponytail. The endearing gesture made Lucas's stomach hurt.

Charlotte skipped into the house, clacking and stumbling, while calling for Aunt Flora.

"Thank you," Lucas said, finding sincerity among the churning in his gut. God, she looked so beautiful…even in a pair of old sweats, her hair pulled back in a pink ribbon.

"You're welcome," she said, dropping her eyes.

"Okay, I gotta run. Don't want Michael to be late for his date with Hannah."

Addy lifted her eyebrows. "He's got a date? He's only thirteen."

"Not a date-date. It's a supervised dance."

"Good for him," Addy said, starting to close the door as soon as Lucas headed toward the steps. "Tell Chris I wish him luck."

Lucas raised a hand in acknowledgment but said nothing further. His pride still felt bruised and it felt awkward between them.

He climbed into the truck with kids full of adrenaline and backed out of the drive, reaching for his cell to check his parents' ETA. His mom hadn't texted him. "Here, call Gran and tell her the neighbor has Charlotte."

"Dude, we're so late." Michael fastened his seat belt and reached for Lucas's phone. "Hannah's meeting me there in twenty minutes and it's going to take at least fifteen to get to Charlie's house."

"Hold on to your cojones 'cause I got this," Lucas said, gunning the truck, shooting out into the narrow street, nearly hitting another truck parked across from his brother's house. "Shit."

"Ooooh," Chris said from the backseat. "That's a really bad word."

"Sorry, I'll put ten bucks in the swear jar," Lucas said, putting the truck in Drive and heading toward Claiborne. He needed to avoid I-10, but somehow manage to get to the Crescent City Connection. Of course, the race would *have* to be on the west bank.

"We don't have a swear jar," Chris said.

"Well, you probably need one." Lucas pushed the call button on his phone and handed it to Michael. "I've known your Dad well enough to guarantee you could make dime if you got one."

Michael laughed at that one before leaving a message on his grandmother's cell phone, telling her where to find Charlotte. Lucas stomped on the accelerator and did what he'd been doing for the past two and a half weeks—ran himself ragged to accommodate his brother's children.

Tomorrow, Ben would come home—he'd already prepared the children for seeing their father and his injury, even though Charlotte hadn't quite understood. But all three were looking forward to being reunited with their parents.

But was Lucas ready to face his past?

Didn't matter because tomorrow he faced his brother and the woman who had betrayed him, breaking his heart for the first time.

Of course, he'd never expected to fall in love a second time, but Addy had proved his hypothesis about love false. It wasn't about choosing to love…that shit just happened, and when it didn't work out, it left a man bitter.

Half broken with no expectation of being whole for the near future. But he could heal. He'd been hurt before and found comfort in his work.

He'd make his peace with Ben, go back to Texas and try to forget Addy Toussant.

UNFORTUNATELY, AUNT FLORA had taken the cookies she'd baked to her friends at Crescent Gardens that afternoon for a rousing game of bingo, which left Addy trying to console a sad little moppet.

"We could make our own," Addy said as Charlotte sat at the kitchen table looking like someone had taken all her toys. She swung her little legs, causing one of her heeled slippers to clatter to the floor.

Aunt Flora poured some milk into the little girl's cup and spread her hands. "I'm so sorry, pumpkin. I think I have some fig cookies in the pantry."

Addy made a face. "I tell you what, let's put on your video in my room. You can snuggle in my fluffy blankie and we'll bake cookies. I bought some dough from Michael's lacrosse team and it's still in the freezer. Sound good?"

"Okay," Charlotte said, brightening.

"She can watch it in the living room," Flora said.

"That's a VCR. She needs a DVD player." Addy grabbed the backpack and took Charlotte's hand. "Heat up the oven and I'll get her settled. Her grandparents should be here in a little while. Lucas said no more than half an hour."

Leaving her aunt to start the cookies, Addy led Charlotte upstairs after urging her to take the slippers off. Last thing Addy needed was to have to make a trip to the hospital. Lucas would—

Addy shut down her mind when she thought about him…or rather she wished she could shut her mind down. For the past three days, she'd been near to mourning over the way she'd ended things between them, but she couldn't bring herself to make it right. How did one undo a goodbye? How did she unsay what she'd blurted out?

So she'd cried in between bouts of glancing over her shoulder, triple-checking locks and praying Robbie would get on with his life, leaving her behind.

But she knew he wouldn't.

On the outside Robbie had always been unassuming, cute and normal in a Kevin Bacon sort of way…but inside he was full-on sociopath.

And he would come.

Someday.

It was for the best she'd ended things with Lucas.

"Here we go," Addy said, entering her room behind Charlotte. She turned on the lamp before lifting Charlotte onto her bed and grabbing her fluffiest throw. After finding the DVD in the bag, she turned on the TV and started setting up the movie.

"Do you like Creampie? She's my favorite." Charlotte flopped onto the pillows on Addy's bed.

"Sure. I like the pink bow she wears in her hair."

"It's not pink, it's wed," Charlotte said, pointing to the picture of the cat on her backpack.

"Not all the time. See?" Addy lifted the DVD case and pointed to the pink bow.

"Oh, yeah," Charlotte said.

The doorbell rang as Addy slid the disk into the player.

"I'll get it," Aunt Flora called up the stairs.

No need to put the video in. Addy turned to tell Charlotte her grandparents were here when a strange feeling hit her. She could hear Flora disarming the alarm as if it were in slow motion.

"No," Addy yelled, but she knew it was too late. She could hear the door open.

She heard Flora say in a friendly voice, "Hey—"

And then she heard her aunt scream.

Oh, dear God, no.

He was here.

Like a monster, fear unleashed inside Addy, choking her, lurching around destroying any sanity she possessed. She was crippled and couldn't move. Her mind flipped through every possible scenario before pausing on the truth—Robbie was downstairs and he'd already hurt Aunt Flora.

Addy pulled out her phone and dialed 911.

"I wanna watch Creampie," Charlotte complained.

"Shh!" Addy turned and shook her head at Charlotte, praying the little girl understood. Charlotte made a face and looked as if she might cry.

"911...what's your emergency?"

"Get to 309 Orchard Street. Hurry!" Addy threw the

phone onto the dresser, leaving the line on, praying the woman traced it or sent a car or something. She could hear her aunt moaning and then heard another crash. Addy felt her heart speed and adrenaline flow out to her limbs, making her arms and legs suddenly heavy. Her vision sharpened as she walked to the door and peered down the hall toward the top of the stairs.

She could lock both her and Charlotte inside her room. Momentary guilt flashed over her aunt, but she had to protect Charlotte. Maybe she could hide her in the closet…

"Addy." Robbie's voice rose like a balloon in singsong madness. "Come out and play."

Swallowing, Addy looked back at Charlotte.

"If you aren't down here in five seconds, I'll use the old lady as a sharpening stone. Get my drift?"

Addy didn't have time to think, grabbing Charlotte while simultaneously slapping a hand over the wriggling child's mouth and lifting her off the bed.

"Charlotte, there's a bad man downstairs," she whispered. "I want you to hide in my closet and be very, very quiet, okay? Don't come out for anything."

Charlotte struggled.

"Do what Addy says, Charlotte," she said, opening the door and literally dumping the girl within. Placing a finger over her mouth, Addy shushed her.

Charlotte's eyes filled with fear as she fell against Addy's shoe boxes but she didn't make a noise. Addy grabbed the backpack and tossed it inside, praying the little girl understood enough to stay put. Addy knew fear sheeted off her and hoped the kid could read it.

She didn't have much more time to think about anything other than her aunt and Robbie with a knife. Switching the TV off, she looked around for a weapon. Her pepper spray was in the kitchen. She'd lent Chris her wooden bat last Sunday when he'd wanted to see the Louisville Slugger her baseball coach brother had brought her from his trip to the factory. Why hadn't she placed it back under her bed?

Addy steeled herself for dealing with the man who wanted to hurt her with only her wits as a defense.

"Addy!" This time no singsong. Anger. "Get your ass down here or I stick the old lady."

Addy walked down the stairs, fear her companion but somehow oddly calm about what she needed to do. Stay between him and Charlotte. Protect Flora as best she could.

She'd made it halfway down, when she saw him.

"Ah, there's my brown-eyed girl. Daddy's home, punkin'."

Bile rose in Addy's throat and she closed her eyes for a brief moment, then opened them. "Robbie."

"Yeah, Robbie. Who'd ya think?"

Swallowing, she forced nonchalance. "What are you doing here? I heard you got out and figured you'd be ready to get on with your life."

"Did ya? Well, I am. And guess what? It starts with you, so get your ass down here," he said, fury glowing in his lurid eyes. He held a large hunting knife and he gestured with it. "Come to me. Now."

Addy didn't want to go, but she could see Aunt Flora's legs out of the corner of her eye. She stepped down slowly, noting her aunt lay motionless and the small marble table just inside the living room had been knocked to the floor. He'd shoved her aunt and Flora wasn't moving. A vise squeezed Addy's heart and she prayed her aunt was merely unconscious.

Robbie wore camouflage pants, a black T-shirt and work boots. A scruffy goatee and bald head made him look nothing like the man she'd once had a crush on. No boyishness or charm. Prison had made his edges razor sharp and eaten away at his mental stability.

"You thought I'd forget about you?" He tsked, moving

forward, shaking his head like a father facing a recalcitrant teen. Behind him the red light of the alarm system blinked, silently mocking her.

She'd never been safe. What a fool she'd been.

Motionless, she stood at the base of the stairs as Robbie walked, almost leisurely, her way. "Of course. You have a life to live after all."

He smiled, lifting the knife so he could study his reflection in the shiny blade. "My little brown-eyed Susan thought I'd forgotten her. Isn't that sad?"

Robbie's cheese had really slid off his cracker. He was going to hurt her. Badly. Panic welled, but she fought it, listening to her internals, remembering that remaining calm and focused was her best chance of saving herself.

Of saving Charlotte.

He moved closer, his nostrils widening as he inhaled her scent. Addy's heart slammed against her ribs and her legs felt rubbery, but she remained a statue, refusing to scurry from him.

She needed to move him from where he might hear Charlotte, perhaps into the living room. Or the kitchen where her pepper spray hung near the phone.

"You look well." She managed to control her breathing, which threatened to gallop out of control. "Would you like a drink? I have some beer."

His laughter made her knees buckle. Madness had carved a home inside him.

Addy slid toward the kitchen, holding out a hand in invitation. "You like Miller Lite if I recall."

"Yeah, you like it in the kitchen, don't cha?" His smile wasn't pretty…wasn't even close.

Shaking, she turned her back to him, closing her eyes as if she could wish this all away. She needed to buy time, protect Charlotte and keep Robbie from escalating the violence.

She entered the kitchen, glancing around for a weapon, but Robbie grabbed her elbow. "Don't get any ideas like last time."

He shoved her sleeve up, revealing the scars, tracing them with the handle of the knife. "Yeah, last time didn't go so well for you, did it?"

"It landed you in prison." She jerked away.

An explosion of a million stars and then the floor rushed up to meet her. Addy fell hard, her head thumping against the tile. She scrabbled on all fours to get away from him. He'd grown stronger in prison and the smack he'd given her made her face throb.

He reached for her and pulled her up.

Addy cradled her cheek and glared at him, trying not to cry out, refusing to give him that pleasure.

Robbie backed her against the counter, his entire body pressing into hers. She could smell his cologne mixed with sweat…and his rage. Reaching behind her she clutched the edge of the granite.

He moved his face closer. "See what you did? Reminding me of all the years I wasted in prison? You really should shut up and get me that beer."

He lifted a hand to caress her cheek and she felt his breath on her neck as she turned her head away from him. Hot lips slid against the cheek he'd hit. "Kissin' it better," he whispered.

Bile churned in her stomach.

"Oh, sweet Addy, I missed you. Feel." He ground against her and she felt his erection. The panic she'd held at bay broke loose, rampaging inside her.

"Robbie, please," she moaned, pleading with him despite her resolve to remain calm.

"Oh, you want it now, darlin'? 'Cause I love when you say my name."

He was going to rape her, that was assured, and he'd

probably kill her. She'd seen homicidal rage in his dark eyes. She wedged a hand between them and pushed. "Stop."

Robbie looked down and laughed before running the flat of the knife's blade over her exposed collarbone. "Ah, yeah, I like this kind of foreplay, Addy. I've been waiting so long for you. I want to savor every second." He snapped his teeth at her like a dog and then laughed.

Out of the corner of her eye, Addy saw Charlotte.

Oh, shit. No. No, no, no.

"Addy?" the little girl called uncertainly.

Robbie spun, tucking the knife behind his back. "Oh, who's this?" he said in the same singsong voice he'd used earlier.

Charlotte's blue eyes grew the size of half dollars as she watched the man move toward her.

"No," Addy shouted. Why had the little girl left the closet? "Go upstairs, Charlotte. Miss Addy is visiting with an old friend."

Charlotte never took her eyes off Robbie and in a quiet voice she said, "But I wanna watch Creampie."

Addy moved quicker than a cat and put herself between the girl and Robbie. "She's my neighbor. No need to involve her in this, Robbie."

He tore his gaze from Charlotte and looked at Addy, a crazy gleam in his eye. "That wouldn't be fun, now would it?"

CHAPTER TWENTY-ONE

WHEN LUCAS ARRIVED at the arena hosting the motocross races, he got an earful from Chris's coach whose supercilious attitude pissed him off. He'd already felt bad about Michael being late, but nothing compared to the way Addy had treated him. Like a damn stranger.

He stomped toward the concession stand to buy a beer, hoping it would make the sting of failure and the stress of driving like a stuntman fade.

After a few sips he set down the beer. Wasn't working. His gut still churned with acid. And his ticker had gotten sucker punched all over again…

Lucas sank onto a metal bench and plopped earplugs in his ears to protect from all the loud engine revving and feedback from the sound system. Thank God he'd prepared for it after going to Chris's practice a few nights ago.

He'd just pulled his phone out to check with his parents and be sure they'd gotten Charlotte when he saw his father walk into the arena entrance.

What the hell?

Rising, he made his way down to where his parents stood. "Dad!"

His father turned, tugging on his mother's arm and waved.

Lucas jogged down. "What are y'all doing here? Where's Charlotte?"

His mother looked up from her phone. "You have Charlotte."

"You didn't get my message?"

His mother shook her head, her light brown hair brushing her thin shoulders. "No. You didn't call us back. We assumed you had her with you."

"I left a message." Lucas pointed at her phone.

"Well, it's a new phone." His mother looked at it with a frown.

"Check it again, Fran," John said, tapping one of the icons.

His mother shook her head and made an apologetic face and handed it to her husband. "I'm no good with these smartphones. They confuse me."

"Ah, hell, I screwed up," Lucas breathed, dropping a perfunctory kiss on his mother's cheek. "I'll call Addy and tell her it will be a bit longer. You might as well stay."

His father didn't look up, just kept pressing buttons and frowning at Fran's phone.

"Surely she'll understand," Fran said with an encouraging smile. "And at the least we'll get to watch Chris attempt to break his neck."

Lucas pulled out his own phone and dialed Addy's number. He knew she wouldn't be pissed, but hated the added complication of dealing with her yet again. He'd told himself if he stayed away from her, his pride could start the healing process. Throwing himself into her path with watching Charlotte had been a mistake. He should have brought the girl with him and done what his parents had suggested.

He waited for the phone to connect, but it went directly to Addy's voice mail.

Hmm…strange. Addy always had her phone with her, and it was always charged. She'd told him it was one of her protocols for safety.

He tried again.

Same result.

His father handed the phone to his mother. "I miss the days when phones had a cord."

His mother smiled. "Yes, but what would you do without your satellite radio and GPS?"

John's eyes held tenderness for her. "You know me too well."

"I can't get in touch with Addy. I'll try Aunt Flora while you two go sit. I'll step out in the corridor," he yelled as a dissonance of engines revved.

His parents nodded and moved toward the stands. Lucas headed toward the entrance, scrolling to Flora's cell phone number.

He called her phone three times, alternating with Addy's, which still went directly to voice mail.

On the forth call, a man answered. "Addy's busy right now." Then the line went dead.

Lucas lowered the phone, first confused by a man answering Flora's phone and then wondering why he'd answered as if it were Addy's phone.

Something was wrong.

And then it hit him like a train.

The dude who had tried to hurt her fifteen years ago—he was out on parole. The image of the white truck he nearly hit—a vehicle out of place. A man waiting until the neighbor left to make his move.

Lucas didn't bother returning to the bleachers. He ran toward the front of the building, pushing out the glass doors, nearly knocking down a man entering.

"Watch it, asshole," the man yelled.

But Lucas didn't stop. He ran toward his truck, dialing 911 as he ran.

"911. What's your emergency?"

"Send someone to 307 Orchard Street. No, wait. 309. 309 Orchard," he said, jogging toward his truck, clicking the truck locks and wrenching the door open.

"Calm down, sir, and give me your name."

"My name is not important. I need you to send a car to 309 Orchard Street, home of Flora… Oh, God, what's her last name? I can't remember, but Addy Toussant lives there and her stalker just got out of prison. Something's wrong there."

He backed out of the lot as the woman asked his name again. "I'm Lucas Finlay. My brother lives at 307. Send a car now. Hurry." He clicked the phone and tossed it in the seat, jetting into the intersection, searching the streets before him. Luckily, the traffic was lighter. He headed toward the Crescent City Connection glowing on the horizon, trying not to kill anyone on his way to get to Addy and Charlotte. His heart raced and he felt as if panic choked him.

"Get out of my way, get out of my way" was the mantra he repeated as he sped toward Uptown.

In his head he prayed. *Dear Lord, please don't let me be too late. Please. I love her. I love them both.*

Never had he felt so helpless. To be six foot four and able to lift sixty-pound bags of feed two at a time, able to wrestle a steer to the ground, able to crush a can in one hand…but not able to stop what was going down in Addy's world.

All he could do was drive like the hounds of hell were on him and pray to a God he'd ignored too often.

AUNT FLORA'S PHONE kept ringing on the granite, jittering like a dancing chicken, the ringtone something she'd heard by Bruno Mars. It seemed to really piss Robbie off.

"Why does that goddamn phone keep ringing?" he shouted before grabbing Addy by her hair and dragging her toward one of the kitchen chairs. He shoved her toward the chair. "Sit down."

Addy stumbled and fell against the chair, the sound screeching against the tile before the chair clattered to the floor. She popped up fast and reached toward Charlotte, who'd darted toward her.

Robbie made a grab for Charlotte but came up with air. He grinned at the little girl who'd wrapped herself around Addy's legs. "Oh, little girl. Been so long since I've seen such innocence. Bet you'll be the sweetest thing I've ever had."

The phone kept ringing and he cast an annoyed look at where it jangled near the coffeepot. Then he turned to Addy and leered. "Two for one deal, huh?"

"You sick bastard," Addy said, lifting her chin. Terror ate away at her insides, but somehow she found her calm. She had no clue how she was able to even speak she was so afraid, but she found her voice again. "Your issue is with me. Not Charlotte."

He cocked his head. "True, but I can't turn down a gift like that, my brown-eyed girl."

Addy did her best to look sad for the man. "What a pitiful man you are. Didn't you realize all these years as you've sent those things, I wasn't interested? What part of no don't you understand?"

He literally growled at her, but the phone rang yet again. He snatched it up. "Addy's busy right now."

Addy's mind flipped through the possibilities of the caller. No one Aunt Flora knew would continue to call over and over again. Maybe her father? And why weren't the Finlays here already? Maybe Lucas's parents would see the door open, catch a glimpse of Flora lying on the floor, and call the police.

Maybe the police were already on their way.

Please let them be on their way.

She glanced again at the pepper spray on her key ring. If only she could slide over...

Robbie tossed the phone onto the counter and advanced toward her. "You didn't like my presents?"

She pushed Charlotte back and squared herself against him, paralyzed at the thought of him using the knife on her again, but not ready to cower. Not ready to give him what he craved—her power.

"No. Why would I want presents from someone who means nothing to me?"

He slapped her again and Charlotte screamed, ducking under the table. "You're pissing me off, Addy."

Addy turned her head so she could look him in the eye. "You may take me down, but I'm not scared of you, you pinky-dicked piece of scum."

The knife flashed in the kitchen light as he slid it to her throat. "You liked my dick at one point if I remember."

Addy swallowed, feeling hot tears slid down her face. "You wish."

She saw the hatred in his eyes, the near insanity as he slid the point of the knife across her throat, lightly like a caress. Then she felt his other hand move downward and heard him unfasten his belt buckle. "Let's find out."

Just as Addy closed her eyes, preparing herself to fight him for her life…for Charlotte's life…she felt two things at once—another presence and Robbie stiffening against her.

Addy opened her eyes.

Aunt Flora stood behind Robbie, a .38 Special pointed at the back of his head.

"Aunt Flora," Addy cried, stepping back, pushing the table aside with a screech.

"That's right," Aunt Flora said, calm as dawn on the bayou. "It's the old lady, and I got my friend with me."

Robbie made a slight move and Aunt Flora cocked the gun. "Go ahead. Give me a good reason."

The man dropped his hands, the knife falling to the floor. Addy reacted without thinking, kicking the weapon across the room.

"I may be easy to knock down, but I got a steady hand,

Mr. Guidry," Aunt Flora said, pressing the gun to the back of his head.

Addy had never seen her aunt look so intent, so absolutely terrifying. It was strange.

"Go call the police, Addy," Aunt Flora said, her hand not wavering, her eyes focused on Robbie.

Robbie's eyes narrowed and Addy slipped around him, going for the phone he'd tossed down seconds ago. Charlotte had curled into a ball under the table, her wails of terror ripping at Addy's heart. She'd just picked up the phone when she heard the sirens.

Relief stole over her. "The police are here."

Robbie's response wasn't fit for polite company.

"Take the baby and go let the police in. I've got this piece of crap under control," Flora said like she was an arresting officer on *Law & Order*.

Addy pulled Charlotte out from under the table, cradling the child in her arms. Charlotte locked her arms around Addy's neck like a vise. "Shh, shh, Charlotte, it's okay now. It's okay."

Addy was afraid to leave Aunt Flora in case Robbie tried to flee, or even worse…take the gun from her. Addy had learned the hard way how easy it was for a perpetrator to take a weapon from a victim and use it on her. So she stood in the doorway, holding Charlotte and waiting on the first officer to arrive on the scene.

She didn't wait long.

With one eye on Flora, Addy motioned the officer inside. "He's in the kitchen. My aunt has a gun."

"Ma'am, step back, please," the female officer said, gun drawn and her eyes focused on the kitchen doorway. "Jeter, cover the back!"

Addy scooted to the side, worried sick about Flora, but wanting the officer to be able to do her job. The policewoman entered the kitchen and Addy heard her say, "Okay, ma'am. I want you to step back and lower your weapon."

Aunt Flora answered, "You put your gun on this piece of shit, and I'll be happy to step away."

"Do as I say," the officer said again and Addy heard the back door burst open.

And that was when the shaking started. Her whole body shook violently as her legs buckled. Addy sank against the wall, lowering herself to the ground, clutching Charlotte, who still clung to her making mewling sounds like a little kitten.

In the background she heard a male voice reading Robbie his rights and felt Flora's cool hand against her neck.

"Addy, you're okay, honey," Aunt Flora said, but Addy couldn't stop shaking. "Let me take Charlotte."

Releasing Charlotte, Addy finally lifted her head. Her teeth chattered and she wrapped her arms around herself, looking up at Flora who still looked cool as ice. "Where did you get that gun?"

"I've had that thing under my mattress for twenty years. Bought it when we had some gang trouble in the area around the shop, then brought it home." Flora stroked Charlotte's hair.

"Dear God, if you hadn't—" The sound of footsteps coming from the kitchen stopped Addy. Seconds later the other officer marched a cuffed Robbie past them. Robbie looked at her and sneered.

Addy turned away, unable to look at him one second longer.

She closed her eyes and all she could see was her life as empty as it ever was. She'd pushed Lucas away—pushed everyone away—thinking she could protect herself, but she hadn't been able to. She'd nearly died, nearly erased the life she could have had with Lucas because she'd been afraid. She'd stood outside life, her nose pressed to the window rather than opening the door and joining it. Well, she'd actually opened the door and stuck her head in…and then pulled it back out when things got too scary.

What good was a life unlived worth?

She needed Lucas beside her. She needed to take a chance on love.

Addy opened her eyes. Aunt Flora soothed Charlotte. Lights from the cruiser flashed like a strobe on the wood floor, and the female officer called numbers into a microphone thing on her shoulder.

"Ma'am, medical assistance is on its way," she said, looking from Addy to Aunt Flora. "But I also need to ask some questions about what happened."

Flora nodded, looking down at Addy. "Can you stand up, sweetheart?"

Addy nodded and began to push herself up…and that was when Lucas arrived.

WHEN LUCAS PULLED onto Orchard Street, he was met with the flashing blue and red lights of a police car. Behind him, he could see the lights of an ambulance making its way from the other direction.

His heart hit his churning stomach, and like a man possessed he hurtled toward Addy's house. With a squeal of tires, he skidded into his brother's driveway, leaping from the truck and running toward the house next door. Out of the corner of his eye, he saw a police officer loading a man in cuffs into the cruiser. Part of Lucas wanted to veer toward the asshole and use him as a punching bag, but the other part needed to get to Addy and Charlotte.

He took the front steps two at a time and burst through the open front door.

"Addy!"

She sat on the floor at the feet of Flora and a police officer. Charlotte wiggled out of Flora's arms and ran to him. She launched herself at him and he snatched her up, hugging her to him as he moved toward Addy. He'd never thought baby shampoo smelled better than it did at that moment.

"Uncle Wucas, there was a bad man who tried to hurt me." Her small voice muffled by his shirt.

He hugged tight the snot-streaked, sweaty little girl. "You're safe, Lottie. You're safe," he crooned, walking toward the women clustered in the small hallway between the living area and kitchen.

He processed everything about the woman he loved. Addy's hair tangled around her ashen face, strands stuck to one cheek where a purpling bruise emerged. A small smear of blood was beneath her nose and when her eyes met his, he saw her terror.

Not thinking twice, he handed the child to the police officer, reached down and picked up Addy, wrapping her in his arms as he had Charlotte.

"Oh, God, Lucas," she said, her body trembling. She clung to him, fisting her hands in his shirt.

"Shh, baby. It's okay. You're okay," he said low in her ear, turning and walking into the living room, sinking onto the couch, cradling her like a child. Her body shook hard, but no tears emerged, making him wonder if she was in shock.

He glanced at the officer who'd followed them, still holding Charlotte, and saw understanding in her eyes. Flora also followed, sinking into a chair and pressing her hands against her face.

Finally, Addy lifted her head. "Oh, Lucas, I'm so sorry Charlotte had to be part of this. I should have said no. I had no idea—"

"It's all right, Addy. None of this was your fault," he said, smoothing her hair.

Paramedics arrived, rolling a yellow-framed gurney inside, carrying huge medical cases.

The officer called them inside the living area.

"I'm okay," Addy said, sitting up. "But you need to check Aunt Flora. Robbie knocked her unconscious."

Flora snorted. "No, he didn't. I was playing possum. I watch plenty of police shows, and I've read enough books to know that playing dead's a strategy."

Addy managed a smile. "Only you would see watching *Hawaii Five-O* as preparation. I'm so glad you're okay."

Flora winked, looking ready to take on anyone else who came through the door ready to do harm to those she loved.

Over the next hour Lucas marveled at the tale that unfolded—one of a brave woman standing up against her attacker, a little girl who never stayed where she was told to stay and an older gun-toting lady who saved the day. All the while Addy sat next to him, pressed tight as if she took comfort in his presence.

In between taking statements, collecting evidence and allowing the EMT to check her over, Addy kept her composure. Lucas fielded phone calls from his parents, Michael's friend's parents and finally Addy's father who was en route.

Lucas cornered the officers on the scene and asked to move Addy, Flora and Charlotte over to the house next door while the scene was processed.

So over they went. Flora made coffee, strangely looking very much unaffected by the whole event. Charlotte clung to the nearest adult and Addy had gotten back some of her color.

With only a few moments before Addy's parents descended on them, his parents arrived and the detective who investigated the first case showed up, Lucas held Addy. "Are you really okay?"

She nodded against his chest. "Oddly enough, I am. I

can't say I wasn't scared, but I didn't let him win. I didn't allow him any satisfaction."

"No, you didn't." He cupped her head and held her tighter. "I'm sorry I didn't believe you. I had no clue he was so dangerous."

She pulled back, her eyes apologetic. "I never told you about the threats he sent me. You couldn't have understood because I didn't let you."

"Why?"

"When we first met, I wanted to protect myself. I didn't want you to see how much baggage I came with. I guess subconsciously I thought you'd think me not worth the trouble."

"Never."

"You say that now, but it's like the divorced gal who finally finds someone to love—she doesn't tell her new boyfriend about her crazy-train ex until she has to. I didn't want you to walk away before we started."

"But we started," he murmured.

"Yeah, but when things got serious between us, I didn't tell you because you were leaving."

"Addy," he whispered against her hair, "don't you know I want to know all of you? Can't you see how much I care?"

She nodded. "I should have told you about the threats, should have shared what I knew about him, about his pro-file and why he wasn't going to stop. I could have protected Charlotte. I never should have let her stay here knowing Robbie was out there."

"But you couldn't have known he'd come tonight."

She shook her head. "But I could have spared her the trauma. She's going to be scared for a long time, and that breaks my heart."

"She's young and she's learned there are people who won't let evil win. Robbie is history—they'll put him away for a long time."

"I hope," she said, her voice fading.

"And if he ever gets out, I'll kill him."

"And how will you know? You won't be here—"

"I'll know. I love you, Addy, and if he even thinks to harm one hair on your head, he'd regret ever being born."

Lifting a trembling hand to her bruised cheek, she looked away. "You love me?"

Lucas turned her face gently so her whiskey eyes met his. "I do love you. I didn't expect it to happen, and I know things aren't ideal, but I can't deny the way I feel. It's okay if you don't feel the same, but one thing I've learned over the past few weeks is when you have the chance to say I love you, you should take it. I'm not asking you to—"

"Shut up," she said, jerking his head down and rising on her tiptoes so she could kiss him.

Lucas felt something inside him release as their lips met. He didn't know if it was because his rollicking emotions had been granted reprieve or if the adrenaline high had faded or if the searing anger for the man who'd hit his Addy had been abated, but at that moment, he was finally content. He accepted what had been growing inside him for the past week—the knowledge he and Addy were meant to be together. And though it might be hard to figure out how their relationship would work logistically, he would make sure they stayed together.

Softly he kissed her, cradling her head in his hands, embracing the love swelling inside.

She ended the kiss and stared up at him, her eyes velvet in the low counter light. "I love you, too, Lucas. I do. I was stupid the other night. Too scared to trust you. I'm sorry."

"Me, too. I don't want to waste any more time denying you were made for me, and I for you."

For several moments they stood content to hold one another. Finally, Lucas gave her a squeeze. "This might be both the worst and best night of my life."

Addy reached up and brushed her hand against his face. "Weird, but true."

"Grammy and Grampy are here!" Charlotte shouted from where she sat with Flora.

Lucas sighed. "Miles to go before I sleep."

"And that's why I love you. You can bake brownies, clean up vomit and do Robert Frost."

Lucas's eyes sparked. "Who are you talking about? I'm a tough cowboy. I eat little kids for breakfast and rope steers. Brownies aren't even in my vocabulary. Maybe we better get those paramedics to come back and check your noggin 'cause you think you're in love with Mr. Mom."

"I'll take both the guys inside of you as long as you'll take the Addy who dresses in frumpy clothes along with the Addy who doesn't wear underwear beneath them."

"Fine, but I want more of the second Addy." He took her hand and it fit like a key in a lock.

In truth, Addy Toussant had been made for him.

CHAPTER TWENTY-TWO

ADDY SPENT THE NIGHT at the Finlay house, wrapped in Lucas's arms on the couch. Since Flora hadn't wanted to sleep in her house alone and Addy was unwilling to leave the protection of Lucas's arms, her aunt went home with Addy's parents while a still freaked-out Charlotte loaded up with Lucas's parents. That left Addy and Lucas with a not-so-surly-anymore teen and a jubilant motocross champ of the junior division. Since everyone was exhausted by the night's drama, all crashed and slept until the doorbell woke them.

Lucas didn't move at the insistent sound, so Addy struggled from the depths of the plush couch to answer the door. Looking out the spy hole, she saw Lucas's mother on the stoop holding balloons and a cake. Charlotte skipped up and down the front pavers, looking none the worse for wear. Thank God.

Kids…she wished she had their resiliency.

Opening the door, Addy ran a hand through her hair and squinted against the morning sun. She tried not to blush at being caught in the same clothes as last night, with her hair knotted and her eyes swollen. She resisted the urge to wipe the sleep from her eyes. "Mrs. Finlay."

"Good morning, dear, and call me Fran, please," she said, pushing past Addy. Charlotte jumped up the steps, Creampie backpack slapping a rhythm. She held her hands up to Addy.

"Good morning, Brave Charlotte," Addy murmured

into the girl's curls. The child smelled like clean cotton and sunshine. Addy set her down so she wasn't tempted to hoof the child like some nut ball, but the clean smell of innocence was addictive.

A balloon snagged around Addy's neck and she pulled it free as Lucas's head emerged over the back of the sofa. Seemed a shame the first time they'd literally slept together had been platonic and on his brother's couch, but it hadn't seemed right to share a bed with two impressionable boys in the house.

"Mom? What are you doing here? What time is it?"

"I'm preparing for your brother to come home, of course. And it's nine-thirty," Fran trilled, bypassing Lucas and heading for the kitchen.

Lucas scrambled off the couch, kicking the fluffy throw they'd been wrapped in to the floor. He rose, clad only in his plaid boxers and a T-shirt. Stretching, he turned to her with a sleepy smile. Something wonderful fluttered in her stomach when she realized this was the first of many smiles she'd wake up to. "Morning, Addy girl."

Addy closed the door and tugged her T-shirt around from where it had twisted under her arms. "Morning, babe."

She heard him sigh and that caused another flood of warmth. For a moment they beamed at one another.

And then they heard the thump, thump, thump of not-so-little feet tromping down the stairs. Michael appeared first, hair sticking up, shoulders slumped. "I smell doughnuts."

"It's a cake your grandmother brought."

Chris came next, sticking his head over the banister as he took the stairs at double time. "Mom and Dad are coming home today!"

"Yes, they are." Fran popped her head back into the foyer. "And we all need to get ready. Your grandfather is on his way to Belle Chasse to pick them up, so we need to make our beds, pick up and tack these balloons on the porch. Lucas, get some britches on and grab the banner out of the car. Your aunt Camille made it."

Addy moved toward the kitchen. "I'll be glad to help, but first I need to grab a shower at my place."

"I better help her." Lucas wiggled his eyebrows.

His mother gave him a blank stare…but Addy saw the twinkle in her eye before she turned around. "Forget about it. I know last night was, well, traumatic, and you two need some time together, but it will have to be later. Today, we're focusing on Benjamin's welcome home. Snap to it, mister."

Addy looked about for her flip-flops and slid a glance toward where Lucas stood still stretching. "I wouldn't mind some company on my walk over. I know it's silly, but the thought of taking a shower alone in that house after Robbie attacked me last night gives me the willies."

Lucas dropped his arms. "Let me grab a few things for Mom and make sure the kids are set, then I'll walk over with you."

Minutes later, hand in hand, they headed silently toward her house.

She pulled the damaged back door open, punched in the code for the alarm and looked at her kitchen. The police had left it as it was, chairs scattered, table shoved out of its normal spot. The pan for cookies still sat on the counter, but thankfully someone had turned the oven off. Addy felt as if she was having an out-of-body experience. It was her kitchen…yet a stranger's kitchen.

Lucas slid his hands to her shoulders and she jumped. "Hey, it's over," he said.

She nodded. "The rational me knows that, but I still feel all quivery in my skin. The only good thing is now I have you beside me."

He wrapped his arms around her and calmed her soul. It had been that way from the beginning—Lucas sooth-

ing her fears with his touch, his smile, his very presence.
She should have trusted that instinct.

Turning, she laid her head against his broad chest, whis-
pering a prayer of thanks. "It's over for me, but what about
you?"

"What do you mean?"

"Ben and Courtney will be here in a few hours."

He pulled away and glanced out the back window.
"Yeah, there's that."

"You want to tell me about what really happened? The
non-kid version?"

He shrugged those massive shoulders, his head tilting
forward enough to give him vulnerability in the morning
light. "Just a major screwup."

Addy didn't say anything, just hooked her foot around
the same chair she'd crashed into the night before and
pulled it to her. She sat...and waited.

"Courtney was my best friend, first girlfriend, first
lover and I had assumed my future," he said, his dark
eyes trained on some unseen horizon outside her kitchen
window.

He sank into a chair. "You plan things, you know? I was
attending Tulane Law, Courtney at University of New Orleans working on her business degree. We were comfortable and I thought happy, even if I studied too much. She
was lonely and when Ben came home for Christmas and
stayed to find a job, he took her to the movies, for drinks
with friends and they job hunted together. I was relieved
because I didn't have her nagging me about ignoring her,
but the joke was on me—they fell in love."

Addy made a sympathetic sound in her throat.

"No, it was partly my fault. I took her for granted, and
she was lonely. Ben didn't intend to betray me. I could see
that in his eyes. He was torn up about it, but I guess they
couldn't stop it. I had saved for a ring and planned to pro-

pose to Courtney. I'd booked a condo in Destin, picked out the Gulf View Grill for the proposal and sent in my resumes to intern at some big law offices. All planned out... except Courtney was pregnant with Michael."

"Oh, Lucas," she murmured, stretching out a hand. He pushed it away, lifting fierce eyes that still mirrored pain.

"A real Jerry Springer special and it killed me. I couldn't believe they'd done something like that behind my back. I dropped out of law school and left New Orleans. You know the rest."

"So why did you come back?"

"I don't know."

"I think you do," she said, seeing straight into his heart.

He shook his head. "When mom called me about Ben getting hurt in Afghanistan, something tore loose inside me. All that bitterness and hate rusting away inside me just broke away. I took a ride on Cisco—"

She lifted her eyebrows.

"That's my horse. And as I stared across the grassland, I knew it was time to let the hatred, the shame of losing out to Ben, go."

"Did you love Courtney?"

"Yeah, of course. You know her. She's hard not to love. But I think it was more a comfort thing. We'd both decided we were better together than apart. She just hadn't banked on finding true love instead." His words fell soft on her and she could feel the change in him even as he spoke.

"You don't ever plan on true love, do you?"

"I kind of figured that out. That's what I wanted to tell you earlier—that when you asked me about love, I froze and panicked."

Addy smiled.

"Fate brought me home. Now I know what it's like to find the person you're meant to be with. I know what real love is."

Addy clasped his hands. "You came home for me."

"I did." He set his forehead against hers. "We don't have time for more, but I'll take a kiss before you go."

"I'm not leaving. Just taking a shower."

He looked at her, the devil in his eyes. "Want me to wash your back?"

Addy's kiss told him all he needed to know.

LUCAS WATCHED as Courtney rolled Ben up the ramp he'd installed after painting the porch. His brother wore a gray sweat suit with his unit's emblem on the front. Very noticeable was the empty right pant leg. He tried not the look, but it drew the eye…and made his heart clench.

The kids hung back watching their father move toward them in a wheelchair. Fran gave Michael a push, but he resisted.

"Look at the porch," Courtney breathed, stroking the glossy satin of the rail, looking up with a pasted-on smile. Her eyes pleaded with her children. "And who put the ramp in?"

"It's temporary," Lucas said. "I figured Ben wouldn't be in a wheelchair long."

At hearing his voice, Ben looked up to where Lucas stood behind their parents. His dark eyes were unfathomable, his expression fierce. Courtney's eyes reflected gratitude…and a certain wariness. He didn't blame her. The situation was awkward and carried enough tension to smother the neighborhood.

With another small push from Fran, Michael moved toward his father. The other two followed clustering around Ben, hugging him, chattering about winning races, making the lacrosse team and getting a new Creampie stuffed kitten. Ben's smile lit up the porch, and though he'd lost much weight and looked older than his thirty-five years, Lucas could see a glimpse of the old Ben within his face.

"Let's all go inside," Fran said, opening the front door. The kids tumbled in, Chris already asking about cutting the cake.

"You haven't had lunch yet," Fran admonished. Lucas glanced over at his father who stood holding the door. The older man nodded and left him on the porch with Ben and Courtney.

Lucas swallowed the sudden emotion that stuck in his throat as the click of the door sounded like thunder.

Ben sighed. "I guess we're doing this."

Courtney rubbed his shoulders and his brother lifted a hand to pat one of her hands. And Lucas got it—they were united in solidarity.

Lucas kicked at the runner of the freshly painted rocker. "I think it's time we did."

A few seconds ticked by.

"What do you want us to say we haven't already," Ben asked, anger still lurking in his tone. "We're sorry for the millionth time?"

Lucas didn't say anything for a moment. "No, you've already apologized."

"Then what?" Courtney sank onto the rocker. "We wronged you. Everybody knows, and we've had to live with it. It's a crappy cloud over your head…and though it's very accurate, it's also not fair because people see only what they want to see. They don't see inside us to the feelings within, to the—"

She shook her head. "I'm so sorry for what happened between us. I wish in one way I could undo how it went down. If I had only told you how I felt instead of hiding from what was happening, things would have been easier."

Lucas nodded. "You're right."

"What more can we do to make things right with you, Luke?" his brother asked.

"You can't make things right," Lucas paused for a moment, eyeing each of the people who'd once been such a part of his life. He didn't know them any longer...but he wanted to. "But we can start over."

Courtney's eyes widened. "How? There's too much hurt. Too many years gone by."

"So we don't try to be a family?" Lucas asked. "The years have given me wisdom. Time has revealed you and I weren't right for each other, Courtney. I understand what happened between us...and what grew between you and Ben. It hurt. But now I see with different eyes."

Ben jerked his head away, aiming his gaze at the recently trimmed azaleas. He remained silent.

"Why now?" Courtney's eyes searched his.

"Why not?"

"Doesn't make sense," Ben said.

"Maybe not, but life doesn't make sense, does it? Does that war you fought make sense? Does the fact you and Courtney ended up together make sense? Christ, does that Creampie movie even remotely make sense?"

A snort escaped Courtney.

He continued, "No, because life is not something to be figured out. It's not fair. It's not easy. And sometimes it sucks. But it's what we have, and if we can find love, if we can grab on to a piece of happiness, we should. And if we can forgive each other for the wrongs in the past, it's a no-brainer."

"What's caused this change in you?" Courtney asked. "The kids?"

Lucas nodded. "But it started long before. I couldn't seem to find a reason to reach out to either of you. You needing me was the catalyst."

Ben's eyes glittered. "Don't do this because you feel sorry for me. Don't come in here painting my house, playing the hero, making me feel guilty all over again for what happened between us years ago."

"Is that what you think? I feel sorry for you?"

Ben held his gaze. "Yeah, I think you love to be the good guy."

"And you're the bad guy?"

Ben jerked away. "I've been the bad guy since I fell in love with your girl."

Lucas snorted. "You're going to play the martyr now? Your leg gets blown off and you survived knocking at death's door, so you're done fighting? You want to continue sticking your head in the sand?"

"Bullshit," his brother said, squaring his shoulders.

"Yeah, that's what I thought. Nothing worth doing is easy, Ben. It's going to be hell to learn to walk on that prosthetic, to be the man you've always been, but you'll do it. That's who you are. And it's not easy for me to stand here, remembering the past, but I'll do it. Because that's who've I've grown to be."

The seconds ticked by again and Lucas struggled for his thoughts. "I don't want to be the man I've spent the past decade being. I don't want to miss out on this family. I'm tired of being angry. I'm tired of weathering life alone, shrouded in my lonely house on my lonely prairie. I want more."

"So you and I forget about everything and go out for beers like nothing happened?" Ben asked.

"No, we'll need time, but I'd rather have you in my life in a somewhat uncomfortable way than to not have you at all."

Courtney looked down at her hands. "And me?"

"The same. We've been friends ever since you fell from that tree. I hated you for a long time, but those bonds didn't break. When you called, I came...because I still care about both of you. Under the anger sat love."

Tears shimmered in Courtney's eyes and she reached for Ben's hand, twining her fingers with his.

At one time that image would have hurt him.

But no longer.

He was over her. He was over being angry at Ben.

"It won't be easy, but I think it's time, for all our sakes, that we bury the hatchet and get on with living." Lucas extended his hand to his brother.

For a moment, Ben studied his hand, dark eyes just matching Lucas's zoning in. Then he lifted his eyes to Lucas's gaze, holding it, allowing Lucas to see the relief, to see the longing.

Ben lifted his hand and put it in Lucas's. It was a firm handshake, full of resolve, full of regret, but most of all it was a forgiving.

Courtney placed her hand atop theirs, the tears shimmering in her eyes now falling on her cheeks.

When Lucas looked up, Addy stood in the door.

He smiled at her and the look in her eyes told him he was truly home.

Courtney's eyes widened as Addy, clad in her pretty green-striped dress, stepped out and accepted his outstretched arm. She snuggled against him, looking as pretty as she had last Sunday when she'd first worn the dress. Of course this time she'd worn it with underwear—he'd watched her put the lacy panties on. It had been a sweet sight.

Courtney wiped her cheeks and arched an eyebrow. "Addy?"

Lucas looked down at the small woman who'd seeped into his heart and shown him what real love was. "Yeah. Addy."

Courtney laughed, a delighted tinkle. "Well, isn't that something. You have a really good reason for sticking around, huh?"

As the kids trooped out onto the porch, complaining about their grandmother refusing to cut the cake, Lucas smiled even bigger. "She's the best reason, but not the only one."

"I'm hungry," Chris complained, kicking his father's chair wheel.

"Stop," Ben said, rolling toward the door. "If anyone needs cake, it's me. Let's cut the damn thing."

The kids cheered and everyone left, leaving Lucas and Addy on the porch alone.

The sun slanted in, falling in golden slants across the white boards. Addy looked up at Lucas.

"A kiss before we eat cake?"

He kissed her nose. "How about a kiss to celebrate spending my tomorrow with you?"

She lifted onto her tiptoes and brushed her lips against his. "Best kiss ever."

* * * * *

*Look for the next Harlequin Superromance by
Liz Talley! Coming in February 2014.*

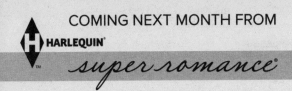
Available November 5, 2013

#1884 BRINGING MADDIE HOME
The Mysteries of Angel Butte • by Janice Kay Johnson

Colin McAllister always believed he would bring Maddie Dubeau home. Then he finds her. Except she's now Nell Smith and has little memory of her past. He must find her abductor, keep her safe...and not fall for her!

#1885 ADVENTURES IN PARENTHOOD
by Dawn Atkins

Aubrey Hanson is an ordinary woman trying extraordinary adventures. But she's unprepared for helping raise her orphaned twin nieces. Luckily she's not alone. Dixon Carter seems to have it all under control—except their attraction!

#1886 NOW YOU SEE ME • by Kris Fletcher

Lydia Brewster longs to shake her "poor widow" image. But reputations die hard in Comeback Cove. No one understands that better than J. T. Delaney. Suddenly Lyddie's ticket to reclaiming her life has appeared in a tempting package....

#1887 THAT RECKLESS NIGHT
The Sinclairs of Alaska • by Kimberly Van Meter

Miranda Sinclair, reeling on the anniversary of her sister's death, has a passionate night with a stranger. The next day she's shocked to discover the man is her new boss, Jeremiah Burke!

#1888 BETTER THAN GOLD
The Legend of Bailey's Cove • by Mary Brady

In Bailey's Cove, Maine, restaurateur Mia Parker and anthropologist Daniel MacCarey discover each other while dealing with a two-hundred-year-old skeleton found in her wall. Their attraction is irresistible, but his past stands between them and love.

#1889 THE MOMENT OF TRUTH
Shelter Valley Stories • by Tara Taylor Quinn

When Dana discovers that her whole life has been based on a lie, she escapes by accepting an opportunity in Shelter Valley. When Josh realizes that *his* whole life has been a selfish pursuit of pleasure, he wants to change—and comes to this town to do it. And when they meet, both their lives are transformed....

That Reckless Night
By Kimberly Van Meter

"You're as stubborn as your old man and just as mean," Russ,
the bartender, said, setting up her drink. "Why do you do this
to yourself, girl? It ain't gonna bring Simone back."

Miranda stilled. "Not allowed, Russ," she warned him
quietly. "Not allowed." Today was the anniversary of her
youngest sister's death. And most people knew better than to
bring up Simone's name.

This, Miranda thought as she stared at the glass, was how
she chose to cope with Simone's death, and no one would
convince her otherwise. What did they know anyway? They
didn't know of the bone-crushing guilt that Miranda carried

every day, or the pain of regret and loss that dogged her nights and chased her days. Nobody knew. Nobody understood. And that was just fine. Miranda wasn't inviting anyone to offer their opinion.

Russ sighed. "One of these days you're going to realize this isn't helping."

"Maybe. But not today." She tossed the shot down her throat. The sudden blast of arctic air chilled the closed-in heat of The Anchor, and Miranda gave a cursory glance at who had walked through the front door.

And suddenly her mood took a turn for the better.

A curve settled on her mouth as she appraised the newcomer. The liquor coursing through her system made her feel loose and wild, and that broad-shouldered specimen shaking the snow from his jacket and stamping his booted feet was going to serve her needs perfectly.

"Hey, Russ…who's he?" she asked.

Russ shrugged. "Never seen him before. By the looks of him, probably a tourist who got lost on his way to Anchorage."

A tourist? Here today, gone tomorrow. "He'll do," she murmured.

But what if the stranger is not a tourist?
Find out in THAT RECKLESS NIGHT
by Kimberly Van Meter, available November 2013
from Harlequin® Superromance®.
And be sure to look for the other books in
Kimberly's The Sinclairs of Alaska series.

REQUEST YOUR FREE BOOKS!
2 FREE NOVELS PLUS 2 FREE GIFTS!

HARLEQUIN®

super romance®

More Story...More Romance

YES! Please send me 2 FREE Harlequin® Superromance® novels and my 2 FREE gifts (gifts are worth about $10). After receiving them, if I don't wish to receive any more books, I can return the shipping statement marked "cancel." If I don't cancel, I will receive 6 brand-new novels every month and be billed just $4.94 per book in the U.S. or $5.24 per book in Canada. That's a savings of at least 14% off the cover price! It's quite a bargain! Shipping and handling is just 50¢ per book in the U.S. and 75¢ per book in Canada.* I understand that accepting the 2 free books and gifts places me under no obligation to buy anything. I can always return a shipment and cancel at any time. Even if I never buy another book, the two free books and gifts are mine to keep forever.

135/336 HDN F46N

Name _____ (PLEASE PRINT) _____

Address _____ Apt. # _____

City _____ State/Prov. _____ Zip/Postal Code _____

Signature (if under 18, a parent or guardian must sign)

Mail to the Harlequin® Reader Service:
IN U.S.A.: P.O. Box 1867, Buffalo, NY 14240-1867
IN CANADA: P.O. Box 609, Fort Erie, Ontario L2A 5X3

**Are you a current subscriber to Harlequin Superromance books
and want to receive the larger-print edition?
Call 1-800-873-8635 or visit www.ReaderService.com.**

* Terms and prices subject to change without notice. Prices do not include applicable taxes. Sales tax applicable in N.Y. Canadian residents will be charged applicable taxes. Offer not valid in Quebec. This offer is limited to one order per household. Not valid for current subscribers to Harlequin Superromance books. All orders subject to credit approval. Credit or debit balances in a customer's account(s) may be offset by any other outstanding balance owed by or to the customer. Please allow 4 to 6 weeks for delivery. Offer available while quantities last.

Your Privacy—The Harlequin® Reader Service is committed to protecting your privacy. Our Privacy Policy is available online at www.ReaderService.com or upon request from the Harlequin Reader Service.

We make a portion of our mailing list available to reputable third parties that offer products we believe may interest you. If you prefer that we not exchange your name with third parties, or if you wish to clarify or modify your communication preferences, please visit us at www.ReaderService.com/consumerschoice or write to us at Harlequin Reader Service Preference Service, P.O. Box 9062, Buffalo, NY 14269. Include your complete name and address.

HSR13R